喚醒你的英文語感 ！

Get a Feel for English !

喚醒你的英文語感！

Get a Feel for English !

全民英檢 '寫作破關'

WRITING

MASTER GEPT WRITING : ELEMENTARY

初級

由句子改寫到段落寫作，
名師完全掌握命題方向，
誘導式教法，
不但幫助寫作破關，
實力並能更上層樓。

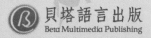

貝塔語言出版
Beta Multimedia Publishing

總編審⊙王復國　作　者⊙艾菱

全民英語分級能力檢定測驗簡介

測驗特色

全民英語能力分級檢定測驗 (General English Proficiency Test) 為教育部指導，財團法人語言訓練中心 (http://www.lttc.ntu.edu.tw) 主辦。本測驗共分 5 級，每級各有明確能力標準。詳細內容請參照下表：

「全民英語能力檢定分級測驗」各級綜合能力說明

級　數	綜　合　能　力	備　　註 建議下列人員宜具有該級英語能力		
初　級	具有基礎英語能力，能理解和使用淺易日常用語，英語能力相當於國中畢業者。	百貨業 餐飲業	旅館業或 觀光景點 服務人員	一般行政助理 維修技術人員 計程車駕駛
中　級	具有使用簡單英語進行溝通的能力，英語能力相當於高中職畢業者。	業　務 餐飲業 旅館業	一般行政 總機人員 銷售人員 警政人員	旅遊從業人員 旅館、飯店接待人員
中高級	通過中高級測驗者英語能力逐漸成熟，應用的領域擴大，雖有錯誤，但無礙溝通，英語能力相當於大學非英語主修系所畢業者。	商　務 秘　書 導　遊 工程師 空服人員	航管人員 航空機師 海關人員 研究助理 企劃人員	新聞從業人員 外事警政人員 資訊管理人員
高　級	英語流利順暢，僅有少許錯誤，應用能力擴及學術或專業領域，英語能力相當於國內大學英語主修系所或曾赴英語系國家大學或研究所進修並取得學位者。	翻譯人員 外交人員 研究人員	協商談判人員 英語教學人員 高級商務人員 國際新聞從業人員	
優　級	英語能力接近受過高等教育之母語人士，各種場合均能使用適當策略作最有效的溝通。	外交官員	專業翻譯人員 國際新聞特派人員 協商談判主談人員	

初級檢定

初試－聽力測驗、閱讀能力測驗、寫作能力測驗
複試－口說能力測驗
※ 初試通過者始能參加複試；初、複試皆通過者發
　給合格證書。

初級考試測驗內容

	測驗項目	題	型	題　數		測驗時間
初 試	聽力測驗	第一部分	看圖辨義	10 題	30 題	約20 分鐘
		第二部分	問答	10 題		
		第三部分	簡短對話	10 題		
	閱讀能力 測驗	第一部分	詞彙和結構	15 題	35 題	35 分鐘
		第二部分	段落填空	10 題		
		第三部分	閱讀理解	10 題		
	寫作能力 測驗	第一部分 單句寫作	句子改寫	5 題	16 題	40 分鐘
			句子合併	5 題		
			重組	5 題		
		第二部分 段落寫作	依題目要求 寫一篇約50 字的短文	1 題		
複 試	口說能力 測驗	第一部分	複誦	5 題	18 題	約10 分鐘
		第二部分	朗讀句子 朗讀短文	5個句子 1篇短文		
		第三部分	回答問題	7 題		

資料來源：財團法人語言訓練中心。

CONTENTS

第二部分：全真模擬試題&解析

前言

全民英文能力分級檢定測驗（以下簡稱「全民英檢」）分為兩階段進行：包括「初試」與「複試」，必須通過初試，方得參加複試。其中，全民英檢「初級」之初試考試項目包括：聽力測驗、閱讀能力測驗及寫作能力測驗等三項，前兩項通過標準為67%（總分120，80分以上算通過），寫作能力測驗的要求較高，為70%；複試項目為口說能力測驗，通過標準更提高為80%。換句話說，全民英檢考試項目涵括聽、說、讀、寫等四項技能，並以設定合格標準的方式，分階段考試，全部通過者始發給合格證書。由於其所要求的是四項技能兼具之「通才」，因此報考者不可偏廢任何一項英文技能。

然而，在讀者所認識諸多報考全民英檢初級的同學當中，未通過者落敗的項目以「寫作能力測驗」居多，原因何在？筆者認為可由外在的英語學習環境與學習者本身的內在條件兩項因素來思考。

首先，初級英文教學較不重視結構的認識。近年來國人開始學習英文之年齡層降至小學、甚至幼稚園階段；此外，拜民間英文教學普及、坊間書報雜誌垂手可得之賜，國小學童或國中生接觸英文機會增多，更塑造了全民學習英文的環境，相當可喜可賀。然而，在部份學童的學習階段中，因為教學與考試方式間的落差，造成了「Broken English（破碎的英文）」的現象。也就是同學對於日常生活字彙、詞彙的掌握度雖強，卻較缺乏對英文此語言結構方面的認識，致使現今國中階段的學童閱讀及寫作能力普遍不佳。

其次，孩童語言分析能力較弱，此項原因間接造成前述現象。因為國中小階段的學童記憶力強、分析能力較弱。因此，對於英語此一外國語言的學習，老師所能要求的不外乎多背單字、片語及日常生活用法。受限於國中小學生語言發展的先天條件，學習者接觸的多為點向與線向的英語，較少接受面向的英文閱讀洗禮，寫作層面的認知更是少之又

少。

提及寫作，無論中文或英文，多數人都有「舉筆千斤重」的感嘆。的確！從閱讀所認知的詞彙，到寫作的應用層次間的落差極大。比方說，一位懂得2000個詞彙的英文學習者，在寫作的輸出方面，能運用的詞彙可能不及200個。所幸全民英檢初級寫作所要求的僅止於單句的「改寫、合併與重組」，以及一篇50字的「段落寫作」。針對前述兩項讓同學的初級寫作無法「破關」的因素，本書提出兩大方向供讀者參考：一為廣泛閱讀，日積月累，自然就能培養語感，並增強對英文結構的認知；二為多練習，所謂 Practice makes perfect. （熟能生巧）正是這個道理。同時，本書在編撰時分為二大部分，即：「應考技巧篇」及「模擬試題篇」。前者在於提供讀者全面性的結構認識，包括各類型單句寫作及段落寫作之要領；後者則作為讀者檢驗自身實力及考前熱身之用。

本書使用方法

按本書之編排，第一部分為【應考技巧】及第二部分為【全真模擬試題&解析】。建議使用方式如下：

1. 對於久未接觸英文的讀者，建議可自第一部分逐章讀起，以達溫故知新之效。

2. 程度較好的同學，不妨自第二部分開始著手，遇到不太理解之處，再回頭查閱第一部分的解說。

3. 而時間不太充裕，馬上得應試的同學，做法可仿照前一類讀者，自模擬題開始做起。

為了讓同學方便查閱，本書特於【全真模擬試題&解析】的解析部份詳列該題與【應考技巧】相對應之單元。

準備方向

當同學問及全民英檢的準備方式時，筆者仍要不厭其煩地提醒同學寫作無法一蹴可幾；因此，及早養成閱讀英文的習慣，除了可以增加語感外，亦可替未來的寫作奠定基礎。因為唯有不斷地觀摩別人的好文章，不斷地輸入（被動層面），到了實際寫作（主動層面）時才能信手

拈來，揮灑自如。舉凡國內風行一時的全民英檢、公務員考試，到留學考試的托福、IELTS，以及其他各類型的英文考試，都紛紛將寫作列入考核的項目之一，顯見英文寫作的重要性。畢竟在全球化的年代中，身為地球村一員的我們，要的不只是用英語跟外國人說說話或者只要聽得懂就好了。文字的溝通與透過文字記錄、獲取最新訊息與知識，亦即英文的閱讀與寫作能力更是同學未來不可或缺的謀生技能。

本書特色

1. 兼顧實力培養與應考訓練
2. 細分題目類型，分單元解說
3. 練習題最多，各個擊破
4. 寫作範文充份，分析詳盡
5. 模擬題型眾多，熟能生巧
6. 解析條理分明，易讀易懂

推薦序

英語一直是身為地球村一員的現代人應具備的基本工具。在這個資訊爆炸、知識經濟掛帥的二十一世紀，有好的英語能力更是一項個人的資產與利器。有鑑於此，政府於 2000 年起開始定期舉辦「全民英語能力分級檢定測驗考試」，讓有需要的人參與以測定自己的英語能力。

貝塔語言出版針對全民英檢考試編著一系列叢書，而本書《全民英檢寫作破關——初級》乃針對英檢初級測驗所編寫。就短期來看，可幫助讀者有效準備並通過英檢初級考試；就長遠來看，則可奠定並增強讀者英語寫作能力之基礎。本書特色：

四大題型各個擊破

題型設計依照全民英檢初級寫作之測驗形式，單句寫作部份包含句子改寫、句子合併和重組等三題型，另加上段落寫作，共計有四大題型，作者艾菱老師依其多年教學經驗歸納出各題型命題方向，並教授詳細的應考技巧，幫助讀者系統化學習、寫作輕鬆破關拿高分。

全真模擬試題，反覆練習

依照全民英檢初級寫作測驗題型而設計的十回全真模擬試題，可供讀者反覆練習、提升應考實戰能力。每回試題均附詳盡解析，提供讀者再次學習機會，針對不足之處再補強，應考實力再上層樓。

應考技巧

Write

單句寫作篇

單元一 句子改寫

直述句改疑問句

範例

1 Charles is visiting in the United States.

→ _____?

→ Where _____?

ANS 1) *Is Charles visiting in the United States*?
查爾斯在美國觀光嗎？

2) Where *is Charles visiting*?
查爾斯去哪裡觀光？

2 Albert passed the GEPT last year.

→ _____?

→ When _____?

ANS 1) *Did Albert pass the GEPT last year*?
艾伯特去年通過全民英檢嗎？

2) When *did Albert pass the GEPT*?
艾伯特何時通過全民英檢的？

3 Gina has traveled to many countries in the past few years.

→ _____?

→ How many _____?

ANS 1) *Has Gina traveled to many countries in the past few years*?
吉娜過去幾年去過很多國家旅行嗎？

2) How many *countries has Gina traveled in the past few years*?
吉娜過去幾年旅行過多少個國家？

4 Students should study Chinese and English in high school.

→ _____?

→ What _____?

ANS 1) *Should students study Chinese and English in high school?*
中學生應該學中文和英文嗎？

2) *What should students study in high school?*
中學生應該學些什麼？

🔹 基本概念

　　「直述句」改為「疑問句」，亦即將一般的敘述句改為問句。問句可分為兩類：一為以Yes/No回答者，稱之為「一般問句」；另一類則為以疑問詞 (who, what, when, where, which, why, how) 為首之問句。二者改為問句之步驟相同，惟後者於更改過程中，往往涉及人、事、時、地、物、原因、方法、程度等，因此，在更改前，需先了解問句所要問的重點；同時，亦須注意原有敘述句所提供之線索。

　　各疑問詞所要問的重點如下：

Who: 　問「什麼人」。

Whose: 問「誰的」，用於人或事物均可。

What: 　問做「什麼」事、買了「什麼」東西、說了「什麼」話等。

Which: 問「哪一個選項」。

When: 　問「時間」，可能是幾點鐘、早上、下午或晚上、上個禮拜或去年等。

Where: 問「地點」，如學校、機場、某個國家等。

Why: 　問「原因」或「理由」。

How: 　問方法、程度 (how well)、時間 (how long)、多少 (how many, how much) 等。

🔹 應考要訣

1️⃣ 將Be動詞或助動詞提至主詞之前，形成倒裝句構：

　1) Be動詞類型→（疑問詞）＋Be＋S（＋補語）？

　2) 其他類型→（疑問詞）＋助動詞＋S＋原形動詞／本動詞（＋受詞）？

2️⃣ 改為以疑問詞為首之問句，需刪除該疑問詞所代替之名詞。

3️⃣ 其餘字詞照抄，句尾加上問號。

簡言之，直述句改為疑問句時，第一步驟即為尋找句中之 Be 動詞或助動詞（包括：一般助動詞、時態助動詞及模態助動詞），並將之提至主詞之前。以下按前述四者歸類，詳述直述句改疑問句之步驟，並提供試題演練。

I. Be 動詞型

（疑問詞）＋ Be ＋ S（＋補語）？
（疑問詞）＋ Be ＋ S ＋ Ving／Vpp？

　　直述句中動詞為 Be 動詞類，包括 Be 動詞後接「補語型」或「分詞型」（包括現在分詞 Ving 及過去分詞 Vpp）兩類。二者改寫為疑問句之步驟相同──亦即將 Be 提至主詞之前，其他字詞不變，字尾加上問號（？）。

◆ 範例分析

1. Nancy is in school.

　　hint 改為一般問句

　→ *Is Nancy in school?*
　　南茜在學校嗎？

　說明
　　本句中出現 Be 動詞 is，改寫為問句時，需將 is 提至主詞之前，形成倒裝，句尾加上問號。

　　hint 改為以疑問詞 where 為首之問句

　→ **Where** *is Nancy?*
　　南茜在哪裡？

　說明
　　本句疑問詞 where 所代替者，即為表地點之 in school，在改寫為疑問句時，必須刪除之。其餘步驟同上。

2 Charles is visiting in the United States.

hint 改為一般問句

→ *Is Charles visiting in the United States?*

查爾斯正在美國觀光嗎？

說明

本句中出現 Be 動詞 is，改為問句時，需將 is 提至主詞之前，形成倒裝；與 is 搭配之現在分詞 visiting 及其後之地方副詞 in the United States 位置不變，惟句尾須加上問號。

hint 改為以疑問詞 where 為首之問句

→ Where *is Charles visiting?*

查爾斯去哪裡觀光？

說明

本句疑問詞 where 所代替者，即為表地點之 in the United States，在改寫為疑問句時，必須刪除。其餘步驟同上。

◆ 試題演練

請將下列直述句更改為疑問句

① Wendy and her family are in Hong Kong.

→ _____?

→ Where _____?

② The students were late for school because they missed the bus.

→ _____?

→ Why _____?

③ My sister is listening to the radio at home.

→ _____?

→ What _____?

④ The little boy was crying because he was very hungry.

→ _____ ?

→ Why _____ ?

⑤ Many people were out of work last year.

→ _____ ?

→ When _____ ?

II. 一般動詞型

（疑問詞）＋助動詞＋S＋原形動詞（＋虛詞）？

　　直述句中動詞為一般動詞類，於改寫為疑問句時，係將相對應之助動詞（do、does 或過去式之 did）附加在主詞之前，一般動詞保持原有位置，但須還原為原形動詞；其他字詞不變，句尾加上問號（？）。

◆ 範例分析

3) Peter likes to play basketball after school.

　hint 改為一般問句

→ *Does Peter like to play basketball after school?*
　彼得喜歡在放學後打籃球嗎？

說明

Likes 為一般動詞之現在式，改為問句時，必須將其對應之助動詞 (does) 附加於主詞之前，並將 likes 改為原形之 like，其他字詞不變，句尾加上問號。

　hint 改為以疑問詞 when 為首之問句

→ When *does Peter like to play basketball?*
　彼得喜歡在什麼時候打籃球？

說明

> 本句疑問詞 when 所代替者為 after school，改為疑問句時須刪除
> 之。其他步驟同上。

hint 改為以疑問詞 what 為首之問句

→ What *does Peter like to do after school?*
彼得放學後喜歡做什麼？

說明

> 本句疑問詞 what 所代替者為 to play basketball，改為疑問句時
> 須刪除之，惟原句中 like 之受詞 to play basketball 應改為 to do。
> 其他步驟同上。

4) The couple traveled to some foreign countries in 1999.

hint 改為一般問句

→ *Did the couple travel to any foreign countries in 1999?*
這對夫婦在 1999 年中去過任何國家旅行嗎？

說明

> Traveled 為一般動詞之過去式，改為問句時，必須將其對應之助
> 動詞 (did) 附加於主詞 the couple 之前，並將 traveled 改為原形之
> travel；some 改為疑問句時更改為 any（任何），其他字詞不
> 變，句尾加上問號。

hint 改為以疑問詞 where 為首之問句

→ Where *did the couple travel in 1999?*
這對夫婦在 1999 年時去了哪裡旅行？

說明

> 本句疑問詞 where 所代替者為 to many foreign countries，改為
> 疑問句時須刪除之。其他步驟同上。

◆ 試題演練

請將下列直述句更改為疑問句

⑥ Tammy likes to read in her free time.

→ _____ ?

→ What _____ ?

⑦ Sarah usually stays up very late on weekends.

→ _____ ?

→ When _____ ?

⑧ Albert passed the GEPT last year.

→ _____ ?

→ When _____ ?

⑨ Joanne goes to school by subway.

→ _____ ?

→ How _____ ?

⑩ Andy's father quit his job last week.

→ _____ ?

→ When _____ ?

III. 時態助動詞型

（疑問詞）＋時態助動詞＋S＋本動詞（＋諭詞）？

所謂「時態助動詞」即構成完成式之 has、have、had，具有完成式功能，但無語意（或可譯為「已經」），其後所接之本動詞為過去分詞 Vpp。

本句型改寫為疑問句的方法同前句型「一般動詞型」，亦即將助動詞提至主詞 S 之前，Vpp 及其後之受詞位置等不變，句尾加上問號（？）。

◆ 範例分析

5 Gina has traveled to many countries in the past few years.

　hint 改為一般問句

→ Has Gina traveled to many countries in the past few years?

吉娜過去幾年去過許多國家旅行嗎？

說明

　在此 has 為時態助動詞，改為問句時，需提至主詞之前。

　hint 改為以疑問詞 how many 為首之問句

→ How many countries has Gina traveled in the past few years?

吉娜過去幾年去過幾個國家旅行？

說明

　本句疑問詞 how many 所問即為直述句中之 many countries，改寫為疑問句時將之刪除。

◆ 試題演練

請將下列直述句更改為疑問句

⑪ He has played on-line games for three hours.

→ _____?

→ How long _____?

⑫ Danny had left town when his girlfriend called.

→ _____?

→ Where _____?

⑬ Karen has spent NT$30,000 on clothes at this department store.

→ _____?

→ How much _____?

⑭ They have had dinner with their manager.

→ _____?

→ With whom _____?

⑮ They have lived in this small town for ten years.

→ _____?

→ How long _____?

IV. 模態助動詞型

（疑問詞）＋模態助動詞＋S＋原形動詞（＋謂詞）？

所謂「模態助動詞」包括：can、could、will、would、shall、should、may、might、had better、must、ought to等，在句中具有不同語意，其後須接原形動詞。

本句型改寫為疑問句的方法同「一般動詞句型」，亦即將模態助動詞提至主詞S之前，其他字詞位置不變，句尾加上問號（？）。

◆ 範例分析

6⃝ Students should study many subjects in high school.

hint 改為一般問句

→ *Should students study many subjects in high school?*

中學生應該唸很多科目嗎？

說明

Should為模態助動詞，改寫為疑問句時，須將之提至主詞前；其他字詞位置不變，並於句尾加上問號。

hint 改為以疑問詞 what 為首之問句

→ What *should students study in high school?*

中學生應該學些什麼？

說明

> **What** 所代替者為 many subjects，改寫為疑問句時須刪除。其他步驟同上。

◆ 試題演練

請將下列直述句更改為疑問句

⑯ Jenny can speak Japanese very well.

→ _____?

→ How well _____?

⑰ Mary will marry George in church next year.

→ _____?

→ Where _____?

⑱ Anne would move to a quieter and unpolluted place.

→ _____?

→ Where _____?

⑲ Celina might go abroad to study this summer.

→ _____?

→ What _____?

⑳ Strong typhoons may cause floods and mudslides.

→ _____?

→ What _____?

解答

① 1) Are Wendy and her family in Hong Kong?
   溫蒂和她的家人在香港嗎？

2) **Where** are Wendy and her family?
   溫蒂和她的家人在哪裡？

② 1) Were the students late for school because they missed the bus?
   這些學生因為錯過了公車而上學遲到嗎？

2) **Why** were the students late for school?
   這些學生為什麼遲到？

③ 1) Is my sister listening to the radio at home?
   我姊姊在家裡聽收音機嗎？

2) **What** is my sister listening to at home?
   我姊姊在家裡聽什麼？

④ 1) Was the little boy crying because he was very hungry?
   這個小男孩是因為太餓了才哭的嗎？

2) **Why** was the little boy crying?
   這個小男孩為什麼哭？

⑤ 1) Were many people out of work last year?
   去年有很多人失業嗎？

2) **When** were many people out of work?
   很多人在什麼時候失業？

⑥ 1) Does Tammy like to read in her free time?
   譚美閒暇之餘喜歡閱讀嗎？

2) **What** does Tammy like to do in her free time?
   譚美閒暇之餘喜歡做些什麼？

⑦ 1) Does Sarah usually stay up very late on weekends?
   莎拉週末的時候通常很晚睡嗎？

2) **When** does Sarah usually stay up very late?
莎拉通常什麼時候會很晚睡？

⑧ 1) **Did** Albert pass the GEPT last year?
艾伯特去年通過全民英檢了嗎？

2) **When** did Albert pass the GEPT?
艾伯特何時通過全民英檢的？

⑨ 1) **Does** Joanne go to school by subway?
瓊安搭地鐵去上學嗎？

2) **How** does Joanne go to school?
瓊安怎麼去上學的？

⑩ 1) **Did** Andy's father quit his job last week?
安迪的爸爸上個禮拜辭職的嗎？

2) **When** did Andy's father quit his job?
安迪的爸爸什麼時候辭職的？

⑪ 1) **Has** he played on-line games for three hours?
他已經玩了三個小時的線上遊戲嗎？

2) **How long** has he played on-line games?
他已經玩了多久的線上遊戲？

⑫ 1) **Had** Danny left town when his girlfriend called?
丹尼在他女朋友打電話來時就已經出城了嗎？

2) **Where** had Danny left when his girlfriend called?
丹尼在他女朋友打電話來時就已離開了哪裡？

⑬ 1) **Has** Karen spent NT$30,000 on clothes at this department store?
凱倫在這家百貨公司買了三萬塊台幣的衣服嗎？

2) **How much** has Karen spent on clothes at this department store?
凱倫在這家百貨公司花了多少錢買衣服？

⑭ 1) **Have** they had dinner with their manager?
他們有跟經理吃晚餐嗎？

2) **With whom** have they had dinner?
　　他們跟誰吃晚餐？

⑮ 1) Have they lived in this small town for ten years?
　　他們在這個小城鎮已住了十年嗎？

　 2) **How long** have they lived in this small town?
　　他們在這個小城鎮住了多久？

⑯ 1) Can Jenny speak Japanese very well?
　　珍妮日語說得很好嗎？

　 2) **How well** can Jenny speak Japanese?
　　珍妮的日語說得怎麼樣？

⑰ 1) Will Mary marry George in church next year?
　　瑪麗跟喬治明年會在教堂結婚嗎？

　 2) **Where** will Mary marry George next year?
　　瑪麗和喬治明年會在哪裡結婚？

⑱ 1) Would Anne move to a quieter and unpolluted place?
　　安會搬去一個較安靜又無污染的地方嗎？

　 2) **Where** would Anne move?
　　安會搬去哪裡？

⑲ 1) Might Celina go abroad to study this summer?
　　席琳娜今年夏天會出國唸書嗎？

　 2) **What** might Celina do this summer?
　　席琳娜今年夏天可能會做什麼？

⑳ 1) **May** strong typhoons cause floods and mudslides?
　　強烈颱風會引起水災和土石流嗎？

　 2) **What** may strong typhoons cause?
　　強烈颱風可能會引起什麼？

直接問句改間接問句

範例

1
Bill asked Judy, "Can you please speak a little louder?"

→ Bill asked Judy if she _____.

ANS Bill asked Judy if she *could please speak a little louder.*
比爾問茱蒂她可不可以說大聲一點。

2
Bob asked his girlfriend, "When will you arrive at the theater?"

→ Bob asked his girlfriend when _____.

ANS Bob asked his girlfriend when *she would arrive at the theater.*
鮑伯問他女朋友什麼時候會抵達戲院。

3
"What did you have in mind?" Write and tell me.

→ Write and tell me _____.

ANS Write and tell me *what you had in mind.*
寫下來並告訴我你心中的想法。

🔷 基本概念

　　本單元係探討如何將「直接問句」(在英文中以引號 "..." 型態呈現的疑問句) 改為名詞子句型態之「間接問句」(即帶有連接詞之直述句)。在間接問句之前的主要子句常見者有兩類:一為以 ask、tell、say 等為動詞者;另一類則為祈使句。

　　以下將直接問句區分為一般問句及疑問詞為首之問句,逐項說明之;此外,並說明祈使句型態間接問句之處理原則。

🔷 應考要訣

1) 將直接問句之逗號及引號去除。

2) 處理直接問句,過程如下:

1) 主詞改爲與主要子句吻合者。

2) 動詞與主要子句動詞時態一致。

3) 其他──若有受詞或所有格,需作適當之處理。

3 將疑問句更改爲直述句

1) 一般問句──先加上連接詞 if 或 whether...(or not),表「是否」,再更改爲直述句。

2) 疑問詞爲首之問句──不需加任何連接詞,直接更改爲直述句。

3) 直述句之詞序爲 S+V+(補語)(參考直述句改疑問句)。

4) 問號改爲句點。

I. 一般問句型

◆ 範例分析

1 Bill asked Judy, "Can you speak a little louder?"

hint 將直接問句更改爲間接問句

→ Bill asked Judy **if** she *could speak a little louder.*

比爾問茱蒂她可不可以說大聲一點?

說明
1 刪除直接問句之引號及問號,調整主詞與動詞位置,改爲直述句 you can speak a little louder。
2 在間接問句前加上連接詞 if 或 whether... (or not)。
3 原句中之 you 爲主要子句動詞 asked 之接受對象,顯然應爲 Judy,因此間接問句的主詞改爲 she。
4 將原句中之助動詞 can 改爲與主要子句動詞 asked 同時態之 could。
5 形成間接問句 if she could speak a little louder。

2 Tammy wondered, "Should I open the present in front of my friends?"

〔hint〕將直接問句更改為間接問句

→Tammy wondered **whether** she should open the present in front of her friends (or not).

譚美心想她是否該在朋友面前打開禮物。

說明

1 刪除直接問句之引號及問號，調整主詞與動詞位置，改為直述句 I should open the present in front of my friends.。

2 在間接問句前加上連接詞 if 或 whether... (or not)。

3 原句中之 I＝主要子句主詞 Tammy＝she；同時將原句之所有格 my 改為與 she 搭配之 her。

4 形成間接問句 whether she should open the present in front of her friends (or not)。

◆ 試題演練

請將句中之直接問句更改為間接問句

① Vicky said to John, "Could you do me a favor?"

→ Vicky asked John if _____ do her a favor.

② Dennis asked me, "Would you like to join us?"

→ Dennis asked me whether _____ to join them or not.

③ Jeff called Patricia and asked her, "Do you feel like seeing a movie?"

→ Jeff called and asked Patricia if _____.

④ I asked Jeanine, "Have you been to Europe?"

→ I asked Jeanine whether she _____.

⑤ I asked my cousin, "Did you enjoy the trip to London?"

→ I asked my cousin if she _____.

⑥ Amy said to Ray, "Why are you in such a hurry?"

→ Amy asked Ray _____.

II. 疑問詞為首型

◆ **範例分析**

③ Bob asked his girlfriend, "When will you arrive at the theater?"

　　hint 將直接問句更改為間接問句

　→Bob asked his girlfriend when *she would arrive at the theater.*

　　鮑伯問他女朋友什麼時候會抵達戲院。

　　說明

　　1 去除逗點及引號。
　　2 You 為主要子句動詞 asked 的接受對象,顯然 his girlfriend ＝ she。
　　3 將助動詞改為與主要子句動詞 asked 同時態之 would。
　　4 改為直述句時,倒裝句型需還原為 S ＋ V。
　　5 形成 when she would arrive at the theater 之間接問句。

◆ **試題演練**

　請將句中之直接問句更改為間接問句

⑦ "How old are you?" Beatrice asked the little boy.

　→ Beatrice asked the little boy ＿＿＿＿＿＿＿＿＿＿＿＿＿＿＿.

⑧ "How do you like Ireland?" my Irish friend asked.

　→ My Irish friend asked me ＿＿＿＿＿＿＿＿＿＿＿＿＿＿＿.

⑨ The mother asked her son, "What would you like to eat?"

　→ The mother asked her son ＿＿＿＿＿＿＿＿＿＿＿＿＿＿＿.

⑩ "Which college did you go to?" the boss asked John.

　→ The boss asked John ＿＿＿＿＿＿＿＿＿＿＿＿＿＿＿.

⑪ "Which season do you like best?" asked my teacher.

　→ My teacher asked me ＿＿＿＿＿＿＿＿＿＿＿＿＿＿＿.

⑫ "Where did she go?" said Joe.

→ Joe asked _____.

III. 祈使句型

◆ 範例分析

④ "What did you have in mind?" Write and tell me.

hint 將祈使句中之直接問句更改為間接問句

→ Write and tell me *what you had in mind.*

寫下來並告訴我你心中的想法。

說明

1 去除引號。

2 在祈使句中之直接問句改間接問句時，時態保持不變。

3 一般問句還原為直述句 S + V，並刪除助動詞 did，將 have 改為
過去式 had，形成 what you had in mind 之間接問句。

◆ 試題演練

請將句中之直接問句更改為祈使句間接問句

⑬ "What day is today?"

→ Tell me _____.

⑭ "When did Steve arrive in Taipei?"

→ Ask them _____.

⑮ "How does your sister go to school?"

→ Tell the teacher _____.

解答

① Vicky asked John if he could do her a favor.
維琪問約翰是否能幫她個忙。

② Dennis asked me whether I would like to join them or not.
丹尼斯問我是否願意加入他們。

③ Jeff called and asked Patricia if she felt like seeing a movie.
傑夫打電話問派翠西雅想不想去看電影。

④ I asked Jeanine whether she had been to Europe.
我問金妮有沒有去過歐洲。

⑤ I asked my cousin if she enjoyed the trip to London.
我問我表妹倫敦之旅好玩嗎。

⑥ Amy asked Ray why he was in such a hurry.
艾咪問雷為什麼行色匆匆。

⑦ Beatrice asked the little boy how old he was.
碧翠絲問小男孩他幾歲了。

⑧ My Irish friend asked me how I liked Ireland.
我的愛爾蘭朋友問我覺得愛爾蘭怎麼樣。

⑨ The mother asked her son what he would like to eat.
那個媽媽問她兒子想吃什麼。

⑩ The boss asked John which college he went to.
老闆問約翰他唸哪一所大學。

⑪ My teacher asked me which season I liked best.
老師問我最喜歡哪個季節。

⑫ Joe asked where she went.
喬問她去哪裡了。

⑬ Tell me what day today is.
告訴我今天幾月幾號。

⑭ Ask them when Steve arrived in Taipei.
問他們史蒂芬什麼時候抵達台北。

⑮ Tell the teacher how your sister goes to school.
告訴老師你姊姊／妹妹怎麼去學校的。

改為虛主詞的句型

1 That Lily has had two children is unbelievable.

→ It _____.

ANS It *is unbelievable that Lily has had two children.*
真不敢相信莉莉已經有兩個小孩了。

2 To study in college has been my dream.

→ It _____.

ANS It *has been my dream to study in college.*
上大學一直都是我的夢想。

3 Crying over spilt milk is useless.

→ It _____.

ANS It *is useless crying over spilt milk.*
覆水難收。

🔖 基本概念

　　所謂改為虛主詞的句型，係將原句中之「子句或片語型的主詞」以 it 代替，形成以「虛主詞」it 為主要子句主詞之句構。一般而言，虛主詞 it 所代替之真正主詞，可區分為三類：名詞子句、不定詞片語及動名詞片語。

🔖 應考要訣

① 找尋名詞子句、不定詞或動名詞片語。

② 將前述子句或片語置換為 it。

③ 將前述子句或片語移至主要子句之後。

I. 名詞子句型

◆ **範例分析**

1) That Lily has had two children is unbelievable.

> **hint** 改為虛主詞之句型

> → It *is unbelievable that Lily has had two children.*
> 真不敢相信莉莉已經有兩個小孩了。

> **說明**
> 1 以 it 代替名詞子句型之主詞 that Lily has had two children。
> 2 將原句改成 It is unbelievable. 後,再併入上述名詞子句。

◆ **試題演練**

請更改為虛主詞之句型

① That Billy's two-year-old son can tell time is surprising.

→ It _____.

② That practice makes perfect is true.

→ It _____.

③ That you eat a lot of junk food is not good.

→ It _____.

II. 不定詞片語型

◆ **範例分析**

2) To study abroad has been my dream.

> **hint** 改為虛主詞之句型

> → It *has been my dream to study abroad.*
> 出國唸書一直是我的夢想。

說明

1 以 it 代替不定詞片語型之主詞 to study abroad。

2 將原句改成 It has been my dream. 後,再併入該不定詞片語。

◆ **試題演練**

請更改為虛主詞之句型

④ To do this will be a waste of time.

　→ It ＿＿＿＿＿＿＿＿＿＿＿＿＿＿＿＿＿＿＿＿＿.

⑤ To meet people from other countries is interesting.

　→ It ＿＿＿＿＿＿＿＿＿＿＿＿＿＿＿＿＿＿＿＿＿.

⑥ To study in a quiet library is a good idea.

　→ It ＿＿＿＿＿＿＿＿＿＿＿＿＿＿＿＿＿＿＿＿＿.

⑦ To take vitamins every day is good to your health.

　→ It ＿＿＿＿＿＿＿＿＿＿＿＿＿＿＿＿＿＿＿＿＿.

III. 動名詞片語型

◆ **範例分析**

3 Spending some time exercising every day is worthwhile.

　hint 改為虛主詞之句型

　→ It *is worthwhile spending some time exercising every day*.

　每天花點時間做運動是很值得的。

說明

1 以 it 代替動名詞片語型之主詞 spending some time exercising every day。

2 將原句改成 It is worthwhile.,再併入上述動名詞片語。

◆ **試題演練**
　請更改為虛主詞之句型

⑧ Living in the countryside can do you good.

　→ It _____.

⑨ Running after a bus is no use.

　→ It _____.

⑩ Studying hard before an exam is worthwhile.

　→ It _____.

解答

① It is surprising that Billy's two-year-old son can tell time.
比利兩歲的兒子會看時間真是令人驚訝。

② It is true that practice makes perfect.
「熟能生巧」一點也沒錯。

③ It is not good that you eat a lot of junk food.
你吃很多的垃圾食物是不好的。

④ It will be a waste of time to do this.
做這件事是浪費時間。

⑤ It is interesting to meet people from other countries.
認識其他國家的人很有趣。

⑥ It is a good idea to study in a quiet library.
在安靜的圖書館唸書是個好主意。

⑦ It is good to your health to take vitamins every day.
每天吃維他命有益健康。

⑧ It can do you good living in the countryside.
住在鄉下對你有益。

⑨ It is no use running after a bus.
追公車也沒用。

⑩ It is worthwhile studying hard before an exam.
考試前努力唸書是很值得的。

不定詞或動名詞片語當受詞

範例	
1	Judy: What is your decision?
	Gina: I will study Arts in college.
→	Gina decides _____.
ANS	Gina decides *to study Arts in college.*
	吉娜決定在大學裡唸文科。
2	Jack: Do you cook dinner for your family?
	Ann: Yeah, I enjoy it very much.
→	Anne enjoys _____ for her family very much.
ANS	Ann enjoys *cooking dinner* for her family very much.
	安十分喜歡為家人煮晚餐。
3	Peggy: Jeanine plays the violin very well.
	Fred:　Yeah, she is pretty good at it.
→	Jeanine is good at _____ the violin.
ANS	Jeanine is good at *playing* the violin.
	金妮很會拉小提琴。

🔷 基本概念

　　及物動詞後之受詞，除了典型的名詞或名詞片語外，常見者還包括「不定詞片語」及「動名詞片語」兩種型態，二者兼具名詞功能，惟性質相異。

　　※ 不定詞：表動作尚未執行；

　　※ 動名詞：表動作已執行或表過去的經驗。

　　上述兩類片語出現於特定動詞之後，以下羅列常見者：

1️⃣ 以不定詞片語為受詞之動詞

　　want, ask, plan, hope, decide, learn, prepare, fail, agree, would like,

expect, promise, refuse

2 以動名詞片語為受詞之動詞

enjoy, finish, mind, practice, quit, imagine, keep, avoid, consider, discuss, suggest, waste, feel like, give up

　　除上述動詞外，動名詞片語亦可能出現於介系詞之後，常見片語如下：

be good at	**be busy (in)**	**have trouble (in)**
be interested in	**succeed in**	**participate in**
apologize for	**thank s.b. for**	**have a reason for**
have an excuse for	**be excited about**	**be worried about**
dream of	**complain of**	**think of**
be capable of	**take care of**	**be tired of**
keep from	**stop from**	**prevent from**
look forward to	**be used to**	**object to**

3 以不定詞或動名詞片語為受詞之動詞

1) 以下動詞可搭配不定詞或動名詞，且句意不變

begin, start, continue

2) 以下動詞可搭配不定詞或動名詞，但句意相異

forget, remember, stop

應考要訣

1 判斷動詞為上述何種類型，決定受詞採用的型態（不定詞或動名詞）。

2 如屬前述第一型之動詞組別，於第二個動詞前加上 to，並還原為原形動詞，形成不定詞片語。

3 如屬前述第二型之動詞組別或在介系詞之後，將第二個動詞改為 Ving 型態，形成動名詞片語。

4 如屬前述第三型，可搭配不定詞或動名詞之動詞，須注意改寫後句子之句意是否變動，以決定受詞採不定詞或動名詞。

I. 不定詞片語型

◆ 範例分析

1 Judy: What is your decision?

Gina: I will study computer science in college.

→ Gina decides _____.

hint 以不定詞改寫

→ Gina decides *to study computer science in college.*

吉娜決定在大學裡讀電腦科技。

說明

1 Decide 後有動詞時，需將該動詞改為不定詞型態。

2 將 will study computer science in college 改為不定詞片語，將 will study 還原為原形之 study，並在 study 前加上 to，形成 to study computer science in college。

◆ 試題演練

請更改為不定詞之句型

① Ting: Did you help Sonia with her assignments?

Sam: I said no to her.

→ Sam refused _____ with her assignments.

② George: Want to go for a ride?

Teddy: No, I'll stay at home.

→ Teddy would like _____.

③ Jeff: Could I use your car?

Bill: Sure. Go ahead.

→ Bill agrees _____ lend his car to Jeff.

④ Tony: Did you arrive at the airport in time?

David: No, I didn't.

→ David failed _____ in time.

⑤ Oscar: What is good about living in Italy?

Cathy: Besides meeting different people, I can cook Italian food very
 well.

→ Cathy learned _____ and met different people in Italy.

⑥ Tina: Can you do me a favor?

Dennis: Not a problem.

→ Dennis agrees _____ Tina a favor.

⑦ Teacher: What do you want to be in the future?

Ray: A lawyer.

→ Ray hopes _____ a lawyer in the future.

⑧ Peter: Do you have any plan after graduation?

Mei: I want to travel to Europe.

→ Mei plans _____ to Europe after graduation.

⑨ Wendy: Will you return my money?

Billy: I will. Don't worry.

→ Billy promises _____ Wendy's money.

⑩ Emma: What is the purpose of your exercising?

Vicky: I want to wear a tight dress on my birthday party.

→ Vicky prepares _____ on her birthday party.

II. 動名詞片語型

◆ 範例分析

2 Jack: Do you cook dinner for your family?

Ann: Yeah, I enjoy it very much.

→ Ann enjoys _____ for her family very much.

→ Ann enjoys *cooking dinner* for her family very much.

安十分喜歡為家人煮晚餐。

說明

1 enjoy 後有動詞時，需將該動詞改為動名詞型態。

2 將第一句之 cook dinner 改成動名詞，形成 cooking dinner。

3) Peggy: Jeanine plays the violin very well.

Fred: She is pretty good at it.

→ Jeanine is good at _____ the violin.

→ Jeanine is good at *playing* the violin.

金妮很會拉小提琴。

說明

1 at 為介系詞，後有動詞時，需將該動詞改為動名詞型態。

2 將第一句之 plays the violin 改成動名詞，形成 playing the violin。

◆ 試題演練

請更改為動名詞之句型

⑪ Emma: Could you speak more slowly?

Joanne: Sure. No problem.

→ Joanne does not mind _____ more slowly.

⑫ Wendy: Wow, you got up so early today.

Billy: Now I know it's not good to stay up late. I'm going to change my habit.

→ Billy wants to quit _____ late.

⑬ Peter: You're not supposed to watch TV.

Mei: Why not? My homework is done.

→ Mei has finished _____ her homework.

⑭ Teacher: You have to spend more time on English.

  Ray:　　I know. I will practice it every day.

  → Ray has to keep ＿＿＿＿＿＿＿＿＿＿＿＿＿ English every day.

⑮ Tina:　　I want to lose some weight by this summer.

  Dennis: Then, you cannot eat fast food. And remember, no more snacks.

  → Tina has to avoid ＿＿＿＿＿＿＿＿＿＿＿ fast food and snacks.

⑯ Greg is very excited.

  He is going to attend the Dragon Boat Race.

  → Greg is excited about ＿＿＿＿＿＿＿＿＿ the Dragon Boat Race.

⑰ Tony:　I don't like to travel by air.

  David: It has never been a problem for me.

  → David is used to ＿＿＿＿＿＿＿＿＿＿＿＿＿＿＿ by air.

⑱ Ting: Will you study computer science in college?

  Sam: Yes, it really interests me.

  → Sam is interested in ＿＿＿＿＿＿＿ computer science in college.

⑲ Judy: You're putting on weight.

  Joe:　You're right. I'd better not eat any more junk food.

  → Joe is going to stop ＿＿＿＿＿＿＿＿＿＿＿＿ junk food.

解答

① Sam refused to help Sonia with her assignments.
山姆拒絕幫蘇菲雅做作業。

② Teddy would like to stay at home.
泰迪想待在家裡。

③ Bill agrees to lend his car to Jeff.
比爾同意把車子借給傑夫。

④ David failed to arrive at the airport in time.
大衛沒能來得及趕到機場。

⑤ Cathy learned to cook Italian food and met different people in Italy.
凱西在義大利學會了煮義大利菜，而且認識了不同的人。

⑥ Dennis agrees to do Tina a favor.
丹尼斯答應幫提娜的忙。

⑦ Ray hopes to be a lawyer in the future.
雷希望將來當個律師。

⑧ Mei plans to travel to Europe after graduation.
梅計畫畢業後去歐洲旅行。

⑨ Billy promises to return Wendy's money.
比利承諾會還溫蒂錢。

⑩ Vicky prepares to wear a tight dress on her birthday party.
維琪準備在她生日宴會上穿緊身洋裝。

⑪ Joanne does not mind speaking more slowly.
瓊安不介意講慢一點。

⑫ Billy wants to quit staying up late.
比利想要戒掉熬夜。

⑬ Mei has finished doing her homework.
梅已經完成了作業。

⑭ Ray has to keep practicing English everyday.
雷必須每天持續練習英文。

⑮ Tina has to avoid eating fast food and snacks.
提娜得避免吃速食和點心。

⑯ Greg is excited about attending the Dragon Boat Race.
奎格對於參加龍舟比賽感到很興奮。

⑰ David is used to traveling by air.
大衛習慣搭飛機旅行。

⑱ Sam is interested in studying computer science in college.
山姆對在大學讀電腦科技有興趣。

⑲ Joe is going to stop eating junk food.
喬將會停止吃垃圾食物。

比較級與最高級的句型切換

範例

1 James is the best player on the team.

→ James is _____ than any other _____ on the team.

ANS James is *better* than any other *player* on the team.
詹姆士比隊上任何一個球員都還棒。

→ James is _____ than all the other _____ on the team.

ANS James is *better* than all the other *players* on the team.
詹姆士比隊上所有其他的球員都還棒。

2 No other sea animal in the world is as big as whales.

→ Whales are the _____ sea animals in the world.

ANS Whales are the *biggest* sea animals in the world.
鯨魚是世界上最大的海洋動物。

🟦 基本概念

處理比較級與最高級題型前，必須先釐清一個重要概念：只有形容詞與副詞才有三級（原級－比較級－最高級）。

1. 原級：形容詞或副詞未加工前的原始型態。如：tall 及 important。

2. 比較級：在原級後附加 er，或在原級前另加一字 more，形成【原級-er】或【more 原級】兩種型態。特別注意，二者只能選其一使用，不可混合使用。原則上單音節用 er，多音節則用 more。

    如：tall 之比較級為 taller；important 之比較級為 more important。
    比較級後須搭配 than，以比較兩事（物）之異同。

3. 最高級：在原級後附加 est，或在原級前另加一字 most，形成【原級-est】或【most 原級】兩種型態。二者只能選其一使用，不可混用。選擇方式與比較級同。

    如：tall 之比較級為 tallest；important 之比較級為 most important。

特別注意,最高級後若有名詞,則必須添加冠詞 the 於該最高級之前端,以表示該事(物)之唯一性。

常見不規則型態之比較級與最高級如下表,讀者務必牢記,以免錯用。

原級	比較級	最高級
many, much	more	most
little	less	least
good, well	better	well
bad	worse	worst

以下列舉兩種切換題型:一為比較級與最高級切換,其二為原級與最高級切換,供讀者參考與練習。

💎 應考要訣

1. 找尋句中之形容詞或副詞。
2. 填入適當的級數,常見規則如下:
   句中若出現 than,採比較級;句中出現 the,表唯一或有排他性之概念時,採最高級。
3. 片語 as...as 中之形容詞或副詞,採原級,即【as +形容詞或副詞+ as】。
4. 比較級後所比較之事物,所指若為全體,則該事物須以複數型態呈現。

I. 比較級與最高級之切換

◆ 範例分析

1. James is the best player on the team.
   → James is _____ than any other _____ on the team.
   → James is _____ than all the other _____ on the team.

以比較級改寫

→ James is *better* than any other *player* on the team.

詹姆士比隊上任何一個球員都還棒。

→ James is *better* than all the other *players* on the team.

詹姆士比隊上所有其他的球員都還棒。

說明

1 原句出現最高級 best 其形容詞為 good。

2 改寫句中出現 than，前方必定有 good 之比較級 better。

3 改寫句第一句中出現 any other，所指為「任何一個」，其後之名詞採單數型。即【比較級 than any other＋單數 N】

4 改寫句第二句中出現 all the other，所指為「所有其他的」，其後方名詞採複數型。即【比較級 than all the other＋複數 N】

II. 原級與最高級之切換

◆ 範例分析

2) No other sea animal in the world is as big as whales.

→ Whales are the ＿＿＿＿＿＿＿ sea animals in the world.

hint 以最高級改寫

→ Whales are the *biggest* sea animals in the world.

鯨魚是世界上最大的海洋動物。

說明

1 原句出現形容詞 big 之原級。

2 原句以【as＋原級＋as】之否定句型呈現 whales 與其他 sea animal 之間的比較，表示「沒有其他海洋動物比鯨魚更大」。

3 改寫句中出現 the，後又有名詞 sea animals，因而在該名詞之前加入 big 之最高級 biggest，以表示「鯨魚是海洋動物中體型最大者」。

◆ **試題演練**

　　請更改為比較級或最高級之句型

① Julie is taller than any other girl in her class.

　　→ Julie is _____ girl in her class.

② Practice is the most important part in one's learning.

　　→ Practice is _____ than any other _____ in one's
　　learning.

③ No other sports are as enjoyable as tennis for Tiffany.

　　→ Tennis is the _____ sport for Tiffany.

④ Christmas is the most important holiday for westerners.

　　→ Christmas is _____ than all the other _____ for
　　westerners.

⑤ For Rita, no one is as important as her mother.

　　→ For Rita, her mother is _____ than all the other people.

⑥ Susan thinks watermelon is the most delicious fruit.

　　→ Susan thinks watermelon is _____ than any other
　　_____.

⑦ Robert runs faster than any of his family members.

　　→ Robert is the _____ runner in his family.

⑧ Washington D.C. has the most interesting museums in the U.S.

　　→ Washington D.C. has _____ than all the other cities in
　　the U.S.

⑨ No one in Wendy's family is as rich as she (is).

　　→ Wendy is _____ than anyone else in her family.

⑩ No other restaurant in this town has as many customers as Bruno's
　　(does).

　　→ Bruno's has _____ than all the other _____ in this town.

解答

① Julie is the tallest girl in her class.
茉莉是她班上最高的女生。

② Practice is more important than any other part in one's learning.
在學習中練習比什麼都重要。

③ Tennis is the most enjoyable sport for Tiffany.
對蒂芬妮來說網球是最好玩的運動。

④ Christmas is more important than all the other holidays for westerners.
對西方人來說聖誕節比所有其他的節日都來得重要。

⑤ For Rita, her mother is more important than all the other people.
對麗妲來說，她的媽媽比所有其它的人更重要。

⑥ Susan thinks watermelon is more delicious than any other fruit.
蘇珊認為西瓜比任何一種水果都好吃。

⑦ Robert is the fastest runner in his family.
羅伯特是家裡面跑得最快的。

⑧ Washington D.C. has more interesting museums than all the other cities in the U.S.
華盛頓有比美國所有其它城市有更多有趣的博物館。

⑨ Wendy is richer than anyone else in her family.
溫蒂比她家中的其他任何一個人都有錢。

⑩ Bruno's has more customers than all the other restaurants in this town.
布魯諾有比鎮上所有其它餐廳都還多的顧客。

時態的切換

範例

1	Johnny walked to school this morning.
→	Johnny usually _____ in the morning.
ANS	Johnny usually *walks to school* in the morning.
	強尼早上通常走路去學校。
2	Tony lost his cell phone yesterday.
→	Tony found he _____ when he wanted to call Gina this morning.
ANS	Tony found he *had lost his cell phone* when he wanted to call Gina this morning.
	東尼今天早上想打電話給吉娜時發現他把手機弄丟了。

◆ 基本概念

　　動詞的時態係由三種「時間」與四種「時貌」所組成，如下：

※ 時間：過去、現在與未來時間。

※ 時貌：

　　1 簡單貌。

　　2 進行貌，強調當下進行的動作，其型態為 Be ＋ Ving。

　　3 完成貌，強調到某一時間點已完成的動作，其型態為

　　　 has/have/had/will have ＋ Vpp

　　4 完成進行貌，係前二者之組合，其型態為

　　　 has/have/had/will have ＋ been ＋ Ving

　　處理時態切換之題型時，第一要務便是尋找時間副詞；若句中無時間副詞，則由主要或附屬子句之動詞判斷時態。常見之線索與其配合之時態如下：

　　1 句中出現頻率副詞 always、usually、often 等時，採現在簡單式。

2 時間副詞為過去時間，如 last week、yesterday、this morning等，採過去簡單式。

3 時間副詞為未來時間，如 tomorrow、next year等，採未來式。

4 句中出現時間副詞 right now，採現在進行式。

5 句中出現從屬連接詞 since，表持續性的時間。其主要子句以現在完成式呈現；since 後可能為名詞（為明確的過去時間）或子句型態（時態採過去簡單式）。

6 介系詞 for 之後接一段時間，如 for ten years，表持續性的時間，時態採現在完成式。

◆ 應考要訣

1 找尋時間副詞；若無時間副詞，則觀察主要或附屬子句之動詞時態。

2 以表時間之從屬連接詞，如 before、after、when等，可判斷時間發生之先後。在過去時間中先發生者，須以過去完成式呈現。

3 注意第三人稱單數在現在式句中當主詞，須在動詞字尾加上(e)s。

◆ 範例分析

1 Johnny walked to school this morning.

→ Johnny usually _____ in the morning.

hint 改為現在簡單式之句型

→ Johnny **usually** *walks to school* in the morning.
強尼早上通常走路去上學。

說明

1 改寫句中出現頻率副詞 usually，時態採簡單現在式即可。

2 將原句中之動詞 walked 更改為 walks，其餘字詞不變。

2 Tony lost his cell phone yesterday.

→ Tony found he _____ when he wanted to call Gina this morning.

hint 改為過去完成式之句型

→Tony found he *had lost his cell phone* **when** he wanted to call Gina this morning.

東尼早上想打電話給吉娜時發現他把手機弄丟了。

說明

1 從屬連接詞 when 引導之附屬子句 when he wanted to call Gina this morning 使主要與附屬子句間產生時間先後關係。

2 「遺失手機」的發生時間，經判斷應在「他想打電話給 Gina」之前。因而，主要子句表「遺失手機」之動詞時態，應採過去完成式，即 had lost his cell phone。

◆ **試題演練**

請更改為適當之動詞時態

① I have fast food for lunch every day.

→ I ＿＿＿＿＿＿＿＿＿＿＿＿＿＿＿＿＿ yesterday.

② Irene lives in Taipei.

→ Irene ＿＿＿＿＿＿＿＿＿＿＿＿＿＿＿ since 1983.

③ Betty studied abroad three years ago.

→ Betty ＿＿＿＿＿＿＿＿＿＿＿＿＿＿＿ next year.

④ I do my laundry and sing songs.

→ I sing songs while I ＿＿＿＿＿＿＿＿＿＿＿＿＿＿.

⑤ Angela is taking some courses at New York University.

→ Angela ＿＿＿＿＿＿＿＿ at New York University last summer.

⑥ Christine introduced Michael to Elaine.

→ Christine ＿＿＿＿＿＿＿＿＿＿ at tomorrow's meeting.

⑦ May reads novels on Sundays.

→ May ＿＿＿＿＿＿＿＿ when she lived on her aunt's farm.

⑧ Vincent is gaining some weight.

→ Vincent ＿＿＿＿＿＿＿＿＿＿＿＿ since he got married.

⑨ I am having a good time at the picnic.

→ I _____ at the picnic yesterday.

⑩ Kevin studied English last night.

→ Kevin _____ for ten years.

解答

① I had fast food for lunch **yesterday.**
我昨天午餐吃速食。

② Irene **has lived** in Taipei **since 1983.**
艾琳從 1983 年就住在台北了。

③ Betty **will/is going to study** abroad **next year.**
貝蒂明年會出國唸書。

④ **I sing songs while** I **do/am doing** my laundry.
我洗衣服時會一邊唱歌。

⑤ Angela **took some courses** at New York University **last summer.**
安琪拉去年夏天在紐約大學修了一些課程。

⑥ Christine **will/is going to introduce** Michael to Elaine **at tomorrow's meeting.**
克莉斯汀會在明天會面時把麥可介紹給伊蘭妮。

⑦ **May read novels when** she lived on her aunt's farm.
住在她嬸嬸農場的時候，梅閱讀小說。

⑧ Vincent **has gained** some weight **since he got married.**
文森自從結婚以後就變胖了。

⑨ **I had a good time** at the picnic **yesterday.**
我昨天去郊遊時玩得很愉快。

⑩ Kevin **has studied** English **for ten years.**
凱文已經學了十年的英文了。

用特定片語改寫

💎 基本概念

本單元收納初級寫作常見的 11 類特定片語，並以例句說明其用法如下：

◆ 範例分析

not...until（直到……時候，才）

1️⃣ It was not until I met Ann that I realized how important one's health was.

→I did not realize ＿＿＿＿＿＿＿＿＿ until ＿＿＿＿＿.

> hint 以特定片語改寫之

→I did **not** realize *how important one's health was* **until** *I met Ann.*

一直到遇見了安，我才瞭解到健康有多重要。

> **說明**
>
> 1 改寫句中出現 not...until 之句型。
>
> 2 與原句 It was not until...that 比較，not...until 前後兩子句之順序恰好相反。亦即【It was not until ＋ A ＋ that ＋ B】＝【B ＋否定 V ＋ until ＋ A】。
>
> 3 改寫時，將原句中 that 所引導之子句，移至主要子句位置。並將第一句之動詞 realized 更改為否定型態之 didn't realize。realize 後接其受詞 how important one's health was。
>
> 4 從屬連接詞 until 所引導之附屬子句不變，直接抄自原句 I met Ann。

not...enough (N) to/too...to（不足以……）與 cannot afford 之切換

2. Lesley cannot afford an air-conditioner.

→Lesley _____ have enough money _____ buy an air-conditioner.

→Lesley _____ too little money _____ buy an air-conditioner.

hint 以特定片語改寫之

→Lesley *does not* have enough money *to* buy an air-conditioner.

萊斯利沒有足夠的錢買冷氣機。

→Lesley *has* too little money *to* buy an air-conditioner.

萊斯利的錢太少，買不起冷氣機。

說明

1 改寫句第一句中出現 enough，可改寫為 not...enough (N) to 之句型。

2 改寫句第二句中出現 too，可改寫為「too ＋形容詞＋ to ＋原形動詞」之句型。

3 原句與兩改寫句之關係，如下：

cannot afford「無法負擔」

= does not have enough money to buy「沒有足夠的錢購買」

= has too little money to buy「錢太少不夠買」

4 須特別注意：在【too ＋形容詞或副詞＋ to ＋原形動詞】句型中，to 之後雖無任何否定字眼，但具否定意味，因此無須再加 not。

5 Lesley 為第三人稱，一般動詞改為否定，須加上 does not；動詞 have 之第三人稱單數型為 has。

too...to... 與 so...that... 句型之切換

3 Celina was too smart to argue with her boss.

→Celina was so _____ she _____ argue with her boss.

hint 以特定片語改寫之

→Celina was so *smart that* she *did not* argue with her boss.

席琳娜聰明地不與老闆爭執。

說明

1 改寫句第一個子句中出現 so，整句可改寫為 so...that 之句型。

2 原句 too...to 句型中之 to argue with her boss，含有否定意味，即「未與她的老闆爭執」。

3 改寫為 so...that 句型時，須將 that 所引導之子句改為否定型，亦即將 argue with her boss 改為 did not argue with her boss。

immediately when 與 as soon as 句型之切換

4 Peter turned the TV off immediately when he heard his parents opening the door.

→Peter turned the TV off _____ he heard his parents opening the door.

hint 以特定片語改寫之

→Peter turned the TV off *as soon as* he heard his parents opening the door.

彼得一聽到爸媽開門的聲音就馬上關掉電視。

說明

1 原句中 immediately when = as soon as。

2 須特別注意：as soon as 為片語型之連接詞，表「一……就……」，其後無須再加 when。

so ＋ adj./adv. 與 such ＋ N 句型之切換

5 A-Mei sings so well that she soon became popular.

→A-Mei is such ＿＿＿＿＿＿＿ that she soon became popular.

hint 以特定片語改寫之

→Ah-Mei is such *a good singer* that she soon became popular.

阿妹是這麼棒的歌手，所以她很快就紅了。

說明

1 原句中一般動詞型態之「sings so well」改寫為 Be 動詞型態之「is such ＋ N」。

2 sing 之名詞型態為 singer，副詞 well 所對應之形容詞為 good。

3 須特別注意：such 後之名詞若為可數名詞單數，須加上冠詞 a 或 an。如本句中之 such a good singer。

so that 與 in order that/in order to（為了……目的）之切換

6 Tony goes jogging every morning so that he can stay healthy.

→Tony goes jogging every morning ＿＿＿＿ he can stay healthy.

→Tony goes jogging every morning ＿＿＿＿ to stay healthy.

hint 以特定片語改寫之

→Tony goes jogging every morning *in order that* he can stay healthy.

為了能保持健康，東尼每天早上慢跑。

→Tony goes jogging every morning *in order* to stay healthy.

為了保持健康，東尼每天早上慢跑。

説明

1 so that = in order that 為片語型之連接詞，其所引導的子句為主
要子句之「目的」。

2 改寫句第二句中之 in order to stay healthy，亦可改寫為不定詞
to stay healthy；二者都表示「目的」。

include 與 including（包括／包含）之切換

7 The music styles that Jeanine enjoys include pop music,
classic music, and jazz.

→Jeanine enjoys music, _____ pop music, classic
music, and jazz.

hint 以特定片語改寫之

→Jeanine enjoys music, *including* pop music, classic
music, and jazz.

金妮喜歡音樂，包括流行音樂、古典樂、還有爵士樂。

説明

改寫句將動詞 include 改成分詞形式；即將原複雜句改成簡單句。

be good at（擅長）之句型

8 Yo-Yo Ma plays the cello well.

→Yo-Yo Ma is _____ cello.

hint 以特定片語改寫之

→Yo-Yo Ma is *good at* cello.

馬友友擅長拉大提琴。

説明

1 表「擅長」之句型，除了【動詞＋(N) well】外，亦可採用 Be 動
詞型態之 be good at。

2 須特別注意：at 為介系詞，其後之受詞須為名詞型態；若遇動詞
須更改為動名詞。

decide 與 make up one's mind（決定）句型之切換

9 He decided to study math in college.

→He made up _____ math in college.

hint 以特定片語改寫之

→He made up *his mind to study* math in college.

他下定決心大學要讀數學。

說明

1 decide = make up one's mind；二者之後均接不定詞。

have interest in 與 be interested in（對……感興趣）句型之切換

10 Mathew has no interest in physics.

→Mathew is not _____ physics.

hint 以特定片語改寫之

→Mathew is not *interested in* physics.

馬修對物理沒興趣。

說明

1 表「對……不感興趣」之句型，除了 have no interest in 外，亦可採 Be 動詞型之 be not interested in。

2 須特別注意：in 為介系詞，受詞須為名詞型態；若遇動詞須更改為動名詞。

used to ＋ V（過去常常……）之句型

11 I made it a rule to walk my dog in the evening.

→I_____ walk my dog in the evening.

hint 以特定片語改寫之

→I *used to* walk my dog in the evening.

我以前習慣在晚上溜狗。

說明

1 表「過去的習慣」可採用「used to + V」之句型，亦即在 used 後接不定詞型態之受詞。

2 須特別注意：本句型中之 to V 為不定詞；而表「習慣於……」之「be used to」句型中之 to 為介系詞，須以名詞或動名詞為受詞。以上二者必須分辨清楚。

◆ 試題演練

請更改為適當片語或詞組

① It was not until Jill married Sean that she understood the meaning of life.

→ Jill did not understand _____ until _____.

② Emma couldn't afford that expensive sports car.

→ Emma _____ have enough money _____ buy that expensive sports car.

→ Emma _____ too little money _____ buy that expensive sports car.

③ Michael was clever enough not to invest in that project.

→ Michael was so _____ he _____ invest in that project.

④ Joanne jumped out of her bed immediately when she heard her cell phone ring.

→ Joanne jumped out of her bed _____ she heard her cell phone ring.

⑤ Mr. Johnson is so fat that he can't even walk.

→ Mr. Johnson is such _____ that he can't even walk.

⑥ Bob worked very late so that he could get his report done by Friday.

→ Bob worked very late _____ to get his report done by Friday.

⑦ The sports that Paul likes includes jogging and swimming.

→ Paul likes sports, _____ jogging and swimming.

⑧ My sister draws well.

→ My sister is _____ at _____.

⑨ Dennis decided to move to Mexico.

→ Dennis made up _____ move to Mexico.

⑩ Moe had no interest in gambling.

→ Moe _____ not _____ in gambling.

解答

① Jill did not understand the meaning of life until she married Sean.
吉兒一直到嫁給尚恩後才瞭解生命的意義。

② Emma did not have enough money to buy that expensive sports car.
艾瑪沒有足夠的錢買那輛昂貴的跑車。

Emma had too little money to buy that expensive sports car.
艾瑪的錢太少了，買不起那輛昂貴的跑車。

③ Michael was so clever that he did not invest in that project.
麥可聰明地沒有投資那項計畫。

④ Joanne jumped out of her bed as soon as she heard her cell phone ring.
瓊安一聽到她的手機響起就跳下了床。

⑤ Mr. Johnson is such a fat person/man that he can't even walk.
強生先生是如此胖的一個人，以致於他甚至無法走路。

⑥ Bob worked very late in order to get his report done by Friday.
為了在星期五前完成報告，鮑伯一直工作到很晚。

⑦ Paul likes sports, including jogging and swimming.
保羅喜歡運動，包括慢跑和游泳。

⑧ My sister is good at drawing.
我姊姊／妹妹擅長畫畫。

⑨ Dennis made up his mind to move to Mexico.
丹尼斯下定決心搬去墨西哥。

⑩ Moe was not interested in gambling.
莫對賭博沒興趣。

單元二　句子合併

- 用對等連接詞合併
- 用對等相關連接詞合併
- 用名詞子句合併
- 用形容詞子句合併
- 用副詞子句合併
- 用比較句型合併
- 用介系詞合併
- 用使役動詞合併
- 用感官動詞合併
- 用特殊句型合併

用對等連接詞合併

範例

1　Sonia doesn't like fish.
　　Sonia didn't eat the fish at dinner.

→　Sonia doesn't like fish, ＿＿＿＿＿＿＿＿＿＿ at dinner.

ANS　Sonia doesn't like fish, *so she didn't eat the fish* at dinner.
　　蘇妮雅不喜歡魚，所以她晚餐時沒有吃魚。

🔹 基本概念

　　常用的「對等連接詞」有四個：and（表二者均……）、or（表選其一）、but（表相反）及 so（表因果）。

　　顧名思義，「對等連接詞」所連接之結構必須「對等」。換言之，對等連接詞可連接對等、平行的文法結構之單字、片語或子句。用對等連接詞連接，可省略重複字詞，具有簡化句子之功效。

🔹 應考要訣

1 判斷兩句之關聯性，選擇適當之對等連接詞。
2 找尋兩句之共通性，以對等連接詞串連後，可省略重複部份。
3 對等連接詞所連接者為單字或片語時，其前方通常不加逗號。
4 使用 so 時，須注意其句型為「原因，so 結果」。

🔹 範例分析

1 Sonia didn't eat the fish at dinner.
　 The reason is that she doesn't like fish.
　　→ Sonia doesn't like fish, so ＿＿＿＿＿＿ at dinner.

hint 改為對等連接詞之句型

→Sonia doesn't like fish, **so** *she didn't eat the fish* at dinner.

說明

1 經判斷第一句為結果，第二句為其原因。因此以對等連接詞 so 合併兩句。

2 合併後句型為【原因，so 結果】。

試題演練

請更改爲對等連接詞之句型

① Ivory waved.

She drove away.

→ Ivory waved and _____.

② I listen to music in the evening.

I take a long walk in the evening.

→ I _____ or _____ in the evening.

③ Beef is O.K. with me.

I can eat fish, too.

→ I can eat beef _____.

④ Bill painted the house.

He also planted some flowers around the house.

→ Bill painted the house _____ around it.

⑤ Jill didn't notice the time.

She missed the train.

→ Jill didn't notice the time, _____.

⑥ Judy studied very hard for the final exam.

She still failed it.

→ Judy studied very hard for the final exam, _____.

⑦ I heard some noise from my neighbors.

I closed the windows.

→ I heard some noise from my neighbors, _____.

⑧ Sonia slept four hours a day.

It is the reason why she fell ill.

→ Sonia slept four hours a day, _____.

⑨ Alex looked everywhere for his car keys.

He couldn't find them.

→ Alex looked everywhere for his car keys, _____.

⑩ I can clean my room now.

I can go shopping with my mother now.

→ I can clean my room _____ my mother now.

解答

① Ivory waved and drove away.
愛佛瑞揮揮手並開車離開了。

② I listen to music or take a long walk in the evening.
我晚上會聽音樂或散很久的步。

③ I can eat beef or fish.
我可以吃牛肉或魚。

④ Bill painted the house and planted some flowers around it.
比爾粉刷了房子，並且在它周圍種了些花。

⑤ Jill didn't notice the time, so she missed the train.
吉兒沒有留意時間，所以錯過了火車。

⑥ Judy studied very hard for the final exam, but still failed it.
茱蒂非常努力的準備期末考，但還是考不及格。

⑦ I heard some noise from my neighbors, so I closed the windows.
我聽到鄰居傳來一些噪音，所以我把窗戶關上了。

⑧ Sonia slept four hours a day, so she fell ill.
蘇妮雅一天睡四個小時，所以她病倒了。

⑨ Alex looked everywhere for his car keys, but couldn't find them.
愛力克斯找過了每個地方，還是找不到他的車鑰匙。

⑩ I can clean my room or go shopping with my mother now.
我現在可以打掃房間或是和媽媽一起去逛街。

用對等相關連接詞合併

範例

1   Jack is my friend.

Teresa is my friend, too.

→   Both Jack _____ my friends.

[ANS]   Both Jack *and Teresa are* my friends.

傑克和泰瑞莎都是我的朋友。

💬 基本概念

「對等相關連接詞」共有四組，其在功能上與前一單元之「對等連接詞」相同，可連接對等之單字、片語或子句，亦具有簡化句子之功效。惟在型態上係以片語形式呈現：

1. both...and （兩者都……）
2. not only...but also （除了……也……）
3. either...or （二者其一……）
4. neither...nor （兩者都不……）

值得一提的是，使用「對等相關連接詞」連接主詞時，須特別注意主詞與動詞之一致性。

　　※ Both S_1 and S_2 ＋ 複數型態 V

$$※ \left[\begin{array}{l} \text{Not only } S_1 \text{ but also } S_2 \\ \text{Either } S_1 \text{ or } S_2 \\ \text{Neither } S_1 \text{ nor } S_2 \end{array} \right] ＋ \text{V（單複數取決於 } S_2 \text{）}$$

💬 應考要訣

1. 依照句意或提示，選擇適當之對等相關連接詞。
2. 找尋兩句子之共通性，連接時省略重複部份。
3. 注意主動詞的一致性。

4 原句中含有 not 或其他否定字，則選用否定型態之 neither...nor。合併時，因動詞將還原為肯定型態，若遇第三人稱單數主詞在現在式時，須特別注意其型態。

◆ 範例分析

1 Jack is my friend.

Teresa is my friend, too.

→ Both _____ and _____ my friends.

hint 改為對等相關連接詞之句型

→ **Both** *Jack* **and** *Teresa are* my friends.

傑克和泰瑞莎都是我的朋友。

> 說明
>
> 1 依句意與改寫句之提示，對等相關連接詞應選擇 both...and。
>
> 2 原句重複處為 is my friend，經連接後主詞變為 Both Jack and Teresa。
>
> 3 both...and 後要用複數動詞 are。

2 Patricia works part time at a restaurant.

She also works as a volunteer at a hospital.

→ Patricia works not only _____ but also _____ .

hint 改為對等相關連接詞之句型

→ Patricia works **not only** *part time at a restaurant* **but also** *as a volunteer at a hospital.*

派翠西亞不只在餐廳兼差，也在醫院當義工。

③ The change in life style may cause his unhappiness.
Maybe the unfamiliar language causes his unhappiness.
→ Either the change in life style or _____
causes his unhappiness.

hint 改為對等相關連接詞之句型

→ **Either** *the change in life style* **or** *the unfamiliar language*
causes his unhappiness.

是生活型態的改變,抑或不熟悉的語言造成他的不快樂。

④ My next-door neighbor is not generous.
Her friends are not generous.
→ Neither my next-door neighbor _____ generous.

hint 改為對等相關連接詞之句型

→ Neither my next-door neighbor *nor her friends are*
generous.

我的隔壁鄰居和她的朋友都不慷慨。

說明

1 依句意與提示，兩句均含否定字 not，因此選擇 neither...nor。
2 原句重複處為 Be＋not generous，須連接者為兩個主詞：my next-door neighbor 及 her friends。
3 連接後，最靠近動詞之主詞為複數型態之 her friends，動詞應選擇複數型態之 are。

◆ 試題演練

請更改為對等相關連接詞之句型

① I will take a bus to the department store.

Maybe I will take a taxi to get there.

→ I will take either ＿＿＿＿＿＿＿＿＿＿ to the department store.

② Robert is good at basketball.

He also bowls well.

→ Robert is good at both ＿＿＿＿＿＿＿＿＿＿＿ bowling.

③ English is a school subject.

It is also a useful skill.

→ English is not only ＿＿＿＿＿＿＿＿＿＿＿ a useful skill.

④ Melody swims very well.

She runs fast, too.

→ Melody not only ＿＿＿＿＿＿＿＿＿＿＿＿＿.

⑤ My brother helped me move.

My friends also helped me with moving.

→ Not only my brother ＿＿＿＿＿＿＿＿ helped me with moving.

⑥ I may go on a trip to Europe.

Maybe I will visit my parents in the country.

→ I will either go on a trip to Europe ＿＿＿＿＿＿＿ in the country.

⑦ I cannot afford a house.

I do not have enough money to buy a car, either.

→ I can afford neither _____ a car.

⑧ Kay doesn't enjoy playing the piano.

Her sisters do not enjoy it.

→ Neither Kay _____ playing the piano.

⑨ I hate the air pollution in big cities.

I also hate the bad traffic in big cities.

→ I hate both the air pollution _____ in big cities.

⑩ She doesn't go to the gym.

She does not play any sport.

→ She neither _____ nor _____ any sport.

解答

① I will take either a bus or a taxi to the department store.
我會搭公車或計程車去百貨公司。

② Robert is good at both basketball and bowling.
羅伯特籃球和保齡球都很厲害。

③ English is not only a school subject but also a useful skill.
英文不只是學校的一門科目，也是一項很有用的技能。

④ Melody not only swims very well but also runs fast.
美樂蒂不只很會游泳，而且也跑得很快。

⑤ Not only my brother but also my friends helped me with moving.
不只是我哥哥，還有我朋友都來幫我搬家。

⑥ I will either go on a trip to Europe or visit my parents in the country.
我不是去歐洲旅行就是去鄉下探視我父母。

⑦ I can afford neither a house nor a car.
不論是房子或車子我都買不起。

⑧ Neither Kay nor her sisters enjoy playing the piano.
不論是凱或是她姊姊都不喜歡彈鋼琴。

⑨ I hate both the air pollution and the bad traffic in big cities.
大都市的空氣污染和擁擠的交通我都討厭。

⑩ She neither goes to the gym nor plays any sport.
她既不去健身中心也不做任何運動。

用名詞子句合併

範例

1 Something is true.

Working part-time helps you experience life.

→ That _____ is true.

ANS That *working part-time helps you experience life* is true.

打工會幫助你體驗人生這件事是眞的。

2 There is a question.

What should I do to improve my English?

→ The question is _____.

ANS The question is *what I should do to improve my English*.

問題是我該如何做才能讓我的英文進步。

3 Something is still unknown.

Will my father buy me a cell phone?

→ _____ is still unknown.

ANS *Whether my father will buy me a cell phone* is still unknown.

我爸爸是否會買手機給我還是未知數。

🔷 基本概念

「名詞子句」顧名思義爲具有名詞功能的子句。依其型態，可區分
爲以下兩種類型。

1️⃣ 敘述型的名詞子句，表「事實或狀態」，以連接詞 that 引導之。

2️⃣ 問句型的名詞子句，表問題；

　1) 疑問詞爲首之問句，以疑問詞【wh-, how】引導。

　2) 以 Yes/No 爲答句之問句，以連接詞 if 或 whether 引導。

　　就功能言，名詞子句在主要子句中可能扮演之角色有：主詞、主詞
補語及受詞。

1 當主詞

　　1) 主要子句之動詞需採單數型態。

　　2) 連接詞 that 不可省略，否則將造成一句兩動詞之錯誤。

　　3) 名詞子句若過長，往往會以虛主詞代替，而形成以 it 為首之主要子句。

　　如： That working part-time helps you experience life is true.

　　1) 動詞為單數型態之 is

　　2) 連接詞 that 不可省略

　　可更改為： It is true that working part-time helps you experience life.

2 當主詞補語

　　1) 出現於 Be 動詞句中，名詞子句在意義上相當於主詞。

　　2) 連接詞通常不省略。

　　如： The truth is that I don't want to go out with him.

　　（the truth ＝ that I don't want to go out with him）

3 當受詞

　　1) 出現於一般動詞句中，名詞子句當及物動詞之受詞。

　　2) 連接詞通常會被省略。

　　如： Do you know (that) Jill works at a fast-food restaurant?

　　1) that Jill works at a fast-food restaurant 為名詞子句，當 know 之受詞。

　　2) that 經常被省略。

I. 敘述型的名詞子句

應考要訣

1 按提示與句意，判斷兩句重複處之屬性：主詞、主詞補語或受詞。

2 在第二句前加上連接詞 that，形成名詞子句。

3 將第一句（主要子句）重複處置換為上述名詞子句。

4 功能為受詞的名詞子句中之 that 一般多予省略。

◆ 範例分析

that 子句當主詞

1️⃣ Something is true.

Working part-time helps you experience life.

→ That _____ is true.

→ It is true _____.

hint 以名詞子句合併

→ That *working part-time helps you experience life* is true.

　或

→ It is true *that working part-time helps you experience life.*

打工會幫助你體驗人生這件事是真的。

說明

1 名詞 something 為原句第一句之主詞。

2 在第二句前加 that，形成名詞子句 that working part-time helps you experience life。

3 合併時，將主要子句之 something 置換成該名詞子句，其他字詞保持不變。

4 或可改為以虛主詞 it 為首之句構。

that 子句當主詞補語

2️⃣ There is a problem.

I don't have a computer at home.

→ The problem is that _____.

hint 以名詞子句合併

→ The problem is that *I don't have a computer at home.*

問題是我家中沒有電腦。

説明

1 原句中第一句 a problem 為主詞補語。
2 在第二句前加 that，形成名詞子句 that I don't have a computer at home。
3 合併時，將前述名詞子句置於主要子句之主詞補語位置。

that 子句當受詞

3 David told Amy something.

David was not feeling very well.

→ David told Amy (that) _____.

hint 以名詞子句合併

→ David told Amy (that) *he was not feeling very well.*

大衛告訴艾咪他覺得不太舒服。

説明

1 原句中第一句的 something 為受詞，所指為第二句 David was not feeling very well。又，David ＝ he。
2 在第二句前加 that，形成名詞子句 that he was not feeling very well。
3 合併兩句，將 something 置換成前述名詞子句。
4 因該名詞子句在句中扮演受詞角色，故 that 可予以省略。

◆ 試題演練

請以名詞子句合併以下句子

① Something surprises me.

Anne married Sam.

→ It surprises me that _____.

② There is a reason.

I have been there before.

→ The reason is that _____.

③ Shima told me something.

She was introduced to a rich young man.

→ Shima told me _____.

④ People believe something.

Pigs are stupid.

→ It is believed that _____.

⑤ James is an honest and generous guy.

I think the same way.

→ I think that _____.

⑥ Jessie told lies.

I can't believe it.

→ I can't believe _____.

⑦ Something is a long story.

George and Mary became a couple.

→ It is a long story that _____.

⑧ There is a point.

No one has the keys to the house.

→ The point is that _____.

⑨ My mother told me something.

She used to drink snake soup.

→ My mother told me _____.

⑩ There is a fact.

Danny's grandfather was a farmer.

→ The fact is that _____.

II. 問句型的名詞子句—以疑問詞為句首的間接問句

🔷 **應考要訣**

1. 形成名詞子句之過程，需將疑問句更改為直述句（即間接問句形式），去除疑問句之問號，並注意時態與詞序之變化（參考直述句改疑問句）。

2. 因直述句中之疑問詞具有連接詞功能，合併時不需再加任何連接詞。

3. 其餘要訣同第 I 型。

◆ **範例分析**

名詞子句當主詞

4. Something is very clear.
   Who will win the prize?

   →_____ is very clear.

   → It is very clear _____.

   hint 以名詞子句合併

   → *Who will win the prize* is very clear.

   或

   → It is very clear *who will win the prize.*

   誰會得獎已經很明顯了。

   說明

   1 名詞 something 為原句中第一句之主詞。

   2 將第二句改為直述句，詞序為 S + V，形成名詞子句 who will win the prize。（注意，本句的 who 原本就是主詞，因此直接問句與間接問句之字序不變）

   3 合併時，將主要子句之 something 置換成上述名詞子句，其他字詞保持不變。

   4 或可改為以虛主詞 it 為首之句構。

名詞子句當主詞補語

5 There is a question.

What should I do to improve my English?

→ The question is _____.

hint 以名詞子句合併

→ The question is *what I should do to improve my English.*

問題是我該如何做才能讓我的英文進步。

說明

1 原句中第一句之 a question 為主詞補語。

2 將第二句改為直述句,詞序為 S + V,形成名詞子句 what I should do to improve my English。

3 合併時,將上述名詞子句置於主要子句之主詞補語位置。

名詞子句當受詞

6 I don't know something.

Who stole my jewelry?

→ I don't know _____.

hint 以名詞子句合併

→ I don't know *who stole my jewelry.*

我不知道誰偷了我的珠寶。

說明

1 第一句的 something 為受詞,所指為第二句之事。

2 將第二句改為直述句,詞序為 S + V,形成名詞子句 who stole my jewelry。(who 原為主詞,故字序不須改變)

3 合併兩句,將 something 置換成上述名詞子句。

◆ 試題演練

請以名詞子句合併以下句子

⑪ There is a problem.

Who can fix my computer?

→ The problem is _____.

⑫ Something is still unknown.

  When can I take a day off?

  → It is unknown _____.

⑬ I'm not sure about something.

  Where will Tina go for her vacation?

  → I am not sure where _____.

⑭ Something is true.

  What did Teddy say to Chikako?

  → _____ is true.

⑮ I am wondering something.

  Whose garden is it?

  → I am wondering _____.

⑯ Joy told me something.

  What had happened to her the other day?

  → Joy told me _____.

⑰ Who broke the window?

  I don't know, but Peter knows.

  → Peter knows _____, but I don't.

⑱ There is a problem.

  Which class should I take?

  → The problem is _____.

⑲ I have no idea about something.

  When will the weather turn better?

  → I have no idea when _____.

⑳ Please tell me something.

  How much pocket money should I give to my children?

  → Please tell me _____.

III. Yes/No 問句型的名詞子句─以 if 或 whether 引導的間接問句

應考要訣

1. 首先需將一般問句更改為直述句，去除問號，並注意時態與詞序之變化（參考直述句改疑問句）。
2. 在直述句前加上連接詞 if 或 whether... (or not)，以形成名詞子句。
3. 其中 if = whether = whether or not（表「是否」），但當此名詞子句置於句首時，只能使用 whether。
4. 其餘要訣同第 I 及第 II 型。

範例分析

7. Something is still unknown.

Will my father buy me a cell phone?

→ _____ is still unknown.

hint 以名詞子句合併

→ *Whether my father will buy me a cell phone* is still unknown.

我爸爸是否會買手機給我還是未知數。

說明

1. 第一句的 something 為主詞，所指之事為第二句。
2. 將第二句改為直述句，並在句首加上 whether 以形成名詞子句 whether my father will buy me a cell phone。
3. 合併兩句，將 something 置換為前述名詞子句。

試題演練

請以名詞子句合併以下句子

21. Dennis wants to know something.

Will the stock prices go up soon?

→ Dennis wants to know if _____.

㉒ I am wondering something.

Will our team win the football game?

→ I am wondering if _____.

㉓ There is a question.

Will the teacher teach us next semester?

→ The question is whether _____.

㉔ Something does not matter.

Is the beautiful movie star married?

→ It does not matter whether _____.

㉕ I am wondering something.

Will the concert begin by 8:00?

→ I am wondering if _____.

解答

① It surprises me that Anne married Sam.
安嫁給山姆讓我很驚訝。

② The reason is that I have been there before.
原因是我以前已經去過了。

③ Shima told me (that) she was introduced to a rich young man.
西瑪告訴我她被介紹給一位年輕又有錢的男子。

④ It is believed that pigs are stupid.
一般人相信豬很笨。

⑤ I think that James is an honest and generous guy.
我認為詹姆士是個誠實又慷慨的人。

⑥ I can't believe (that) Jessie told lies.
我不敢相信潔西說謊。

⑦ It is a long story that George and Mary became a couple.
喬治和瑪麗結為夫妻的經過說來話長。

⑧ The point is that no one has the keys to the house.
重點是沒有人有那間房子的鑰匙。

⑨ My mother told me (that) she used to drink snake soup.
我媽媽告訴我她過去習慣喝蛇湯。

⑩ The fact is that Danny's grandfather was a farmer.
事實是丹尼的爺爺是個農夫。

⑪ The problem is who can fix my computer.
問題是誰會幫我修電腦。

⑫ It is unknown when I can take a day off.
我何時能請假一天還不知道。

⑬ I am not sure where Tina will go for her vacation.
我不確定提娜會去哪裡度假。

⑭ What Teddy said to Chikako is true.

泰迪跟知佳子說的話是真的。

⑮ I am wondering whose garden it is.

我在想這是誰家的花園。

⑯ Joy told me what had happened to her the other day.

嬌伊告訴我她前幾天發生的事。

⑰ Peter knows who broke the window, but I don't.

彼得知道誰打破了窗戶，但我不知道。

⑱ The problem is which class I should take.

問題是我該選哪一門課。

⑲ I have no idea when the weather will turn better.

我不知道天氣何時會好轉。

⑳ Please tell me how much pocket money I should give to my children.

請告訴我該給我小孩多少零用錢。

㉑ Dennis wants to know if the stock prices will go up soon.

丹尼斯想知道股票價格會不會很快上漲。

㉒ I am wondering if our team will win the football game.

我正在想我們隊會不會贏得這場橄欖球賽。

㉓ The question is whether the teacher will teach us next semester (or not).

問題是老師下學期會不會教我們。

㉔ It does not matter whether the beautiful movie star is married (or not).

那個美麗的電影明星已婚與否一點也不重要。

㉕ I am wondering if the concert will begin by 8:00.

我正在想音樂會是否會在八點開始。

用形容詞子句合併

範例	
1	The artist is very famous.
	She is standing next to Jeff.
→	The artist ＿＿＿＿＿＿＿＿＿＿＿ is very famous.
ANS	The artist *who is standing next to Jeff* is very famous.
	站在傑夫身旁的藝術家很有名。
2	Chris moved to a place.
	There is no air pollution there.
→	Chris moved to a place ＿＿＿＿＿＿＿＿＿＿＿.
ANS	Chris moved to a place *where there is no air pollution.*
	克利斯搬到了一個沒有空氣污染的地方。
3	I have a nephew.
	He goes to kindergarten.
	I sent him a model car for his birthday present.
→	I sent my nephew ＿＿＿＿＿＿＿＿＿＿＿ a model car for his birthday present.
ANS	I sent my nephew, *who goes to kindergarten*, a model car for his birthday present.
	我送給我那讀幼稚園的外甥一輛模型車當他的生日禮物。

🔷 基本概念

「形容詞子句」為具有形容詞功能之子句，位於名詞之後，作為後位修飾。就其型態，可區分為兩種：

1 以關係「代名詞」為句首之形容詞子句

關係代名詞（以下簡稱關代）在子句中扮演名詞之功能，可作為主詞或受詞，並具有主格、受格或所有格的概念，整理如下表。在選用關

代時，必須同時考量其所代替者（為人或事），以及其屬性（主格、受格或所有格）。

關係代名詞	主格	受格	所有格
用於表「人」	who	whom	
用於表「事物」	which	which	whose
以上二者均適用	that	that	

2 以關係「副詞」where，when 或 why 引導的形容詞子句用來修飾其前之地點、時間或原因。

　除上述重點外，將在第 III 部份說明關係子句的限定及補述用法。

I. 關係代名詞為首的形容詞子句

💎 應考要訣

1 找出兩句重複之處，判斷其詞性：為主格、受格或所有格。作受格使用之關代可省略。

2 按前述表格將重複處的詞組以適當之關代置換，形成以關代為首的形容詞子句。

3 合併時，在重複的詞組後加上前述形容詞子句，形成後位修飾。

◆ 範例分析

關係代名詞為主詞

1 The artist is very famous.

　She is standing next to Jeff.

→ The artist ＿＿＿＿＿＿＿＿＿＿＿ is very famous.

hint 以形容詞子句合併

→ The artist *who is standing next to Jeff* is very famous.

　站在傑夫身旁的藝術家很有名。

說明

1 第一句的 The artist ＝ 第二句之主詞 she。
2 將第二句 she 置換為代表人之關代主格 who，形成形容詞子句 who is standing next to Jeff。
3 在第一句的 The artist 後加上前述子句，形成合併句的主詞 The artist who is standing next to Jeff。
4 第一句其他字組不變。

關係代名詞為受詞

2 The report has some mistakes.
Robin handed in the report yesterday.
→ The report ＿＿＿＿＿＿＿＿＿＿ has some mistakes.

> hint 以形容詞子句合併

→ The report *which Robin handed in yesterday* has some mistakes.
→ The report *that Robin handed in yesterday* has some mistakes.
→ The report *Robin handed in yesterday* has some mistakes.

羅賓昨天交的那份報告有一些錯誤。

說明

1 第一句的 The report ＝ 第二句之受詞 the report。
2 將第二句的 the report 置換為代表關代受格之 which 或 that 並移至句首，形成形容詞子句 which/that Robin handed in yesterday。
3 受格之關代 which 或 that 可省略。
4 合併時，在第一句 the report 後加上前述形容詞子句，其他字詞保持不變。

關係代名詞為所有格

3 Mike married a girl.

Her father is a professor.

→ Mike married a girl _____.

hint 以形容詞子句合併

→ Mike married a girl *whose father is a professor.*

麥克娶了一位爸爸是教授的女孩。

說明

1 兩句重複處在：第二句的 her 為第一句 a girl（代名詞為 she）之所有格。

2 將第二句之 her 置換為 whose，形成形容詞子句 whose father is a professor。

3 合併時，在第一句 a girl 後加上前述形容詞子句，其他字組保持不變。

◆ **試題演練**

請以形容詞子句合併以下句子

① I ran into an old friend.

The friend just moved back to Taipei.

→ I ran into an old friend _____.

② I know the woman.

You invited her to the party.

→ I know the woman _____.

③ I like to shop at the store.

The owner of the store has a cute cat.

→ I like to shop at the store _____.

④ Kevin likes the girl.

Her face is round.

→ Kevin likes the girl _____.

⑤ What happened to the woman?

I met her at your wedding.

→ What happened to the woman _____?

II. 關係副詞為首的形容詞子句

🔵 **應考要訣**

① 找出兩句重複之處，判斷為以下何種型態：

　地點=>關係副詞用 where

　時間=>關係副詞用 when

　原因=>關係副詞用 why

② 合併時，在表「地點、時間或原因」之名詞後加上相對應的關係副詞，形成以關副為首之形容詞子句，作為後位修飾。

◆ **範例分析**

　表地點，關係副詞用 where

④ Chris moved to a place.

There is no air pollution there.

→ Chris moved to a place _____.

　hint 以形容詞子句合併

→ Chris moved to a place *where there is no air pollution.*

　克利斯搬到了一個沒有空氣污染的地方。

　說明

1 第一句的 a place ＝ 第二句之 there，表地點。

2 將第二句的 there 置換為表「地點」之關副 where 並移至句首，形成形容詞子句 where there is no air pollution。

3 在第一句的 a place 後併入前述子句，形成合併句 a place where there is no air pollution。

4 第一句其他字組不變。

5 Chikako was working as a waitress at that time.

The war broke out then.

→Chikako worked as a waitress at the time _____.

hint 以形容詞子句合併

→Chikako was working as a waitress at the time *when the war broke out.*

知佳子在戰爭爆發時從事女服務生的工作。

> **說明**
> 1 第一句的 the time ＝ 第二句之 then，表時間。
> 2 將第二句的 then 置換為表「時間」之關副 when 並移至句首，形成形容詞子句 when the war broke out。
> 3 在第一句的 the time 後併入前述子句，形成 the time when the war broke out。
> 4 其他字組不變，將兩句合併。

6 That is the reason.

James put on weight because of the reason.

→That is the reason _____.

hint 以形容詞子句合併

→That is the reason *why James put on weight.*

那就是詹姆士為什麼變胖的原因了。

> **說明**
> 1 第一句的 the reason ＝第二句之 because of the reason，表原因。
> 2 將第二句的 because of the reason 置換為表「原因」之關副 why 並移至句首，形成形容詞子句 why James put on weight。
> 3 在第一句的 the reason 後併入前述子句，形成合併句 the reason why James put on weight。
> 4 其他字組不變，將兩句合併。

◆ **試題演練**

　　請以形容詞子句合併以下句子

⑥ The place is in my dream.

　I can dance with the wind there.

　→ The place _____ is in my dream.

⑦ Irene remembered the day.

　She saw snow in New York then.

　→ Irene remembered the day _____.

⑧ This is the reason.

　Gina became a Christian because of the reason.

　→ This is the reason _____.

⑨ Betty moved back to the city.

　She was born there.

　→ Betty moved back to the city _____.

⑩ Christmas is the holiday.

　Families get together during the holiday.

　→ Christmas is the holiday when _____.

III. 限定或補述作用的關係子句

🧇 **應考要訣**

1️⃣ 判斷限定或補述用法：

　　限定用法=>沒有逗號，直接置於名詞之後作後位修飾，即一般所謂
　　　　　　　之形容詞子句。

　　補述用法=>加上逗號，補充敘述前面的名詞

2️⃣ 明確指某事或某人時，用限定用法；補充說明時，用補述用法。

3️⃣ 其餘有關形容詞子句之用法同第 I 部份。

◆ 範例分析

限定用法

8 John has two sisters.

One is studying in graduate school.

John called her.

→John called his sister _____.

hint 以形容詞子句合併

→John called his sister *who is studying in graduate school.*

約翰打電話給他唸研究所的姊姊。

説明

1 第一句已說明 John 有兩個姊妹，第二句明確指出打電話的對象 her 是 studying in graduate school 的姊妹。合併為形容詞子句時須採限定用法。

2 將第二句之 One 置換為 who，形成形容詞子句 who is studying in graduate school。

補述用法

9 I have a nephew.

He goes to kindergarten.

I sent him a model car for his birthday.

→I sent my nephew _____ a model car for his birthday.

hint 以關係子句合併

→I sent my nephew, *who goes to kindergarten,* a model car for his birthday.

我送給我那讀幼稚園的外甥一輛模型車當他的生日禮物。

寫作破關 ▶ 初級

說明

1 三個句中的 nephew、He、him 均指同一人。
2 第一句已說明只有一個 nephew，無須限定，所以合併為形容詞子句時，用補述用法加以補充說明即可。
3 將第二句的 He 置換為 who，形成形容詞子句 who goes to kindergarten。
4 在合併句 my nephew 後加上前述形容詞子句，並在此子句前後加上逗點，形成補述性質之形容詞子句。

◆ 試題演練

請以關係子句合併以下句子

⑪ Kay's mother usually buys fruit and vegetables at that supermarket.
  She is a housewife.
  → Kay's mother ＿＿＿＿＿＿＿＿＿ usually buys fruit and vegetables at that supermarket.

⑫ My boyfriend bought me a watch in China.
  He took a business trip to China last month.
  → My boyfriend ＿＿＿＿＿＿＿＿＿ bought me a watch there.

⑬ Vicky has three sisters.
  One of them is living in Japan.
  George wants to marry her.
  → George wants to marry Vicky's sister ＿＿＿＿＿＿＿＿＿.

⑭ Lily's father-in-law is a police officer.
  He lives in Tainan.
  → Lily's father-in-law ＿＿＿＿＿＿＿＿＿ is a police officer.

⑮ I have two brothers.
  One is married and I live with him.
  → I live with my brother ＿＿＿＿＿＿＿＿＿.

解答

① I ran into an old friend who just moved back to Taipei.
我偶然遇見一個剛搬回台北的老朋友。

② I know the woman (whom) you invited to the party.
我認識你邀請來參加宴會的那名女子。

③ I like to shop at the store whose owner has a cute cat.
我喜歡在那家老闆有養可愛貓咪的店購物。

④ Kevin likes the girl whose face is round.
凱文喜歡那個臉圓圓的女孩。

⑤ What happened to the woman (whom) I met at your wedding.
我在你婚禮遇到的那個女人發生了什麼事?

⑥ The place where I can dance with the wind is in my dream.
我可以乘風起舞的地方是在我的夢裡。

⑦ Irene remembered the day when she saw snow in New York.
艾琳記得她在紐約看到雪的那一天。

⑧ This is the reason why Gina became a Christian.
這是吉娜成為基督教徒的原因。

⑨ Betty moved back to the city where she was born.
貝蒂搬回到她出生的城市。

⑩ Christmas is the holiday when families get together.
聖誕節是闔家團聚的節日。

⑪ Kay's mother, who is a housewife, usually buys fruit and vegetables at that supermarket.
凱那當家庭主婦的媽媽通常在那間超級市場買水果和蔬菜。

⑫ My boyfriend, who took a business trip to China last month, bought me a watch there.
我男朋友上個月去中國大陸出差,在那裡買了一只手錶給我。

⑬ George wants to marry Vicky's sister who is living in Japan.
喬治想和維琪住在日本的姊姊 / 妹妹結婚。

⑭ Lily's father-in-law, who lives in Tainan, is a police officer.
莉莉住在台南的公公是一位警察。

⑮ I live with my brother who is married.
我跟我已婚的哥哥 / 弟弟住在一起。

用副詞子句合併

1　Harry arrived at the airport late.

　　The plane had taken off.

→　Harry ＿＿＿＿＿＿＿＿＿＿ after ＿＿＿＿＿＿＿＿＿＿.

ANS　Harry *arrived at the airport* after *the plane had taken off.*

　　哈利在飛機起飛之後才抵達機場。

🔷 基本概念

　　「副詞子句」係指由引導副詞子句的「從屬連接詞」所帶領之子句，在功能上作為副詞使用。在合併過程中，必須掌握兩個要點：一為判斷其類型；其次則為標點之使用。

1 副詞子句類型：

　　副詞子句種類繁多，在此僅列舉常見四大類型及其配對之從屬連接詞如下：

副詞子句性質	從屬連接詞
◎表時間	when, while, as, before, after, whenever, since
◎表因果	because, since
◎表條件	if, unless
◎表讓步	though, although, even though

2 副詞子句的標點

　　首先，須判斷何者為主要子句、副詞子句。其原則為：以從屬連接詞為句首者為副詞子句，而主要子句則為完整的句子。其標點用法如下：

1) 副詞子句在前，必須以逗號將兩子句隔開，形成如下句型：

【副詞子句,＋主要子句.】
2) 主要子句在前,不需加逗號,句型如下:
【主要子句＋副詞子句.】

I. 表時間之副詞子句

應考要訣

1. 找尋表時間之從屬連接詞,如:when、after、before 等,該連接詞所引導者為副詞子句。

2. 判斷兩子句的時間發生先後 (可能同時發生)。

   1) when, while, as
      意為「當⋯⋯時」,表兩動作幾乎同時發生,必須進一步分析原句之句意,以決定合併後之主從關係。

   2) before
      意為「在⋯⋯之前」,表副詞子句中之動作後發生。

   3) after
      意為「在⋯⋯之後」,表副詞子句中之動作先發生。

   4) since
      意為「自從」,副詞子句通常採用簡單過去式,主要子句則為現在完成式。

範例分析

1. Harry arrived at the airport.
   The plane had taken off.
   → The plane ＿＿＿＿＿＿＿ when ＿＿＿＿＿＿＿.

   hint 以副詞子句合併

   → The plane *had taken off* **when** *Harry arrived at the airport.*

   當哈利抵達機場時,飛機已經起飛了。

說明

1 句1時態為過去簡單式 arrived，而句2為過去完成式 had taken off。即「飛機起飛」發生在前，「抵達機場」發生在後。

2 when 後所接之子句為後發生之動作，形成副詞子句 when Harry arrived at the airport。

3 附屬子句在後，其前方不須加逗號。

II. 表因果之副詞子句

應考要訣

1 找尋表因果之從屬連接詞。

2 判斷兩子句的因果關係。

  1) 主要子句表動作或事件之「結果」，而副詞子句表「原因」。

  2) 形成如下句構：

    【**Because** 或 **Since** ＋原因, ＋結果.】

    【結果 ＋ **because** 或 **since** ＋ 原因.】

◆ **範例分析**

2 Summer is usually hot and humid.

  So, Steve does not like summer.

  →Steve ＿＿＿＿＿＿＿＿＿ because ＿＿＿＿＿＿＿＿.

  hint 以副詞子句合併

  →Steve *does not like summer* **because** *it is usually hot and humid.*

  史帝夫不喜歡夏天，因為它又濕又熱。

> **說明**
>
> 1 從屬連接詞because後應加上「原因」：it is usually hot and humid。
> 2 附屬子句在後，不須加逗號。

III. 表條件之副詞子句

● 應考要訣

1. 找尋表條件之從屬連接詞，如：if、whether...(or not) 或 unless。
2. 判斷兩子句的關係，以決定主從關係。
   1) 主要子句表「動作或決定」，而副詞子句表「在……條件下」。
   2) if句構：
      【**If**＋條件,＋動作或決定.】
      【動作或決定＋**if**＋條件.】
   3) unless（除非）句構：
      【**Unless**＋不會發生的條件,＋動作或決定.】
      【動作或決定＋**unless**＋不會發生的條件.】
3. 注意：主要子句的時間雖為未來，條件句（副詞子句）仍須採用現在時間之動詞時態。

◆ 範例分析

3. I will go hiking in the mountains tomorrow.
   I will not go if it rains.
   →Unless _____ , I _____.

   > hint 以副詞子句合併

   →**Unless** *it rains,* I *will go hiking in the mountains tomorrow.*
   除非下雨，不然我明天會去山裡健行。

> **說明**
> 1 從屬連接詞 unless 後應加上主要子句動作「不會發生的條件」=
>   it rains，表「假如下雨就不去」。
> 2 從屬連接詞在句首，兩子句間必須加上逗號。
> 3 表條件之副詞子句，採現在時間 rains。

IV. 表讓步之副詞子句

🔵 應考要訣

1. 找尋表讓步之從屬連接詞，如：though、although、even though 等。
2. 所謂「讓步」關係，表「即使在……情況下，主詞仍然……」
3. 判斷兩子句的關係，以決定主從關係：
   主要子句表「讓步」或「非預期」的結果，而副詞子句為讓步的情況
   或條件，表「即使在……情況下」。
4. 須注意：表讓步之從屬連接詞，不可與對等連接詞 but 連用，而形成
   「Although..., but」之錯誤句構。

◆ 範例分析

4. Judy did not feel better.
   She had taken some cold medicine.
   → Judy _____ although _____.

   hint 以副詞子句合併

   → Judy *did not feel better* **although** *she had taken some cold medicine.*
   雖然吃過了感冒藥，茱蒂還是沒有覺得較舒服。

說明

1 從屬連接詞 although 應引出「讓步的情況」：「雖然她已吃了感冒藥」，主要子句為「讓步的結果」或「非預期的結果」：「Judy 並沒有覺得較舒服」。

2 從屬連接詞在後，兩子句間不須加逗號。

◆ **試題演練**

請以副詞子句合併以下句子

① Sally spent an hour dressing up.

Then, she went to a dinner party.

→ Sally _____ before _____.

② Little Eva sits on a high chair.

She always cries out loud.

→ Little Eva _____ whenever _____.

③ Taiwan has entered the WTO.

English has become more important.

→ Since _____ , _____.

④ Sonia quit her job.

Sonia could not get along with her boss.

→ Sonia _____ because _____.

⑤ Julia felt very tired and hungry.

She could not concentrate in class.

→ Julia _____ because _____.

⑥ Irene may go to the herbal teahouse tomorrow.

She will call and tell her friend.

→ If _____ , she _____.

⑦ You will communicate better with foreigners.

You can speak their languages.

→ You _____ if _____.

⑧ Patrick will go on a study tour to London this summer.

He will not go if he cannot get his parents' permission.

→ Patrick ＿＿＿＿＿＿＿＿＿＿＿＿ unless ＿＿＿＿＿＿＿＿＿＿＿＿.

⑨ Jeff ran very quickly to the bus station.

He still missed the bus.

→ Although ＿＿＿＿＿＿＿＿＿＿＿ , ＿＿＿＿＿＿＿＿＿＿＿＿.

⑩ Robert was terribly sick.

He went to school this morning.

→ ＿＿＿＿＿＿＿＿＿＿＿ even though ＿＿＿＿＿＿＿＿＿＿.

解答

① Sally spent an hour dressing up before she went to a dinner party.

莎莉去晚宴之前花了一個小時打扮。

② Little Eva cries out loud whenever she sits on a high chair.

小伊娃每次坐到高椅子上就大聲喊叫。

③ Since Taiwan has entered the WTO, English has become more important.

台灣加入世界貿易組織以後，英文就變得更重要了。

④ Sonia quit her job because she could not get along with her boss.

桑妮雅辭職了，因為她跟老闆處不來。

⑤ Julia could not concentrate in class because she felt very tired and hungry.

茱莉亞上課無法集中精神，因為她又累又餓。

⑥ If Irene goes to the herbal teahouse tomorrow, she will call and tell her friend.

如果艾琳明天要去花草茶店，她會打電話跟她朋友說。

⑦ You will communicate better with foreigners if you can speak their languages.

如果你會說外國人的語言，就會比較容易跟他們溝通。

⑧ Patrick will go on a study tour to London this summer unless he cannot get his parents' permission.

除非無法得到父母的同意，不然派屈克今年夏天會去倫敦遊學。

⑨ Although Jeff ran very quickly to the bus station, he still missed the bus.

雖然傑夫快速地跑去公車站，他還是錯過了公車。

⑩ Robert went to school this morning even though he was terribly sick.

雖然病得很重，羅伯特今天早上還是去上學了。

用比較句型合併

範例

1 Joanne has five thousand dollars.

Jenny has the same amount of money.

→ Jenny has ＿＿＿＿＿＿＿＿＿＿ Joanne.

ANS Jenny has *as much money as* Joanne (does).

珍妮有和瓊安一樣多的錢。

2 Alex and Adam are brothers.

Alex is short and Adam is tall.

→ Adam is ＿＿＿＿＿＿＿＿＿＿ of the two brothers.

ANS Adam is *the taller* of the two brothers.

亞當是兩兄弟中較高的那一個。

🔷 基本概念

　　關於形容詞或副詞之比較級與最高級之概念，本書「比較級與最高級的句型切換」單元已作說明，在此不再贅述。以下區分為「as ＋原級＋ as」及「more/-er...than」兩種型態，說明比較句型之合併題型。

I. 原級型態的比較句型

$$as + \begin{cases} \text{adj. 原級 (＋ N)} \\ \\ \text{adv. 原級} \end{cases} + as = \text{the same N} + as$$

🔷 應考要訣

1️⃣ as...as 之間必須接形容詞或副詞之原級。

2️⃣ 句中之形容詞後若搭配名詞，必須將此 adj. ＋ N 置於 as 與 as 中間。

③ 在原句中若找不到適當之形容詞或副詞，不可數名詞可採用 much，
而可數名詞則以 many 替代。

◆ **範例分析**

1. Joanne has five thousand dollars.

   Jenny has the same amount of money.

   →Jenny has ＿＿＿＿＿＿＿＿＿＿ Joanne (does).

   hint 以形容詞原級改寫

   →Jenny has *as much money as* Joanne (does).

   珍妮有和瓊安一樣多的錢。

說明
1 原句中 Joanne 與 Jenny 有相同數目的錢。
2 原句中無適當之形容詞，不可數名詞可選用形容詞 much，形成 much money。
3 將 much money 套入「as ＋原級形容詞 (+N) ＋ as」句型中。

◆ **試題演練**

請以形容詞原級合併以下句子

① A cat is not like a tiger.

   A tiger is very strong.

   → A cat is not as ＿＿＿＿＿＿＿＿＿＿＿ a tiger.

② Clark is 183 centimeters tall.

   Alex is the same height as Clark.

   → Alex is as ＿＿＿＿＿＿＿＿＿＿＿ Clark.

③ Beatrice does not have much money.

   Her sister doesn't have much money, either.

   → Beatrice's sister has as ＿＿＿＿＿＿＿＿ Beatrice.

④ Sandy is a beautiful girl.

   Sandra has the same good looks.

   → Sandra is as ＿＿＿＿＿＿＿＿＿＿＿ Sandy.

⑤ Lily has five brothers.

Amy has the same number of brothers.

→ Amy has as _____ brothers _____ Lily.

⑥ Vincent is very rich.

He is the richest man in town.

→ No one in town is as _____ Vincent.

⑦ Sean plays football well.

He is the best player on the team.

→ No one on the team plays football as _____ as Sean.

⑧ I got ten emails.

My friend got the same number of emails.

→ I got as _____ emails _____ my friend.

⑨ I drank four cups of coffee.

Kay drank four cups, too.

→ Kay drank as _____ I.

⑩ Sally is very thin.

Her sister has the same weight.

→ Sally's sister is as _____ she.

→ Sally's sister weighs as _____ she.

II. 比較級的比較句型

$$\left[\begin{array}{l} \textbf{adj.-er / adv.-er} \\[2mm] \textbf{more adj. / adv.} \end{array} \right] + \textbf{than}$$

💡 **應考要訣**

1) 句中出現 than，採形容詞或副詞之比較級 more/-er，如下列例句 2 及例句 3。

2) 句中未出現 than 但後有「of＋兩事物」，採比較級句型，形成「the ＋

比較級＋of＋兩事物」之句型，如例句4。

◆ 範例分析

2) Tom is twenty.

Betty is twenty-six years old.

→Betty is six years _____ than Tom.

hint 以形容詞比較級改寫

→Betty is six years *older* than Tom.

貝蒂比湯姆大六歲。

說明

1 原句係比較 Tom 及 Betty 兩人之年紀。

2 合併句使用 older than，表示 Betty 比 Tom 年紀大。

3) The weather in Taipei is not hot.

It is very hot in Kaohsing.

→The weather in Kaohsing is _____ than that in Taipei.

hint 以形容詞比較級改寫

→The weather in Kaohsing is *hotter* than that in Taipei.

高雄的天氣比台北熱。

4) Alex and Adam are brothers.

Alex is short and Adam is tall.

→Adam is _____ of the two brothers.

hint 以形容詞比較級改寫

→Adam is *the taller* of the two brothers.

亞當是兩兄弟中較高的那一個。

說明

1 兩者較高者，採用「the＋比較級＋of＋兩事物」句型。

2 Adam 較 Alex 高，因而將 tall 改為其比較級 taller。

◆ **試題演練**

請以形容詞比較級合併以下句子

⑪ Fred got good grades on the final exam.

Alice did not do well.

→ Fred got _____ grades on the final exam than Alice.

⑫ My school is big.

Your school is small.

→ My school is _____ than yours.

⑬ Rivers in Taiwan are short.

Most rivers in China are long.

→ Most rivers in China are _____ than those in Taiwan.

⑭ The traffic in Taipei is bad.

The traffic in my hometown is good.

→ The traffic in Taipei is _____ than that in my hometown.

⑮ Jessie is a clever girl.

She is the cleverest girl in her class.

→ Jessie is _____ than any other _____ in her class.

⑯ Judy does not sing beautifully.

Kristy sings beautifully.

→ Judy sings _____ than Kristy.

⑰ It is noisy in a big city.

The countryside is quiet.

→ The countryside is _____ than a big city.

⑱ Yvonne earns 80 thousand NT dollars a month.

Her sister earns 50 thousand NT dollars a month.

→ Yvonne's sister earns _____ than she.

⑲ Tom felt a little nervous.

Andy was very nervous.

→ Andy was _____ than Tom.

⑳ My grandfather can speak Japanese.

No one in my family speaks as well as he.

→ My grandfather speaks Japanese _____ than all the other members in my family.

解答

① A cat is not as strong as a tiger.
貓不像老虎一樣勇猛。

② Alex is as tall as Clark.
艾力克斯和克拉克一樣高。

③ Beatrice's sister has as little money as Beatrice.
碧翠絲的姊姊／妹妹有和碧翠絲一樣少的錢。

④ Sandra is as beautiful as Sandy.
珊德拉和姍蒂長得一樣漂亮。

⑤ Amy has as many brothers as Lily.
艾咪有和莉莉一樣多的兄弟。

⑥ No one in town is as rich as Vincent.
鎮上沒有人和文森一樣富有。

⑦ No one on the team plays football as well as Sean.
隊上沒有人足球踢得和西恩一樣好。

⑧ I got as many emails as my friend.
我收到和我朋友一樣多的電子郵件。

⑨ Kay drank as many cups of coffee as I.
凱依喝了和我同樣多杯的咖啡。
Kay drank as much coffee as I.
凱依喝了和我一樣多的咖啡。

⑩ Sally's sister is as thin as she.
莎莉的姊姊／妹妹和她一樣瘦。
Sally's sister weighs as much as she.
莎莉的姊姊／妹妹和她一樣重。

⑪ Fred got better grades on the final exam than Alice.
弗瑞德期末考得到比艾莉絲好的成績。

⑫ My school is bigger than yours.

我的學校比你的學校來得大。

⑬ Most rivers in China are longer than those in Taiwan.

中國境內大多數的河流都比台灣的來得長。

⑭ The traffic in Taipei is worse than that in my hometown.

台北的交通比我家鄉的交通糟糕。

⑮ Jessie is cleverer than any other girl in her class.

潔西比她班上的任何其他女生聰明。

⑯ Judy sings less beautifully than Kristy.

茱蒂歌唱得沒克莉絲蒂好聽。

⑰ The countryside is quieter than a big city.

鄉村地區比大城市安靜。

⑱ Yvonne's sister earns less (money) than she.

伊鳳的姊姊／妹妹賺的錢比她少。

⑲ Andy was more nervous than Tom.

安迪比湯姆還要緊張。

⑳ My grandfather speaks Japanese better than all the other members in my family.

我祖父日文說得比我們家裡任何人都要好。

用介系詞合併

範例

1　Catherine picked up the trash.

The trash was on the floor.

→　Catherine _____ the trash _____ the floor.

ANS　Catherine *picked up* the trash *on* the floor.

凱薩琳撿起地上的垃圾。

🔳 **基本概念**

　　介系詞位於名詞之前，表地點、位置、時間、方法、方向、原因等。以下列舉常見以介系詞合併之句型：

◆ **範例分析**

表地方（常見介系詞，如 on、in、under、from 等）

1. Catherine picked up the trash.

The trash was on the floor.

→ Catherine _____ the trash _____ the floor.

hint 以介系詞片語合併

→ Catherine *picked up* the trash *on* the floor.

凱薩琳撿起地上的垃圾。

說明

1　原句重複之處，為 the trash。

2　合併時在 the trash 後加入介系詞片語 on the floor，表 the trash 所在位置。

2 My father cut the steak.

He used a knife to cut it.

→ My father ＿＿＿＿＿ the steak ＿＿＿＿＿ a knife.

hint 以介系詞片語合併

→ My father *cut* the steak *with* a knife.

我爸爸用刀子切那塊牛排。

說明

1 原句中 cut the steak ＝ cut it。

2 合併後，動詞片語 used a knife 轉化為介系詞片語 with a knife，表 cut the steak 的方法。

3 Vicky dressed herself.

She wore a red dress.

→ Vicky dressed herself ＿＿＿＿＿ red.

hint 以介系詞片語合併

→ Vicky dressed herself *in* red.

維琪穿著一套紅色的衣服。

說明

1 原句中重複之處為 dressed 與 wore。

2 合併後，動詞片語 wore a red dress 轉化為介系詞片語 in red，in 表「方式」。

表屬性（常見介系詞，如 with、of 等）

4 I like the guys.

They have a sense of humor.

→ I like the guys ＿＿＿＿＿ a sense of humor.

hint 以介系詞片語合併

→ I like the guys *with* a sense of humor.

我喜歡那些有幽默感的人。

> **說明**
>
> 1 原句 the guys = They。
>
> 2 合併時，於 guys 後加上 with 以串連 a sense of humor，表 guys 之屬性。

> 表交通方式（常見介系詞為 by，如：by bus、by air、by taxi 等，但 on foot）

5 Tony goes to school.

He takes the bus.

→ Tony goes to school _____ bus.

hint 以介系詞片語合併

→ Tony goes to school *by* bus.

東尼搭巴士去上學。

> **說明**
>
> 1 原句 Tony = He。
>
> 2 合併時，將動詞片語 takes the bus 轉化為介系詞片語 by bus，表交通方式。

> 表原因（常見介系詞為 for）

6 William was punished.

He was late for school.

→ William was punished _____ late for school.

hint 以介系詞片語合併

→ William was punished *for being* late for school.

威廉因為上學遲到而受處罰。

> **說明**
>
> 1 原句 William = He。
>
> 2 合併時，在句 1 之句尾加上表原因之介系詞 for；句 2 之 was late for school 緊接於介系詞之後，was 須變化為其動名詞型態 being，形成介系詞片語 for being late for school。

特定介詞片語

7 Something keeps me busy.

I write my report.

→I am busy _____ my report.

[hint] 以介系詞片語合併

→I am busy *with* my report.

→I am busy *writing* my report.

我忙著寫我的報告。

說明

1 be busy with 為特定片語。

2 本句有兩種改法

  a) 以 be busy ＋介系詞 with ＋名詞＝ be busy with my report 合併之。

  b) 或 be busy ＋動名詞 Ving（＋受詞）＝ be busy writing my report。

◆ 試題演練

請以介系詞合併以下句子

① Irene looked at the poster.

The poster was on the bulletin board.

→ Irene _____ the poster _____ the bulletin board.

② I cannot do it.

I have to use a computer.

→ I cannot do _____ a computer.

③ Taroko National Park is famous.

It has beautiful scenery.

→ Taroko National Park is famous _____ its beautiful scenery.

④ Reading is interesting.

Ting reads lots of books.

→ Ting _____ interested _____ reading books.

⑤ Joe is a leader.

He has a strong sense of responsibility.

→ Joe is a leader _____ a strong sense of responsibility.

⑥ John went to the train station.

He walked there.

→ John went to the train station _____ foot.

⑦ Jason wore a suit.

He wanted to look formal.

→ Jason dressed _____ a formal way.

⑧ Michelle smiled.

She looked very friendly.

→ Michelle smiled _____ a friendly way.

⑨ Calvin was punished.

He stole money.

→ Calvin _____ for _____.

⑩ No one can survive.

Everyone needs water.

→ One cannot survive _____ water.

解答

① Irene looked at the poster on the bulletin board.
艾琳看著佈告欄上的海報。

② I cannot do it without (using) a computer.
沒有電腦我無法做這件事。

③ Taroko National Park is famous for its beautiful scenery.
太魯閣國家公園以漂亮的風景而聞名。

④ Ting is interested in reading books.
婷對閱讀書籍有興趣。

⑤ Joe is a leader with a strong sense of responsibility.
喬是個有強烈責任心的領導者。

⑥ John went to the train station on foot.
約翰步行到火車站。

⑦ Jason dressed in a formal way.
傑森穿著正式服裝。

⑧ Michelle smiled in a friendly way.
蜜雪兒很友善地微笑著。

⑨ Calvin was punished for stealing money.
凱文因為偷錢而被處罰。

⑩ One cannot survive without water.
一個人要是沒有水就無法生存。

用使役動詞合併

範例

1　The teacher had us do something.
　　We mopped the floor.

→　The teacher had us _____ .

ANS　The teacher had us *mop the floor.*
　　老師要我們拖地板。

基本概念

　　「使役動詞」包括：make、have及let，其基本句型為「使役動詞＋受詞＋受詞補語」如下。另，get雖為一般動詞，被動用法與使役動詞類似，在此一併說明。

使役動詞	受詞	受詞補語		
		主動型態	被動型態	
make	受詞	V	Vpp	Adj.
have				
let				
get		to + V		

　　使役動詞後之受詞補語，包括一般動詞及形容詞兩種型態，前者表動作、後者表狀態。當受詞補語為一般動詞時，須判斷其主、被動，以決定採用原形動詞或過去分詞。

　　至於受詞補語之主被動，取決於受詞與受詞補語間之關係；判斷準則在於受詞是否為受詞補語之動作行使者：

①受詞為受詞補語的動作行使者──→表主動，受詞補語採原形動詞。

113

（注意：get後之受詞補語採不定詞to＋V型態）

2 受詞非受詞補語的動作行使者──→表被動，受詞補語採過去分詞 Vpp。

應考要訣

1 判斷該使役動詞的組別（參考上表）。

2 找尋受詞補語（可能為動詞或形容詞兩種型態）。

3 受詞補語為動詞時，需進一步研究其與受詞間之關係，以決定語態：主動採原形動詞、被動則採Vpp。

◆ 範例分析

受詞補語為動詞之主動型態

1 The teacher had us do something.
　 We mopped the floor.

　 →The teacher had us _____.

　 hint 以使役動詞合併

　 →The teacher had us *mop* the floor.
　　 老師要我們拖地板。

說明

1 使役動詞had後，須與動詞mopped作適當結合。

2 檢驗mopped之語態：受詞us為mopped the floor之執行者，故採用主動型態之受詞補語，即其原形mop。

受詞補語為動詞之被動型態

2 Dennis asked Ivy to do something.
　 Ivy typed his letters.

　 →Dennis had his letters _____ by _____.

　 hint 以使役動詞合併

　 →Dennis had his letters *typed* by *Ivy*.
　　 丹尼斯請艾薇幫他打信。

說明

1 使役動詞 had 後，須與動詞 typed 作適當結合。

2 檢驗 typed 之語態：受詞 his letters 非 typed 之執行者，故採用被動型態之受詞補語，即其過去分詞 typed。

受詞補語為形容詞

3 I am tired.

The reason is that I stayed up late last night.

→Staying up late last night makes me _____.

hint 以使役動詞合併

→Staying up late last night makes me *tired.*

昨天晚上熬夜讓我覺得疲倦。

說明

原句中無一般動詞，make 後之受詞補語，採原句之形容詞 tired。

◆ 試題演練

請以使役動詞句型合併以下句子

① Amy called a repairman.

The repairman fixed her TV set.

→ Amy had her TV set _____ by the repairman.

② Jenny asked George for help.

George helped Jenny with her math assignments.

→ Jenny got George _____ her with her math assignments.

③ I felt relaxed.

Listening to music helped.

→ Listening to music made me _____.

④ Jessica cooked dinner for Ray.

Ray asked her to cook.

→ Ray got his dinner _____ by Jessica.

⑤ Billy's wife asked him to do something.

Billy cleaned up the toilet.

→ Billy's wife made him _____ the toilet.

⑥ The boy went straight home after school.

His mother told him to do so.

→ The boy's mother had him _____ after school.

⑦ Annie washed the dishes.

Her mother asked her to do it.

→ Annie's mother got her _____ the dishes.

⑧ I was confused.

Ben married the woman.

→ That Ben married the woman got me _____.

⑨ My mother allowed me to do something.

I worked in a comic bookstore last summer.

→ My mother let me _____ in a comic bookstore last summer.

⑩ Rex sent his computer to the store.

It was repaired.

→ Rex had his computer _____ in the store.

解答

① Amy had her TV set fixed by the repairman.
艾咪請維修工人修好她的電視。

② Jenny got George to help her with her math assignments.
珍妮請喬治來幫她寫數學作業。

③ Listening to music made me feel relaxed.
聽音樂讓我覺得放鬆。

④ Ray got his dinner cooked by Jessica.
瑞讓潔西卡幫他煮晚餐。

⑤ Billy's wife made him clean up the toilet.
比利的老婆要他洗廁所。

⑥ The boy's mother had him go straight home after school.
男孩的媽媽要他放學後直接回家。

⑦ Annie's mother got her to wash the dishes.
安妮的媽媽要她去洗碗盤。

⑧ That Ben married the woman got me confused.
班和那女人結婚的事讓我不解。

⑨ My mother let me work in a comic bookstore last summer.
去年夏天媽媽讓我在一間漫畫書店工作。

⑩ Rex had his computer repaired in the store.
雷克斯讓他的電腦在那間店裡修好了。

用感官動詞合併

範例

1　The boys watched something on TV.
　　Some people played football on TV.

→　The boys watched some people ＿＿＿＿＿＿ on TV.

ANS　The boys watched some people *play football* on TV.
　　男孩們看著電視裡的人踢足球。

🔵 **基本概念**

　　所謂「感官動詞」，係表達視、聽、感覺方面之動詞，常見者如：see、watch、look at、hear、listen to 及 feel等。其基本句型為「感官動詞＋受詞＋受詞補語」。感官動詞之受詞補語有以下兩類，其型態與功能如表所示：

感官動詞之受詞補語	
型態	功能
V	強調事實
Ving	強調進行

🔵 **應考要訣**

1️⃣ 找尋句中之感官動詞與一般動詞

2️⃣ 原句中一般動詞為簡單式，合併後需還原為原形動詞型態。

3️⃣ 原句中一般動詞為進行式，合併則為 Ving 型態。

◆ **範例分析**

受詞補語為原形動詞

1️⃣ The boys watched something on TV.

Some people played football on TV.

→ The boys watched some people ＿＿＿＿＿＿＿＿ on TV.

hint 以感官動詞合併

→ The boys **watched** some people *play football* on TV.

男孩們看著電視裡的人踢足球。

說明

1 第一句中的 watched 為感官動詞，第二句之動詞 played 為簡單過去式。

2 played 作為感官動詞之受詞補語，需還原為原形動詞 watch。

受詞補語為 Ving 型態

2️⃣ I heard some sounds.

The birds were singing.

→ I heard ＿＿＿＿＿＿＿＿＿＿＿＿.

hint 以感官動詞合併

→ I **heard** the birds *singing*.

我聽到鳥在唱歌。

說明

1 第一句中的 heard 為感官動詞，第二句之動詞 were singing 為進行式。

2 合併時感官動詞後之受詞補語須採 Ving 型態，即 singing。

◆ **試題演練**

請以感官動詞的句型合併以下句子

① The teacher saw something.

Her students were cheating on the exam.

→ The teacher saw her students ＿＿＿＿＿＿＿＿＿ on the exam.

② The house was shaking.

  We felt it.

  → We felt the house _____.

③ Bill saw a dog.

  The dog was wagging its tail.

  → Bill saw a dog _____ its tail.

④ Moe watched something.

  A thief stole her jewelry.

  → Moe watched a thief _____ her jewelry.

⑤ Charlie is looking at something.

  The sun is setting.

  → Charlie is looking at the sun _____.

⑥ I listened to some music.

  The guitarist played in an auditorium.

  → I listened to the guitarist _____.

⑦ Sophia heard some noise.

  The floor was creaking.

  → Sophia heard the floor _____.

⑧ Phil is listening to his teacher.

  The teacher is telling a ghost story.

  → Phil is listening to his teacher _____.

⑨ I saw some children.

  They were dancing on the playground.

  → I saw some children _____.

⑩ Tina's heart was beating faster and faster.

  She felt it.

  → Tina felt her heart _____.

解答

① The teacher saw her students cheating on the exam.
老師看見她的學生考試作弊。

② We felt the house shaking.
我們感覺到房子在震動。

③ Bill saw a dog wagging its tail.
比爾看見一隻狗搖著尾巴。

④ Moe watched a thief steal her jewelry.
摩依看到小偷偷她的珠寶。

⑤ Charlie is looking at the sun setting.
查理正望著日落。

⑥ I listened to the guitarist play in an auditorium.
我在演奏廳裡聽那吉他手表演。

⑦ Sophia heard the floor creaking.
索菲亞聽到地板咯吱作響的聲音。

⑧ Phil is listening to his teacher telling a ghost story.
菲爾正在聽他的老師說鬼故事。

⑨ I saw some children dancing on the playground.
我看到一些孩子在運動場上跳舞。

⑩ Tina felt her heart beating faster and faster.
蒂娜感覺到她的心愈跳愈快。

用特殊句型合併

範例

1　The news is very good.
　　We can't believe the news is true.

→　The news is ＿＿＿＿＿ good to ＿＿＿＿＿ true.

ANS　The news is *too* good to *be* true.
　　這消息好得令人難以置信。

🔷 基本概念

　　以下僅列出兩種以特定片語合併之題型供參考，其他特殊句型之用法請參考本書用特定片語改寫的單元。

◆ 範例分析

1. The news is very good.
   We can't believe the news is true.

   → The news is too ＿＿＿＿＿ to ＿＿＿＿＿ true.

   hint 以特定片語合併

   → The news is *too* good to *be* true.
   這消息好得令人難以置信。

   說明

   1 合併句中出現 to，可合併為 too...to 之句型。
   2 too 後加上形容詞 good，to 後加原形動詞，因而將 is 改成 be。

2. I can do only one thing.
   The thing is to ask for help.

   → All ＿＿＿＿＿＿＿＿＿＿ is ＿＿＿＿＿＿＿＿＿＿.
   → What ＿＿＿＿＿＿＿＿ is ＿＿＿＿＿＿＿＿＿＿.

→ The only thing that _____ is _____.

hint 以特定片語合併

→ **All** *I can do* is *ask for help.*

→ **What** *I can do* is *ask for help.*

→ **The only thing that** *I can do* is *ask for help.*

我所能做的就是請求協助。

> **說明**
>
> 1 以上合併句之三種句型，均採單數動詞 is，其後之主詞補語必須
> 接原形動詞，句構如下：
>
> $\left.\begin{array}{l} \text{All...} \\ \text{What...} \\ \text{The only thing...} \end{array}\right\}$ + is + 原形 V
>
> 2 將原句中不定詞型態之主詞補語改為原形的 ask for help。

◆ **試題演練**

請合併以下句子

① I felt very embarrassed.

I was speechless.

→ I felt so embarrassed _____ I _____.

② I had a habit.

I always walked home after work.

→ I used _____ after work.

③ Alice went to bed late.

It was three o'clock in the morning when she did.

→ Alice didn't _____ until _____ in the morning.

④ The phone rang.

Tom picked up the phone immediately.

→ Tom _____ as soon as _____.

⑤ The teacher always called on Adam.

He was never able to answer the questions.

→ Adam was unable to _____ whenever _____.

⑥ John loves reading magazines.

He reads *Time* magazine sometimes.

→ John loves reading magazines, _____ *Time* magazine.

⑦ I did not know Kim would teach us.

I knew it only when May told me.

→ I did not know _____ until _____.

⑧ Judy does not have enough money.

She cannot buy that coat.

→ Judy does not _____ enough money _____ that coat.

→ Judy has _____ little money to _____ that coat.

⑨ Ming eats little food.

Her purpose is to lose weight.

→ Ming _____ so that she can _____.

→ Ming _____ in order to _____.

⑩ Sean has many very good friends.

He likes Michael very much.

→ Michael _____ one of _____ best friends.

解答

① I felt so embarrassed that I was speechless.
我感到相當尷尬而說不出話來。

② I used to walk home after work.
我以前下班都走路回家。

③ Alice didn't go to bed until three o'clock in the morning.
愛麗絲一直到清晨三點才上床睡覺。

④ Tom picked up the phone as soon as it rang.
電話一響湯姆就接起來。

⑤ Adam was unable to answer the questions whenever the teacher called on him.
每次老師叫到亞當他都回答不出問題。

⑥ John loves reading magazines, including *Time* magazine.
約翰喜歡讀書，包括雜誌。

⑦ I did not know Kim would teach us until May told me.
直到梅告訴我我才知道金要教我們。

⑧ Judy does not have enough money to buy that coat.
茱蒂沒有足夠的錢買那件外套。

Judy has too little money to buy that coat.
茱蒂的錢太少無法買那件外套。

⑨ Ming eats little food so that she can lose weight.
明吃得很少以便她能夠減肥。

Ming eats little food in order to lose weight.
明吃得很少是為了減肥。

⑩ Michael is one of Sean's best friends.
麥可是西恩最好的朋友之一。

單元三 重組

授與動詞的重組

範例

1 I sent _____ during my trip.

(my boyfriend/some photos/to)

ANS I sent *some photos to my boyfriend* during my trip.

旅程中我寄了些照片給我男友。

🔹 基本概念

擁有兩個受詞之及物動詞，稱之為「授與動詞」，如：give、send、lend、sell、buy、bring及ask等。

授與動詞的兩受詞，分別為「直接受詞」(D.O.)與「間接受詞」(I.O.)。直接受詞表示授與動詞的「主要施予對象」，通常為「物」；而「接受直接受詞的對象」即為間接受詞，通常為「人」。兩受詞先後位置不同，形成不同句構如下：

句型1：間接受詞在前，無介系詞

　　　⟶ 授與動詞＋I.O.＋D.O.（通常為「人＋物」）

句型2：直接受詞在前，須加介系詞

　　　⟶ 授與動詞＋D.O.＋介系詞＋I.O.（通常為「物＋介系詞＋人」）

授與動詞常搭配之介系詞，用以表達「直接受詞」傳遞至「間接受詞」之過程或方法，如下：

授與動詞	搭配之介系詞
ask	of
bring, give, lend, send, sell, teach, tell, write	to
bring, buy, choose, do, get, order, cook	for

🔵 應考要訣

1️⃣ 找尋授與動詞後之兩受詞。

2️⃣ 分辨直接受詞 D.O. 與間接受詞 I.O.。

3️⃣ 句中若無介系詞，則選擇上述句型 1：間接受詞在前；句中有介系詞，則選擇上述句型 2：直接受詞在前。

◆ 範例分析

1️⃣ I sent _____ during my trip.
(my boyfriend/some photos/sent/to)

　hint 以授與動詞重組

→ I sent *some photos to my boyfriend* during my trip.

　　旅程中我寄了些照片給我男友。

　說明

1 此句型為「授與 V ＋ D.O.＋介系詞＋ I.O.」。
2 重組字詞中出現介系詞 to，選用第 2 句型：D.O.＋介系詞＋ I.O.。
3 直接受詞為 some photos，間接受詞為 my boyfriend。
4 授與動詞 sent 先接 some photos，再接 to my boyfriend。

2️⃣ Kristy's husband _____ as a birthday gift.
(her/some flowers/bought)

　hint 以授與動詞重組

→ Kristy's husband *bought her some flowers* as a birthday gift.

　　克麗絲提的丈夫買了些花給她當作生日禮物。

　說明

1 重組字詞中無任何介系詞，選用第 1 句型：
　授與動詞＋ I.O.＋ D.O.。
2 間接受詞為 her，直接受詞為 some flowers。
3 授與動詞 bought 後接 her，再接 some flowers。

◆ **試題演練**

請以授與動詞重組以下句子

① The Smiths _____.

   (the kids/some candy/gave/and chocolate)

② Ivy's boyfriend _____.

   (for/bought/a beautiful/her/bracelet)

③ The street vender _____.

   (fake bags/sold/people/to)

④ Joanne always asks _____ in class.

   (questions/her teacher/asks/a lot of)

⑤ Billy _____.

   (a letter/to/wrote/his brother)

⑥ Bob doesn't want to _____.

   (the computer/his little brother/to/lend)

⑦ Ray _____.

   (yesterday/sent/Christmas cards/his friends/some)

⑧ Molly _____ her children.

   (for/some fried chicken/bought/and hamburgers)

⑨ The store _____.

   (pet rabbits/my brother/two/sold)

⑩ The old lady _____.

   (a/for/wonderful/us/cooked/meal)

解答

① The Smiths gave the kids some candy and chocolate.
史密斯一家人給那些孩子一些糖果和巧克力。

② Ivy's boyfriend bought a beautiful bracelet for her.
艾薇的男友買了一只漂亮的手環送她。

③ The street vender sold fake bags to people.
路邊小販販售仿冒皮包給人。

④ Joanne always asks her teacher a lot of questions in class.
瓊安上課時總是問老師很多問題。

⑤ Billy wrote a letter to his brother.
比利寫一封信給他哥哥／弟弟。

⑥ Bob doesn't want to lend the computer to his little brother.
鮑伯不想把電腦借給他弟弟。

⑦ Ray sent his friends some Christmas cards yesterday.
瑞昨天寄了一些聖誕卡給他朋友。

⑧ Molly bought some fried chicken and hamburgers for her children.
莫莉買了些炸雞和漢堡給她的小孩。

⑨ The store sold my brother two pet rabbits.
那間店賣給我哥哥／弟弟兩隻寵物兔。

⑩ The old lady cooked a wonderful meal for us.
這老婦人為我們煮了美味的一餐。

時態的重組

範例

1　Mark _____.

　　(on/was/a book/working/yesterday morning)

ANS　Mark *was working on a book yesterday morning.*

　　馬克昨天早上在寫一本書。

🔖 基本概念

　　本單元主要處理肯定句之時態重組。以下區分為四個主題，概略說明時態重組應注意事項：

1 詞序——➤ S＋V

　　1) 進行式時態——➤ S＋Be＋Ving

　　2) 完成式時態——➤ S＋has/have/had＋Vpp

2 動詞性質

　　觀察動詞為及物動詞或不及物動詞；若為前者，進一步判斷是否為一般動詞、使役、感官或授與動詞。（前述動詞特性與用法，可參考本書各相關單元。）

3 受詞位置

　　位於動詞之後；若為授與動詞，則需判斷其為直接或間接受詞，以決定二者之先後位置。

4 副詞位置

　　表地點或時間之副詞片語，通常置於句尾。

　　頻率副詞置於 Be 動詞和助動詞之後，一般動詞之前。

🔖 應考要訣

1 找尋句中主詞，其次找出主要動詞與助動詞，並分辨動詞性質。

2 將受詞移至動詞之後。

3 片語處理原則

　　V＋介系詞──→形成動詞片語──→置於主詞之後。

　　介系詞＋N──→通常表時間或地點──→一般置於句尾。

◆ 範例分析

進行式之重組

1 Mark ＿＿＿＿＿＿＿＿＿＿＿＿＿＿＿＿＿＿＿＿＿ .

(on/was/a book/working/yesterday morning)

hint 以適當時態重組之

→ Mark *was working on a book yesterday morning.*
馬克昨天早上在寫一本書。

說明

1 主詞之後應為動詞。重組字組中之動詞有 was 及 working，可判斷為進行式。

2 Work 為不及物動詞，後加 on 以連接受詞 a book。 work on 為動詞片語，表「從事……；做……；寫……等」。

3 Yesterday morning 為表時間之副詞片語，應置於句尾。

完成式之重組

2 I ＿＿＿＿＿＿＿＿＿＿＿＿＿＿＿＿＿＿＿＿＿ .

(new/laptop computer/have/for/longed for/a/two years)

hint 以適當時態重組之

→ I *have longed for a new laptop computer for two years.*
這兩年來我一直想要一台新的筆記型電腦。

說明

1 重組字堆中有 have 及 longed，可判斷為完成式。

2 Long 為不及物動詞，後加 for 以連接受詞 a new laptop computer。動詞片語 long for 表「渴望」。

3 For two years 為表持續性時間之副詞片語，應置於句尾。

◆ 試題演練

請以適當的時態重組以下句子

① Jessie _____.

(on the phone/is/with/her friend/talking)

② I _____ the phone rang.

(having/when/at home/was/breakfast)

③ They _____ to catch the last train.

(rushing/the station/to/were)

④ Sunny _____.

(her baby/was/at that time/feeding)

⑤ Patrick _____.

(at home/is/right/math/studying now)

⑥ Kristy _____.

(kept/for/the teddy bear/twelve years/has)

⑦ You _____.

(have/should/the truth/us/told)

⑧ My niece and nephew _____.

(been/in the park/playing/half an hour/for/ have)

⑨ Tony _____.

(worked/for/at the company/fifteen years/has/more than)

⑩ Einstein _____.

(the/considered/one/has been/of/greatest scientists)

解答

① Jessie is talking with her friend on the phone.
潔西正在和她朋友講電話。

② I was having breakfast at home when the phone rang.
電話響時我正在家裡吃早餐。

③ They were rushing to the station to catch the last train.
他們正趕往車站以趕上最後一班火車。

④ Sunny was feeding her baby at that time.
桑妮那時候正在餵孩子吃東西。

⑤ Patrick is studying math at home right now.
派屈克現正在家裡念數學。

⑥ Kristy has kept the teddy bear for twelve years.
克麗絲提已保存那泰迪熊有十二年之久。

⑦ You should have told us the truth.
你應該對我們說實話的。

⑧ My niece and nephew have been playing in the park for half an hour.
我的姪子和姪女已經在公園裡玩了半小時了。

⑨ Tony has worked at the company for more than fifteen years.
東尼已經在那家公司工作超過十五年。

⑩ Einstein has been considered one of the greatest scientists.
愛因斯坦被公認為最偉大的科學家之一。

疑問句的重組

範例

1   Is _____?

(hottest/month/in Taiwan/the/July)

ANS   Is *July the hottest month in Taiwan*?

在台灣七月是最酷熱的一個月嗎？

🔰 基本概念

　　疑問句之基本句型於本書「直述句改疑問句」單元中已作說明，請讀者自行參考，在此不再重述。本單元僅就四種疑問句類型各舉一例說明之。

🔰 應考要訣

1️⃣ 分辨問句之類型，找出句子之主詞與動詞。

2️⃣ 及物動詞及介系詞後須接受詞。

3️⃣ 表地點或時間之副詞片語置於句尾。

I. Be 動詞型問句之重組

　　Be 動詞型之疑問句，主詞與動詞必須倒裝，形成如下句構：

Be ＋ S ＋ (Ving/Vpp) ＋ 補語 ?

◆ 範例分析

1️⃣ Is _____?

(hottest/month/in Taiwan/the/July)

hint Be 動詞型問句之重組

→ Is *July the hottest month in Taiwan*?

在台灣七月是最酷熱的一個月嗎？

> **說明**
>
> 1 July 為本句之主詞。
> 2 Hottest 為形容詞最高級，與定冠詞 the 搭配形成 the hottest，後
> 接名詞 month。
> 3 In Taiwan 為地點片語置於句尾。

◆ 試題演練

請重組以下問句

① Was _____?

(the doorbell/cooking/rang/Susan/when)

② Is _____?

(any/for today/homework/there)

③ When _____?

(your brother/born/was)

④ Where _____?

(the nearest/Taipei Zoo/is/to/bus stop)

⑤ What _____?

(favorite/your/is/sport)

II. 一般動詞型問句之重組

一般動詞型之問句，必須在主詞前加上助動詞 do/does/did，而主詞
之後為原形動詞，句構如下：

$$疑問詞 \begin{bmatrix} do \\ does \\ did \end{bmatrix} + S + V（+ 副詞）?$$

注意，若問句以疑問詞起頭而該疑問詞作為主詞時，其後直接接動
詞，無須加助動詞。

◆ 範例分析

2. Does _____ ?

(to walk/to school/take/it/long)

hint 一般動詞型問句之重組

→ Does *it take long to walk to school*?

走路去學校要花很長的時間嗎?

說明

1 it為本句之主詞,動詞為take,助動詞為does。

2 依【助動詞+S+V】之句構重組,形成 Does it take...。

3 To walk 後接介系詞片語 to school 表地方。

3. Who _____ ?

(my/came/birthday party/last night/to)

hint 一般動詞型問句之重組

→ Who *came to my birthday party last night*?

昨晚誰來參加我的生日派對?

說明

1 疑問詞 Who 為本句之主詞,came 為動詞。

2 介系詞 to 後接 my birthday party,表地點。

◆ 試題演練

請重組以下問句

⑥ Who _____ ?

(Mei-Ting/the party/yesterday/to/took)

⑦ How often _____ ?

(in the gym/exercise/you/do)

⑧ When _____ in your country?

(dating/do/start/most teenagers)

⑨ Did _____ ?

(enjoy/at the restaurant/on the corner/the food/Tina)

⑩ Did _____ when watching _____?
(romantic movie/the/fall/John/asleep)

III. 時態助動詞型問句之重組

時態助動詞型之問句，係在主詞前加上助動詞 has/have/had，形成如下句構：

$$（疑問詞）\begin{bmatrix} \textbf{has} \\ \textbf{have} \\ \textbf{had} \end{bmatrix} + \textbf{S} + \textbf{Vpp} （+ 副詞）？$$

◆ **範例分析**

3） How many _____?
(have/you/in/pounds/the past month/lost)

> hint 時態助動詞型問句之重組

→ How many *pounds have you lost in the past month*?
上個月你減重幾磅？

> **說明**
>
> 1 How many 為表數量之疑問詞，後接名詞 pounds。
> 2 You 為本句之主詞，助動詞為 have，Vpp 為 lost。
> 3 依【時態助動詞 + S + Vpp】之句構，重組為 have you lost...。
> 4 In the last month，為時間片語，置於句尾。

◆ **試題演練**

請重組以下問句

⑪ Has _____?
(a horse/ridden/ever/Alan)

⑫ Have _____?
(waiting/long/you/been)

⑬ Have _____?

(that/new shoes/noticed/Tina/you/is wearing)

⑭ How long _____?

(the/prepared/Joe and Jill/farewell party/have/for)

⑮ What _____?

(you/have/from/learned/the lesson)

IV. 模態助動詞型問句之重組

模態助動詞型之問句，係在主詞前加上模態助動詞 can、could、will、would、should……等，形成如下句構：

（疑問詞）模態助動詞 ＋ S ＋ V（＋謂詞）?

◆ **範例分析**

④ Which major _____?

(I/in college/choose/should)

hint 模態助動詞型問句之重組

→ Which major *should I choose in college*?

我上大學該選什麼作為主修？

說明

1 I 為本句之主詞，模態助動詞為 should，動詞為 choose。

2 依【模態助動詞 ＋ S ＋ V】之句構，重組為 should I choose。

3 in college 表地點，置於句尾。

◆ **試題演練**

請重組以下問句

⑯ Could _____?

(give/you/to Robert/the message)

⑰ What _____?

(do/her school grades/should/to improve/Sonia)

⑱ How much _____?

(us/Gina/give/will/money)

⑲ When _____?

(our class/will/come/the teacher/to)

⑳ May _____?

(email address/your name/have/I/and)

解答

① Was Susan cooking when the doorbell rang?
門鈴響時蘇珊正在做飯嗎？

② Is there any homework for today?
今天有任何作業嗎？

③ When was your brother born?
你哥哥是何時出生的？

④ Where is the nearest bus stop to Taipei Zoo?
到台北市立動物園最近的公車站在哪裡？

⑤ What is your favorite sport?
你最喜歡什麼運動？

⑥ Who took Mei-Ting to the party yesterday?
昨天誰帶美婷去參加舞會？

⑦ How often do you exercise in the gym?
你多常去健身房運動？

⑧ When do most teenagers start dating in your country?
在你的國家，大部分的青少年從什麼時候開始約會？

⑨ Did Tina enjoy the food at the restaurant on the corner?
堤娜喜歡轉角那家餐廳的食物嗎？

⑩ Did John fall asleep when watching the romantic movie?
約翰看那部愛情文藝片時有沒有睡著？

⑪ Has Alan ever ridden a horse?
艾倫有騎過馬嗎？

⑫ Have you been waiting long?
你等了很久嗎？

⑬ Have you noticed that Tina is wearing new shoes?
你有注意到堤娜穿著新鞋嗎？

⑭ How long have Joe and Jill prepared for the farewell party?
喬和吉兒籌畫這場餞別會多久了？

⑮ What have you learned from the lesson?
你從課程中學到了什麼？

⑯ Could you give the message to Robert?
你可以傳話給羅伯特嗎？

⑰ What should Sonia do to improve her school grades?
桑妮亞該怎麼提升她的學業成績？

⑱ How much money will Gina give us?
吉娜會給我們多少錢？

⑲ When will the teacher come to our class?
老師什麼時候會來我們班上？

⑳ May I have your name and email address?
我可以知道你的名字和電子郵件信箱嗎？

間接問句的重組

範例

1 I wondered if ＿＿＿＿＿＿＿＿＿＿＿＿＿＿＿＿＿＿＿.

(be late/the heavy traffic/the bus/because of/would)

ANS I wondered if *the bus would be late because of the heavy traffic.*

我想知道公車會不會因為塞車而晚到。

📦 基本概念

　　間接問句之概念可參考本書「直接問句改間接問句」。間接問句為名詞子句，在結構上與直述句相同：主詞在前，動詞在後（＝S＋V）。處理間接問句之重組，須特別注意：該名詞子句可能為 if 或 whether，或疑問詞 where、when、how、why、what、how 等所引導，分別形成如下兩種句構：

1️⃣ S＋V＋【if/whether＋S＋V＋...】

2️⃣ S＋V＋【疑問詞＋S＋V＋...】

　　「直接問句改間接問句」單元中所提及之祈使句型態之間接問句，除了省略主詞 You 外，與上述兩句構無異。

📦 應考要訣

1️⃣ 看看待重組之字組中是否有主詞與動詞。

2️⃣ 找尋連接主要子句與間接問句之連接詞。

3️⃣ 間接問句之詞序為→連接詞＋S＋V。

4️⃣ 時態助動詞（have/has/had）後搭配 Vpp；模態助動詞（can/will/may/should 等）後搭配原形動詞。

5️⃣ 表地點或時間之單字或片語置於句尾。

◆ 範例分析

1 I wondered if _____.

(be late/the heavy traffic/the bus/because of/would)

hint 間接問句之重組

→I wondered if *the bus would be late because of the heavy traffic.*

我想知道公車會不會因為塞車而晚到。

說明

1 重組字組中有動詞 be late；because of 為介系詞片語，後須接名詞。

2 具主格性質之 the bus 與 the heavy traffic 均為名詞，分別為間接問句之主詞及 because of 之受詞。

3 因 Be 動詞採原形之 be，故將 would 置於 be 之前，形成動詞 would be late。

4 The heavy traffic 置於 because of 之後，表原因。

2 Harry asked his teacher _____.

(his/could/English listening ability/he/improve/how)

hint 間接問句之重組

→Harry asked his teacher *how he could improve his English listening ability.*

哈利問他的老師如何增進他的英文聽力。

說明

1 引導間接問句者為疑問詞 how。

2 間接問句中之主詞為 he，動詞為 could improve。

3 所有格 his 後接名詞 English listening ability，形成 his English listening ability 作為動詞 improve 之受詞。

③ Ask the manager _____.

(could/for two days/sick leave/take/if/Lisa)

hint 間接問句之重組

→ Ask the manager *if Lisa could take sick leave for two days.*

問問看經理麗莎是否可以請病假兩天。

說明

1 引導間接問句者為連接詞 if。

2 重組字組中之主詞為 Lisa，動詞為 take。

3 Lisa 為第三人稱單數主詞，動詞為原形的 take，因而將模態助動詞 could 與 take 搭配，形成 could take。

4 Sick leave 為 take 之受詞，搭配形成片語 take sick leave；for two days 表時間置於句尾。

◆ 試題演練

請重組以下間接問句題型

① Graham is wondering _____.

(for/his birthday/what/will buy/his girlfriend)

② I wonder _____.

(could/schedule/if/the/we/change)

③ Irene asked Jim _____.

(if/give/downtown/he/a/her/ride/could)

④ Kate asked us _____.

(she/should/next semester/what classes/take)

⑤ Teddy was told _____.

(he/the U.S./his aunt/in/could/when/visit)

⑥ Ask the shop assistant _____.

(can/batteries/we/where/find)

⑦ Write and tell _____ for the school.

(do/he/new/what/can/the/principal)

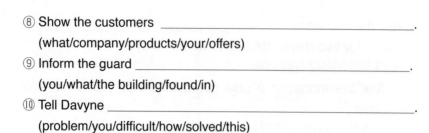

⑧ Show the customers _____.
(what/company/products/your/offers)

⑨ Inform the guard _____.
(you/what/the building/found/in)

⑩ Tell Davyne _____.
(problem/you/difficult/how/solved/this)

解答

① Graham is wondering what his girlfriend will buy for his birthday.
　葛瑞漢想知道他女朋友會為他買什麼生日禮物。

② I wondered if we could change the schedule.
　我不確定我們能否更改時間表。

③ Irene asked Jim if he could give her a ride downtown.
　艾琳問吉姆能否載她到市中心。

④ Kate asked us what classes she should take next semester.
　凱特問我們她下學期該修什麼課。

⑤ Teddy was told when he could visit his aunt in the U.S.
　泰迪被告知何時能探視他在美國的阿姨。

⑥ Ask the shop assistant where we can find batteries.
　問一下店員我們要到哪兒找到電池。

⑦ Write and tell the new principal what he can do for the school.
　寫信告訴那位新校長他所能為學校做的事。

⑧ Show the customers what products your company offers.
　向顧客展示你們公司所提供的產品。

⑨ Inform the guard what you found in the building.
　通知警衛你在大樓裡發現的東西。

⑩ Tell Davyne how you solved this difficult problem.
　告訴戴維你如何解決這困難的問題。

對等相關連接詞的重組

範例

1 Neither _____ the kitchen.

(volunteers/my sister/nor/to clean/I)

ANS Neither *I nor my sister volunteers to clean* the kitchen.

我和姊姊都沒有主動去打掃廚房。

🔷 基本概念

　　本書「用對等相關連接詞合併」單元中已介紹過對等相關連接詞之特性，讀者可自行參考。由於 both...and、not only...but also、either...or 及 neither...nor 等四組對等相關連接詞所連接者為詞性相同之單字、片語或子句，因此重組過程中可先觀察是否有詞性相同之字組。

🔷 應考要訣

⒈ 找尋主詞及動詞，並先行組合可組合之字詞。

⒉ 除 both...and 外，其他三組對等相關連接詞所連接者若為兩個主詞，需注意句中之動詞需與最接近之主詞一致。（見「用對等相關連接詞合併」單元）

◆ 範例分析

⒈ We have to not only _____ in school.

(but also/wear/obey/uniforms/school regulations)

hint 對等相關連接詞之重組

→We have to **not only** *wear uniforms but also obey school regulations* in school.

我們在學校不但要穿制服，還要遵守校規。

> 說明
>
> 1 重組字組中有兩動詞 wear 及 obey、兩受詞 uniforms 及 school regulations。
> 2 Wear uniforms 與 obey school regulations 分別為動詞片語。
> 3 用 not only...but also 連接上述兩動詞片語。

② Neither _____ the kitchen.
(volunteers/my sister/nor/to clean/I)

> hint 對等相關連接詞之重組

→ **Neither** *I nor my sister volunteers to clean* the kitchen.
我和姊姊都沒有主動去打掃廚房。

> 說明
>
> 1 重組字組中有兩主詞 my sister 及 I，動詞為 volunteers。
> 2 由於 volunteers 為第三人稱單數型態，故連接時須將 my sister 置於接近該動詞處，合併後之主詞為 Neither I nor my sister。
> 3 To clean 為不定詞片語作動詞之受詞。

◆ 試題演練

請以對等相關連接詞重組

① Not only _____ to go swimming.
(like/the father/the children/but also)

② Both the teacher _____.
(happy with/and/are/the test results/the students)

③ Either _____ for five years.
(her roommates/have/Catherine/lived/or/in the apartment)

④ Jessica likes _____.
(orange/nor/pink/neither)

⑤ Graham speaks _____.
(and/Chinese/English/both)

⑥ Bob will _____ early next morning.
(in the evening/either/arrive/or/late)

⑦ Neither _____ the door.
(I/nor/want/to answer/Alan)

⑧ Tina enjoys _____.
(seeing/both/musical instruments/movies/and/playing)

⑨ Albert neither _____ at home.
(cooks/goes out/nor/for dinner)

⑩ To keep in good shape, you have to not only _____.
(exercise/but also/carefully/eat/regularly)

解答

① Not only the father but also the children like to go swimming.
不只有父親，小孩也喜歡游泳。

② Both the teacher and the students are happy with the test results.
老師和學生都對這次考試結果很滿意。

③ Either Catherine or her roommates have lived in the apartment for five years.
不是凱薩琳就是她的室友已經住在這公寓裡五年了。

④ Jessica likes neither pink nor orange.
潔西卡不喜歡粉紅色，也不喜歡橘色。

Jessica likes neither orange nor pink.
潔西卡不喜歡橘色，也不喜歡粉紅色。

⑤ Graham speaks both Chinese and English.
葛瑞漢會說中文和英文。

Graham speaks both English and Chinese.
葛瑞漢會說英文和中文。

⑥ Bob will arrive either late in the evening or early next morning.
鮑伯不是晚上晚點到就是隔天一早到。

⑦ Neither Alan nor I want to answer the door.
艾倫和我都不想去應門。

⑧ Tina enjoys both seeing movies and playing musical instruments.
堤娜喜歡看電影和演奏樂器。

Tina enjoys both playing musical instruments and seeing movies.
堤娜喜歡演奏樂器和看電影。

⑨ Albert neither goes out for dinner nor cooks at home.
艾伯特不出去吃晚飯也不在家裡煮飯。

⑩ To keep in good shape, you have to not only eat carefully but also exercise regularly.

要維持好身材，你不但要注意飲食還要持續運動。

To keep in good shape, you have to not only exercise regularly but also eat carefully.

要維持好身材，你不但要持續運動還要注意飲食。

副詞子句的重組

範例

1 I got _____.

(stood/when/cold feet/on the stage/I)

ANS I got *cold feet when I stood on the stage.*
我站在舞台上時很緊張。

🔹 基本概念

　　本書於「用副詞子句合併」單元介紹副詞子句時，已對副詞子句作過初步介紹，以下僅列出兩例句與應考注意事項供讀者參考。

🔹 應考要訣

1. 找尋引導副詞子句之連接詞。
2. 找出主詞與動詞。
3. 依句意，判斷主要子句與時間副詞子句之關係。
4. 將表地點或時間之片語置於句尾。

◆ 範例分析

1. I got _____.

(stood/when/cold feet/on the stage/I)

hint 時間副詞子句之重組

→I got *cold feet when I stood on the stage.*

我站在舞台上時很緊張。

說明

1 重組字組中以 when 引導之副詞子句的主詞為 I，動詞為 stood。

2 On the stage 表地點，置於副詞子句句尾。

3 主要動詞 got 後接 cold feet 為受詞。

153

② You will _____ unless you _____.
   (study hard/the GEPT/you//fail)

   hint 時間副詞子句之重組

   → You will fail the GEPT **unless** you study hard.

   你沒辦法通過全民英檢，除非你好好用功。

   > 說明
   >
   > 1 以 unless 引導副詞子句，表條件，主詞為 you。
   > 2 重組字組中共有兩個動詞片語：study hard 及 fail the GEPT。
   > 3 You study hard 為條件，應置於 unless 之後；will 應與 fail the GEPT 合併，作為主要子句之動詞。

◆ 試題演練

請以對等相關連接詞重組之

① As soon as Emma _____ , she _____.
   (knew/ran/her test results/her mother/to tell)

② Don't forget _____ before _____ the room.
   (the lights/you/turn off/leave/to)

③ Amy's mother _____.
   (until/didn't/turned five/work/Amy)

④ Charlie's cousin decided _____ after _____ college.
   (graduated/around/to travel/she/the world/from)

⑤ Michelle saw _____ while _____.
   (in/she/the backyard/unusual object/was walking/an)

⑥ Jill had _____ while _____ in Mount Ali.
   (she/her grandparents/was visiting/an accident)

⑦ Danny got _____ when _____ with a handsome man.
   (talking/saw/his girlfriend/jealous/he/very)

⑧ Tracy worked part time _____ before _____.
   (she/a convenience store/went to/college/at)

⑨ When Vicky saw _____ , _____.
(got/ran away/the snake/and/scared/she)

⑩ Shima used to _____ when _____.
(play/was/the piano/when/elementary school/she/in)

解答

① **As soon as Emma** knew her test results, **she** ran to tell her mother.
艾瑪一知道考試結果就跑去告訴她媽媽。

② **Don't forget** to turn off the lights **before** you leave the room.
離開房間之前別忘了關燈。

③ **Amy's mother** didn't work until Amy turned five.
艾咪的媽媽等到艾咪五歲時才去工作。

④ **Charlie's cousin decided** to travel around the world **after** she graduated from **college.**
查理的表妹決定大學畢業後要環遊世界。

⑤ **Michelle saw** an unusual object **while** she was walking in the backyard.
蜜雪兒在後院散步時看見不尋常的物體。

⑥ **Jill had** an accident **while** she was visiting her grandparents in Mount Ali.
吉兒去探望住在阿里山的祖父母時發生了意外。

⑦ **Danny got** very jealous **when** he saw his girlfriend talking **with** a handsome man.
丹尼看見她的女友和一個英俊的男生講話時變得很忌妒。

⑧ **Tracy worked part time** at a convenience store **before** she went to college.
崔西念大學前在一家便利商店打工。

⑨ **When Vicky saw** the snake, she got scared and ran away.
維琪看到蛇時，被嚇得逃跑。

⑩ **Shima used to** play the piano **when** she was in elementary school.
詩瑪念小學時經常彈鋼琴。

特殊句型的重組

📦 基本概念

　　關於特殊句型之重組，讀者需掌握幾個要點：先尋找主詞與動詞；注意及物動詞後須接受詞；表時間或地點之片語位置通常位於句末。（特殊句型之概念請參考本書「用特定片語改寫」及「用特殊句型合併」單元）

◆ 試題演練

　　請重組以下句子

① Vincent is too ＿＿＿＿＿＿＿＿＿＿＿＿＿＿＿＿＿＿＿＿＿.

　　(on/the book/short/the shelf/to get)

② John is ＿＿＿＿＿＿＿＿＿＿＿＿＿＿＿＿＿＿ likes him.

　　(generous/that/everyone/so/in his company)

③ I ＿＿＿＿＿＿＿＿＿＿ when I was ＿＿＿＿＿＿＿＿＿＿.

　　(in college/to school/ride/used to/a bicycle)

④ Lisa didn't ＿＿＿＿＿＿＿＿＿＿ until ＿＿＿＿＿＿＿＿＿＿.

　　(crying/came home/stop/her mother)

⑤ Rose ＿＿＿＿＿＿＿＿＿＿＿＿＿＿＿＿＿＿＿＿＿＿＿.

　　(rang/woke up/the alarm clock/as soon/as)

⑥ Jack ＿＿＿＿＿＿＿＿＿＿＿ whenever ＿＿＿＿＿＿＿＿＿.

　　(names/angry/people/gets/very/call him)

⑦ All Mel ＿＿＿＿＿＿＿＿ was ＿＿＿＿＿＿＿＿＿＿＿＿＿.

　　(for/pack/and/did/the coming trip/get ready)

⑧ Debby ＿＿＿＿＿＿＿＿＿＿ , ＿＿＿＿＿＿＿＿＿＿＿＿＿.

　　(and/sports/including/softball/likes/volleyball)

⑨ Flora ＿＿＿＿＿＿＿ in the front so that she could ＿＿＿＿＿＿.

　　(the play/sat/see/more clearly)

⑩ Diving _____.
(one/favorite/David's/activities/is/of)

解答

① Vincent is too short to get the book on the shelf.
　文森太矮了，拿不到書架上的書。

② Johnny is so generous that everyone in his company likes him.
　強尼很大方，以致於公司裡每個人都喜歡他。

③ I used to ride a bicycle to school when I was in college.
　我念大學時經常騎腳踏車上學。

④ Lisa didn't stop crying until her mother came home.
　麗莎一直哭到媽媽回家才停住。

⑤ Rose woke up as soon as the alarm clock rang.
　鬧鐘一響羅絲就馬上起床了。

⑥ Jack gets very angry whenever people call him names.
　每當有人罵他，傑克就會氣得不得了。

⑦ All Mel did was pack and get ready for the coming trip.
　梅爾做的就只是打包為即將到來的旅行做好準備。

⑧ Debby likes sports, including softball and volleyball.
　黛比喜歡運動，包括壘球和排球。

⑨ Flora sat in the front so that she could see the play more clearly.
　佛蘿菈坐在前面以便能把戲看得更清楚。

⑩ Diving is one of David's favorite activities.
　跳水是大衛最喜歡的活動之一。

段落寫作篇

- 段落寫作的文體
- 段落寫作的結構與發展──記述文
- 段落寫作的結構與發展──描寫文
- 變化句構的方式

段落寫作的文體

段落寫作的文體

　　寫作的文體雖然眾多,然而全民英檢初級「段落寫作」係以看圖說故事或描述圖形內容的方式出題,亦即「記述文」(Narration) 與「描寫文」(Description) 兩大類文體。

　　在實際寫作時,一篇文章亦可能為上述兩文體之交替運用。本單元將概述上述兩類文體之特性,並舉例說明之。接下來的兩個單元,將分別針對此二文體說明其文章之結構與發展。最後一個單元則針對初級「段落寫作」可運用的變化句構方式做一整理說明。

Ⅰ. 記述文

　　顧名思義,「記述文」係依據某一個故事為主軸,記下其發展情節。換言之,記述文係以說故事的方式鋪陳,描述事情發生的經過。時間次序佔相當重要的地位;一般而言,以過去式時態呈現居多。以下列舉三篇文章供讀者參考。

範文1 A Subway Ride

One Saturday evening, I took the subway home. While I was trying to find a seat, I ran into a classmate. We were very excited and talked happily on the train. Meanwhile, more and more people got on the train. It became very crowded. Suddenly, we found the train had come to its terminal. We had missed our stops! As a result, we had to wait for the next train back home.

中文翻譯

搭乘地鐵

　　某個週末傍晚我坐地鐵回家。在我忙著找位置時,遇到了一位同

學。我們很興奮地在車上聊著。在那時有愈來愈多的人上了車,車上變得很擁擠。突然間,我們發現我們已經坐到了終點站。我們兩個都錯過了該下車的站,結果只得在月台上等下班車回家。

範文2　A Trip to Hua-lien

Last summer my family went on a trip to Hua-lien. On the first day, we visited the Taroko Gorge. The scenery was terrific and the air was so fresh. The second day was Dolphin Watching. I saw many dolphins jumping in the sea. How beautiful they were! On the last day we were invited to my aunt's farm and had some local food there. We really had a good time.

中文翻譯

花蓮之旅

　　去年暑假我們全家人到花蓮去玩。第一天我們到太魯閣,那兒風景很棒而且空氣很新鮮。第二天是賞豚。我看到很多海豚在海裏跳著,牠們非常漂亮!最後一天姑媽邀請我們到她的農場享用當地的美食。這趟旅程我們玩的非常愉快。

範文3　The Speech Contest I Attended

I attended a speech contest last week. Before the contest, I practiced very hard every day in the hope that I could win it. On that day, I thought I could do very well. However, when it was my turn, I became so nervous that I was speechless on the stage. It was so embarrassing because everyone was looking at me. Finally, I spoke out but the time was up. So, I lost the contest.

中文翻譯

我參加的演講比賽

　　上週我參加一場演講比賽。比賽之前,我每天都很努力練習,希望

能得獎。當天我以為我會表現得很好。然而，輪到我的時候，我變得很緊張，在台上一句話都說不出來。當時真的很尷尬，因為每個人都看著我。最後，我終於開始說話，可是時間已經到了。我就這樣輸了這場比賽。

Ⅱ. 描寫文

「描寫文」所描寫的內容，包括人、事、時、地與物等。亦即在特定的時間架構下，勾勒作者眼睛所見的或內心所感受的「人、事、地點或景物」。除了要描述文章主角（人、地點或景象）靜態的外在之外，同時可表達其動態的一面，讓讀者有親臨其境的感受。

範文4　My Best Friend

My best friend, Gina, means a lot to me. We first met at a party five years ago, and have shared everything in life since then. Gina looks like a model and is very beautiful. Besides, she is popular with her friends because she is caring and always willing to help others. When I am in trouble, Gina is always by my side. The friendship between us is very important for me.

中文翻譯

我最要好的朋友

我的好友吉娜對我而言意義深遠。五年前我們在一次舞會上認識，從那時後開始我們就一直分享生活中的點點滴滴。吉娜看起來像個模特兒，人長得非常漂亮。此外，因為她善解人意而且總是樂於助人，所以人緣很好。當我遇到麻煩時，她總是在我身旁。我們之間的友誼對我來說非常重要。

範文5　The Corner Coffee House

My favorite coffee house is the one on the corner of the street near my school. It sells nice coffee and delicious desserts. I like to read books there because it is quiet and full of the good smell of coffee. Sometimes I sit by the window so that I can watch people passing by. It is very interesting. I enjoy staying in the coffee house very much.

中文翻譯

街角咖啡店

我最喜歡的咖啡店是位於學校附近街角的那一家。那裡賣的咖啡很棒，點心也很可口。因為那家店很安靜而且充滿著咖啡的香味，所以我喜歡到那兒去看書。有時我會坐在窗邊，那樣我就可以看到往來的人們。相當地有趣。我非常喜歡待在那家咖啡店裡。

範文6　The Early Morning

Early in the morning, when most people are still sleeping, some people are already up and starting their day. You may see them dancing or jogging in the park. Some people walk their dogs on the street. In the traditional market, many housewives are busy buying things for their families. They go home even before the city wakes up and starts its busy day.

中文翻譯

清晨

一大清早，當多數人還在睡夢中時，有些人就已經起床開始他們的一天了。在公園可以看到一些人在跳舞或慢跑。有些人則在街上溜狗。在傳統市場裡，許多家庭主婦忙著幫家人買菜。她們甚至在這個城市甦醒、開始忙碌的一天之前，就趕回家了。

段落寫作應考要訣

Ⅰ. 判別文體（記述文或描寫文）

Ⅱ. 界定主題

1. 記述某次演講比賽經驗（我參加的演講比賽）
2. 描寫某位好友的特徵及影響（我最要好的朋友）

Ⅲ. 記錄想法

1. Who?（跟誰？）
2. Where?（去那兒？）
3. When?（何時去的？）
4. Why?（為何選這個地點或日子？）
5. How?（搭乘何種交通工具？）
6. What?（沿途看到什麼景象、目的地的風景如何？）

Ⅳ. 組織文章

1. 文章內容──前言、故事發展及結論
2. 選用適當的時態與字詞
3. 連接詞與轉折語的運用

Ⅴ. 檢查

1. 拼字、時態、詞語
2. 計算字數（英檢初級要求至少50個字）

段落寫作的結構與發展─記述文

I. 文章佈局

　　如「段落寫作的文體」單元所述，記述文係以「說故事」的方式呈現。故事中的佈局通常包括時間、地點及人物，因此在應考要訣中的「記錄想法」步驟中，必須記下三個要點：

　　1. When：各個情節的發生先後。

　　2. Where：空間的轉換。

　　3. Who：人物的特性。

　　最常見的記述文為流水帳表達法，亦即按照事件發生先後呈現所要記述的內容，偶會以倒敘法來表現；其次，作者也可依據空間順序來記述事件。

II. 結構與發展

　　在段落鋪陳方面，可分為三個步驟：

1	前言	事件（故事）發生之前
2	推展	事件本身（即故事的主軸）
3	結論	事件（故事）之後

　　值得注意的是，動詞時態在記述文中扮演極為重要的角色。一般而言，記述文多採過去式，時而配合過去進行與過去完成貌。

說明─範文 1 A Subway Ride（搭乘地鐵）

題目：有天你搭乘地鐵回家時在車上遇到同學。因爲聊得太開心，忘了
下車而坐到終點站。請根據以下圖片，寫一篇約 50 字的短文，描
述那天你搭乘地鐵的經驗。

One Saturday evening, I took the subway home. While I was trying
to find a seat, I ran into a classmate. We were very excited and talked
happily on the train. Meanwhile, more and more people got on the
train. It became very crowded. Suddenly, we found the train had come
to its terminal. We had missed our stops! As a result, we had to wait
for the next train back home.

解析

文章大意：

記述某個週六在地鐵車上所經歷的事件。

文章佈局：

① When ：陳述各個情節的發生先後。

主要時間爲某個週六傍晚 One Saturday evening。

其他時間的切換：運用時間副詞片語，如：

meanwhile 、 suddenly

② Where ：空間轉換。

本文空間爲地鐵車上及月台：

→ We were very excited and talked happily on the train.

→ We had to wait for the next train back home.

③ Who ：人物的特性。

　　　　本文主角為作者及其朋友，配角為車上及月台上的人，因此，
　　　　除故事發展之初，以第一人稱 I 陳述外，整篇以 we 為主軸。

故事的發展：

① 事件發生之前

　　搭地鐵回家（I took the subway home.）

　　在地鐵車上巧遇朋友（I ran into a classmate.）

② 事件的主軸

　　愉快地在車上聊著（We were excited and talked happily on the train.）

　　車子開到終點站，我們忘了下車

　　（The train had come to its terminal. We had missed our stops.）

③ 事件發生之後

　　只好再等下班車回家（We had to wait for the next train back home.）

段落寫作的結構與發展─描寫文

I. 文章佈局

如「段落寫作的文體」中所述，描寫文係以「文字」的方式來描寫作者所見到或感受到的「景像」（人、地點或景物）。為求生動呈現作者所見所聞，應將原本平鋪直敘的靜態表陳，用豐富的詞藻（尤其是形容詞與副詞）轉化為動態的描述以賦予其生命，困難度較前單元記述文文體來得高。

換句話說，描寫文所要描述的包括：客觀的描述（肉眼可見的外在與景物）及主觀的描述（作者對主角的心理感受）。描寫的主角，可能為人、地點或景物，因此在應考要訣中的「記錄想法」步驟中，首先須記下主角：

① Who：人物。

② Where：空間位置。

此外，記錄以下各項也有助於文章的發展。

③ When：何時認識的人、何時發生的事等，有助於時態的選定。

④ What：人物的特性（包括外在與心理層面）或空間內的擺設。

⑤ How：作者對於文章中主角內心的感受為何。

⑥ Why：為什麼選這個主角。

II. 結構與發展

在段落鋪陳方面，可分為三個步驟：

1	前言	說明主角與作者的關係（When & Who/Where）
2	推展	描寫主角的特性（What & How）
3	結論	解釋主角在作者心中的地位（Why）

說明—範文 5　My Best Friend（我最要好的朋友）

題目：描述你的一位好友，包括他／她的外觀、特質及對你的影響。請根據以下圖片，寫一篇約 50 字的短文，描述你的一位好友。

　　My best friend, Gina, means a lot to me. We first met at a party five years ago, and have shared everything in life since then. Gina looks like a model and is very beautiful. Besides, she is popular with her friends because she is caring and always willing to help others. When I am in trouble, Gina is always by my side. The friendship between us is very important for me.

解析

文章大意：

描寫一位好友

文章佈局：

① Who ：主角為Gina。

　　　　配角為與Gina關係密切的作者及Gina週遭的人。因此，描寫
　　　　時前言與結論說明作者的感受以第一人稱呈現，文章主軸以第
　　　　三人稱描寫Gina。

② When ：事實的描述，時態主要以現在式呈現。

③ Where ：並無明顯的空間轉換。

文章的發展：

① 介紹主角並說明與作者之關係

　　介紹主角（My best friend, Gina,...）

　　五年前在舞會上認識（We met at a party five years ago.）

② 主角的特性

　　1) 外觀——為客觀描述

　　　　像模特兒，很漂亮（She looks like a model and is very beautiful.）

　　2) 人格特質——為主觀描述

　　　　很受歡迎（popular）

　　　　善解人意（caring）

③ 主角對作者的意義

　　對我來說意義深遠（She means a lot to me.）

　　這段友誼對我來說很重要（The friendship between us is very important
　　for me.）

變化句構的方式

本單元將列舉全民英檢初級【段落寫作】可運用的幾種變化句構方式，包括：轉折語的運用、時態的變化、副詞子句的運用及描寫性形容詞等。

I. 轉折語的運用

在寫作的過程中，除了詞彙片語的選用、句型的運用以及文章的組織外，巧妙地運用轉折語，可讓文章結構更加緊湊。

在前面單元提及英文寫作中的段落鋪陳，包括前言、推展與結論，其與中文的「起、承、轉、合」概念相近。對應關係如下：

前言	＝	「起」
推展	＝	「承」與「轉」
結論	＝	「合」

因此，在英文段落寫作的推展過程（「承」與「轉」）中，往往需要轉折語作為潤滑劑。轉折語多半出現在句首，同時兼具提示字的導引功效，讓讀者預知故事情節的發展方向。

一般而言，句與句的關係或連接不外乎：時間、空間、因果、舉例或對照。以下列舉9種常見的轉折語表達法，其中第9類為結論之提示字。

① 表時間的轉折語：

a few days later, meanwhile, at that moment, soon, just then, recently

② 表空間的轉折語：

in this area, to the right/left, on the way home

③ 表添加的轉折語：

also, too, again, in addition, besides

④ 表對比的轉折語：

but, however, on the other hand, although

⑤ 表結果的轉折語：

so, therefore, thus

⑥ 表舉例的轉折語：

for instance, for example

⑦ 表重複的轉折語：

in other words, to be sure, that is

⑧ 表強調的轉折語：

in fact, in particular, generally

⑨ 表摘要的轉折語：

in short, in brief, all in all

II. 時態的變化

記述文時態的變化

一般而言，記述文所採用的時態以過去式居多，當中可能出現過去式之進行或完成貌。

① 表過去習慣或事實，採過去簡單

I was tired, so I fell asleep on the train very soon.

（我很疲憊，所以我一上火車很快地就睡著了。）

② 表過去某特定時間點的動作，採過去進行

While I was taking the escalator, I heard a strange sound.

（我在搭手扶梯時，聽到一個很奇怪的聲音。）

③ 表較過去更早發生之動作，採過去完成

The man had been out of work for six months before he found a job.

（這個人找到工作之前已經失業六個月。）

描寫文時態的變化

　　描寫文所採用的時態可能為現在、過去或未來，以簡單式居多，亦可能出現完成貌。

① 表過去的事實，採過去簡單

　　We first met at a New Year celebration party five years ago.

　　（我們是在五年前的一次新年慶祝舞會上認識的。）

② 表現在的事實與狀態，採現在簡單

　　Gina looks like a model and is very beautiful.

　　（吉娜看起來像個模特兒，人長得非常漂亮。）

　　She is caring and always willing to help others.

　　（她善解人意而且總是樂於幫助他人。）

③ 表過去發生到現在的動作，採現在完成

　　Gina has had deep influence on me.

　　（吉娜對我有深遠的影響。）

　　We have shared everything in life since then.

　　（從那時候開始，我們就一直分享生活中的點點滴滴。）

III. 副詞子句的運用

　　副詞子句的型態與功能等概念，詳見本書第一部份「用副詞子句合併」的單元。本單元僅列舉例句供讀者參考。

表原因的副詞子句

　　以 because 所引導者之副詞子句，表「原因」。

　　例：She is popular because she is always willing to help others.

　　　　（因為她總是樂於幫助他人，所以人緣很好。）

　　例：It was so embarrassing because everyone was looking at me.

　　　　（當時真的很尷尬，因為每個人都看著我。）

表時間的副詞子句

① 以 when 所引導者之副詞子句，表「某特定時間」，用簡單式。

　　例：When I am in trouble, she is always by my side.

　　　　（在我遇到麻煩時，她總是在我身旁。）

　　例：When it was my turn, I became so nervous.

　　　　（輪到我的時候，我變得很緊張。）

② 以 while 所引導者之副詞子句，表「某段時間」，用進行式。

　　例：While I was trying to find a seat, I ran into a classmate.

　　　　（在我忙著找位子時，遇到了一位同學。）

　　例：While I was watching TV, I heard the door bell ringing.

　　　　（我在看電視時，聽到門鈴響。）

③ 以 since 所引導者之副詞子句，表「持續性的時間」。主要子句用現在完成式，副詞子句用過去式。

　　例：We have shared everything in life since we first met at a party.

　　　　（自從在一次舞會上初次見面後，我們就一直分享生活中的點點滴滴。）

表讓步

以 although/even though 所引導者之副詞子句，表「讓步」。

　　例：Although I had practiced many times, I still lost the contest.

　　　　（雖然我已經練習很多次了，但還是輸了比賽。）

表條件

以 if 所引導者之副詞子句，表「條件」。

　　例：If I move to Hua-lien, I will find a quiet and clean place.

　　　　（如果我搬到花蓮，我會找個安靜又乾淨的地方。）

IV. 描寫性形容詞

　　以下依人、事物、地點等三個主題，列舉全民英檢初級「描寫文」寫作常用之形容詞供參考。

① 描寫人

　1) 外表

　　　tall, short, thin, fat, beautiful, ugly, black-haired, young, old

　2) 人格

　　　kind, nice, caring, friendly, unfriendly, easy-going, bad-tempered

　3) 情緒

　　　excited, surprised, happy, sad, interested, angry, patient

② 描寫事物

　　square, round, red, blue (color), dirty, clean, beautiful, ugly, cold, hot

③ 描寫地點

　　to the right of the house, under the table, in the room, next to the bank, across the street

全真模擬試題 & 解析

Write

第一回 全真模擬試題

第一部份：單句寫作

請將答案寫在答案紙上對應的題號旁，如有文法、用字、拼字、標點符號、大小寫等之錯誤，將予扣分。

第1-5題：句子改寫

請依題目之提示，將原句改寫成指定型式，並將改寫的句子完整地寫在答案紙上（包括提示之文字及標點符號）。

範例

Q   I like to sing songs.

→   Ted _____.

A   Ted *likes to sing songs.*

---

① Ah-Mei sings very well.

How _____?

② The boss asked, "Where did they go?"

Tell the boss _____.

③ That all birds can fly is not always true.

It is not always true _____.

④ Joanne: What was your decision?

Michael: I didn't take the job.

Michael decided _____.

⑤ Arthur is the best student in his class.

Arthur is _____ than any other _____ in his class.

第6-10題：句子合併

請依題目之提示，將兩句合併成一句，並將合併的句子完整地寫在答案紙上（包括提示之文字及標點符號）。

範例

Q Sophia has a dog.

The dog is black and white.

→ Sophia has a _____ .

A Sophia has a *black and white dog.*

⑥ George took off his shoes.

He entered the room.

George _____ his shoes and _____ .

⑦ Sophia is a secretary.

She also works part-time as an English teacher.

Sophia is not only _____ a part-time English teacher.

⑧ Something is true.

That saying thank you to people can win their respect and friend-ship is true.

It is true that _____ .

⑨ The teacher is celebrating his birthday.

We met the teacher yesterday.

The teacher _____ is celebrating his birthday.

⑩ Albert still went to sleep.

He had drunk a lot of coffee during the daytime.

Albert _____ although he _____ during the daytime.

第11-15題：重組

　　請將題目中所有提示 Words & Phrases 整合成一有意義的句子，並將重組的句子完整地寫在答案紙上（包括提示之文字及標點符號）。答案中必須使用所有提示 Words & Phrases，且不能隨意增加 Words & Phrases，否則不予計分。

範例

Q　Would _____?
　　(like/some/you/coffee)

A　Would *you like some coffee*?

⑪ I _____.
　　(nephew/some souvenirs/brought/my niece/for/and)

⑫ Kevin and Davyne _____.
　　(in New Zealand/were/some relatives/visiting)

⑬ How many _____ in Taiwan?
　　(holidays/in a year/there/are)

⑭ I wondered _____.
　　(over/tonight/if/could/to your place/I/go)

⑮ Not only _____.
　　(was/he/surprised/his parents/at/but also/the news)

第二部份：段落寫作

題目：上個禮拜天早上，Tony 一起床就覺得頭痛，很不舒服。請根據下圖，寫一篇約 50 字的短文，描寫 Tony 生病的經過。

第一回 解析

第一部份：單句寫作

1 Ah-Mei sings very well.

How _____?

ANS **How** does Ah-Mei sing?

（阿妹歌唱得怎麼樣？）

句型 直述句改疑問句 (p. 5)。

解析 由於 sing 爲一般動詞，改爲以疑問詞 how 爲首的問句時，必須在主詞之前加上助動詞 does，形成 V＋S 之倒裝句型。

---

2 The boss asked, "Where did they go?"

Tell the boss _____.

ANS **Tell the boss** where they went.

（跟老闆說他們到那兒去了。）

句型 直接問句改爲間接問句 (p. 18)。

解析 首先須刪除直接問句之引號與問號；其次，直接問句中之疑問詞 where 改爲間接問句時仍保留，改爲【where＋S＋V】的名詞子句。原直接問句中之助動詞 did 與 go，更改爲原過去式動詞 went。

---

3 That all birds can fly is not always true.

It is not always true _____.

ANS **It is not always true** that all birds can fly.

（所有的鳥都會飛未必是真的。）

句型	改爲虛主詞的句型 (p. 25)。
解析	本題改以虛主詞 it 爲首，將眞主詞名詞子句 that all birds can fly 移至句尾。

④ Joanne: What was your decision?

Michael: I didn't take the job.

Michael decided _____.

ANS **Michael decided not to take the job.**

（麥可決定不接受這份差事。）

句型	不定詞片語當受詞 (p. 30)。
解析	本題爲 decide 後接不定詞爲受詞之句型。原句名詞 decision 改以動詞 decide 表達時，其後之受詞須採不定詞型態。亦即在 take 前加上 to，形成不定詞 to take，作爲 decide 之受詞。特別注意：不定詞之否定，須在 to take 之前加上 not。

⑤ Arthur is the best student in his class.

Arthur is _____ than any other _____ in his class.

ANS **Arthur is better than any other student in his class.**

（亞瑟表現得比班上任何一位同學都來得好。）

句型	比較級與最高級的句型切換 (p. 38)。
解析	本句係將最高級句型【the best ＋單數 N】改爲比較級句型【比較級 ＋ than any other ＋單數 N】。原句形容詞最高級 best 之比較級爲 better，the best student 改爲比較級句型後爲 better than any other student。

⑥ George took off his shoes.

He entered the room.

George ＿＿＿＿＿ his shoes and ＿＿＿＿＿＿＿＿＿＿.

ANS **George took off his shoes and entered the room.**

（喬治脫下鞋子，然後進到房間裡面。）

句型 用對等連接詞合併 (p. 58)。

解析 以對等連接詞 and 將兩句合併為 George took off his shoes and he entered the room.。由於兩句主詞相同，即 George ＝ he，為 took off 與 entered 兩個動詞之行使者，因而省略第二個主詞 he。

Words & Phrases

take off *v. phr.* 脫下（衣、鞋、襪等）

enter〔`ɛntɚ〕*v.* 進入

⑦ Sophia is a secretary.

She also works part-time as an English teacher.

Sophia is not only ＿＿＿＿＿＿＿ a part-time English teacher.

ANS **Sophia is not only a secretary but also a part-time English teacher.**

（蘇菲亞不只是個秘書，也是位兼職的英文老師。）

句型 用對等相關連接詞合併 (p. 62)。

解析 合併句中出現 not only 顯然為對等相關連接詞【not only...but also】句型。第二句可改寫為 She is a part-time English teacher.。兩句主詞相同（即 Sophia ＝ she），動詞為 is，因此以 not only...but also 連接 a secretary 與 a part-time English teacher 兩名詞，形成 not only a secretary but also a part-time English teacher，作為主詞補語。

Words & Phrases

part-time　*adj./ adv.* 兼職的；打工的 / 兼職地；打工地

⑧ Something is true.

That saying thank you to people can win their respect and friendship is true.

It is true that _____.

ANS **It is true that saying thank you to people can win their respect and friendship.**

（對別人說「謝謝！」可贏得尊重與友誼是真確的。）

句型　用名詞子句合併 (p. 68)。

解析　第一句 something ＝第二個句子主詞 that saying thank you to peo-ple can win their respect and friendship。再以虛主詞 it 代替之，形成虛主詞為首的句型。

Words & Phrases

respect〔rɪˋspɛkt〕*v., n.* 尊重；敬重

friendship〔ˋfrɛndˌʃɪp〕*n.* 友誼

⑨ The teacher is celebrating his birthday.

We met the teacher yesterday.

The teacher _____ is celebrating his birthday.

ANS **The teacher (whom) we met yesterday is celebrating his birth-day.**

（我們昨天遇到的那位老師正在慶生。）

句型　用形容詞子句合併 (p. 80)。

解析　合併句係將第二句併入第一句，亦即將第二句改為形容詞子句。兩句重複處為 the teacher，以關係代名詞受格 whom 取代第二句中之受詞 the teacher，形成形容詞子句 whom we met yester-day。又，受格關代 whom 可省略。

Words & Phrases

celebrate〔ˋsɛləˏbret〕 v. 慶祝

⑩ Albert still went to sleep.

He had drunk a lot of coffee during the daytime.

Albert _____ although he _____ during the daytime.

ANS **Albert went to sleep although he had drunk a lot of coffee during the daytime.**

（雖然亞伯特白天喝了很多咖啡，但他還是睡著了。）

句型	用副詞子句合併 (p. 91)。
解析	合併句中出現表讓步的從屬連接詞although，其後子句應為讓步的情況，即He had drunk a lot of coffee during the daytime.。

⑪ I _____.

(nephew/some souvenirs/bought/my niece/for/and)

ANS **I bought some souvenirs for my niece and nephew.**

（我為姪女和姪子買了些紀念品。）

句型	授與動詞的重組 (p. 127)。
解析	重組字串中出現授與動詞bought及介系詞for，因而本句為【授與動詞buy＋物 (D.O.) ＋for＋人 (I.O.)】的重組。句中直接受詞 (D.O.) 為some souvenirs，間接受詞 (I.O.) 為my niece and nephew，注意二者不可顛倒。

Words & Phrases

niece〔nis〕 n. 姪女

nephew〔ˋnɛfju〕 n. 姪子

souvenir〔ˏsuvəˋnɪr〕 n. 紀念品；禮物

⑫ Kevin and Davyne _____.

(in New Zealand/were/some relatives/visiting)

ANS **Kevin and Davyne were visiting some relatives in New Zealand.**

（凱文跟黛芬在紐西蘭探望親戚。）

句型	時態的重組 (p. 131)。
解析	主詞之後尋找動詞，Be動詞were與分詞visiting搭配，形成過去進行式were visiting，其受詞為some relatives，地方副詞in New Zealand則置於句尾。

Words & Phrases

visit〔ˋvɪzɪt〕v. 拜訪

relative〔ˋrɛlətɪv〕n. 親戚

⑬ How many _____ in Taiwan?

(holidays/in a year/there/are)

ANS **How many holidays are there in a year in Taiwan?**

（在台灣一年有幾天假？）

句型	疑問句的重組 (p. 135)。
解析	疑問詞how many後需接可數名詞holidays。本疑問句中之虛字主詞there與動詞are必須倒裝（there + be表「有」），時間副詞in a year則置於句尾。

Words & Phrases

holiday〔ˋhɑləˏde〕n. 假期；節日

⑭ I wondered _____.

(over/tonight/if/could/to your place/I/go)

ANS **I wondered** **if I could go over to your place tonight.**

（我在想今晚可不可以到你家去？）

> **句型** 間接問句的重組 (p. 143)。
>
> **解析** 本句間接問句係以連接詞if引導的名詞子句，其後應為S＋V型態（主詞為I、動詞為could go over）。動詞之受詞為介系詞片語 to your place，時間副詞tonight則置於句尾。

Words & Phrases

go over to　*v. phr.*　前往；到

⑮ Not only _____.

(was/he/surprised/his parents/at/but also/the news)

ANS **Not only** **his parents but also he was surprised at the news.**

（不只是他的爸媽，他也為這個消息所震驚。）

> **句型** 對等相關連接詞的重組 (p. 148)。
>
> **解析** 重組句not only與but also搭配以連接主詞，字串中名詞有二（he與his parents）。值得注意的是，以【not only...but also】句型連接兩個主詞時，其動詞單複數取決於靠近動詞之主詞。由於動詞為was surprised，因此合併後之主詞應為not only his parents but also he。

Words & Phrases

be surprised at　*v. phr.*　對……感到吃驚、訝異

第二部份：段落寫作

參考範文

Tom was sick today. First, he woke up with a terrible headache. A sore throat and a runny nose came soon after. He wondered if he should stay home, but finally decided to go to school anyway. However, he could not concentrate in class. After school, Tom went to the doctor. The doctor told him to take medicine and get plenty of rest.

中文翻譯

　　湯姆今天生病了。他剛醒來時就覺得頭很痛；接下來是喉嚨不舒服、流鼻水。他考慮應否待在家裡，但最後決定還是抱病去上學。不過他卻無法專心上課。下課後，湯姆去看了醫生。醫生告訴他要吃藥且多休息。

結構分析

　　本篇為記敘文，涉及時間與空間的轉換。在時間的處理方面，為流水帳描述法，敘述從早上感到不適到放學後看醫生的一連串動作，均採過去簡單式，如：頭痛、上學及醫生叮嚀的話。在空間方面，則涵括了家裡、學校及診所。

在句型運用方面，包含：

（1）名詞子句型的間接問句 if he should stay home。

（2）decide 後用 to go to school 當受詞。

（3）tell 後以不定詞片語 to take medicine and get plenty of rest 作為受詞 him 之補語。

Words & Phrases

terrible〔`tɛrəbḷ〕adj. 糟糕的；可怕的

sore throat〔`sor `θrot〕n. 喉嚨痛

runny nose〔`rʌnɪ `noz〕n. 流鼻水

wonder〔`wʌndɚ〕v. 想著

plenty of phr. 許多的

第二回 全真模擬試題

請將答案寫在答案紙上對應的題號旁，如有文法、用字、拼字、標點符號、大小寫等之錯誤，將予扣分。

第1-5題：句子改寫

請依題目之提示，將原句改寫成指定型式，並將改寫的句子完整地寫在答案紙上（包括提示之文字及標點符號）。

範例

Q I like to sing songs.

→ Ted _____.

A Ted *likes to sing songs.*

① Henry hurried to catch the bus to school.

Henry _____ now.

② It was not until Julia met Sam that she realized how lovely life could be.

Julia didn't _____ until she _____.

③ Vincent is visiting his aunt in Taichung.

Where _____?

④ "Joanne has passed the exam." Tell her.

Tell Joanne that _____.

⑤ Whether being vegetarian is good for one's health is being discussed.

It is being discussed _____.

第6-10題：句子合併

請依題目之提示，將兩句合併成一句，並將合併的句子完整地寫在答案紙上（包括提示之文字及標點符號）。

範例

Q Sophia has a dog.

The dog is black and white.

→ Sophia has a _____.

A Sophia has a *black and white dog.*

⑥ Harry does not study hard.

His sister studies very hard.

Harry _____ study as _____ as his sister does.

⑦ Carol took an umbrella.

The umbrella was from her friend's house.

Carol took _____ her friend's house.

⑧ My teacher asked me to do something.

I rewrote the report.

My teacher had me _____.

⑨ The police saw something on the street.

A man and a woman were fighting.

The police saw _____ on the street.

⑩ "Pocket Monster" is very popular.

Everyone knows it.

"Pocket Monster" is so _____ that _____.

第11-15題：重組

　　請將題目中所有提示 Words & Phrases 整合成一有意義的句子，並將重組的句子完整地寫在答案紙上（包括提示之文字及標點符號）。答案中必須使用所有提示 Words & Phrases，且不能隨意增加 Words & Phrases，否則不予計分。

範例

Q　Would _____?

(like/some/you/coffee)

A　Would *you like some coffee*?

⑪ The girl _____ when _____.
(crying/her bike/when/burst out /from/she/fell down)

⑫ The weather is _____ for us _____.
(camping/go/bad/too/to)

⑬ Bill _____ when he studied _____.
(many letters/in the U.K./his girlfriend/wrote)

⑭ Jeff is _____.
(in/going/big project/invest/the/to)

⑮ Is _____ France?
(most beautiful/the/in/Paris/city)

第二部份：段落寫作

題目： Kate 家在週末時都是全家一起出動做家事，經過一天的辛勞後，爸爸會慰勞全家。請根據以下圖片，寫一篇約50字的短文，描寫 Kate 全家如何度過週末。

_____

_____

_____

_____

_____

第二回 解析

第一部份：單句寫作

① Henry hurried to catch the bus to school.

Henry _____ now.

ANS **Henry is hurrying to catch the bus to school now.**

（亨利正忙著趕公車上學。）

句型 時態的切換 (p. 43)。

解析 改寫句中出現 now，時態改採現在進行式【Be + Ving】表達。

Words & Phrases

hurry〔ˋhɝɪ〕v. 急忙

catch the bus v. phr. 趕公車

② It was not until Julia met Sam that she realized how lovely life could be.

Julia didn't _____ until she _____.

ANS **Julia didn't realize how lovely life could be until she met Sam.**

（直到裘莉遇到山姆後，她才知道生命的可愛。）

句型 用特定片語改寫 (p. 48)。

解析 本句係【It is not until + A + that + B】與【B + not...+ until + A】（直到……時候，某人才……）兩句型之切換。切換時，A (Julia met Sam.) 與 B (She realized how lovely life could be.) 兩句須更換位置。因此，改寫後主要子句應為 B 的否定（即 Julia didn't realize how lovely life could be.）；而以 until 為首之附屬子句則更換為 A（即 She met Sam.）

Words & Phrases

realize〔ˋriəˏlaɪz〕v. 了解;明瞭

lovely〔ˋlʌvlɪ〕adj. 可愛的

③ Vincent is visiting his aunt in Taichung.

Where _____?

ANS **Where is Vincent visiting his aunt?**

(文森去那兒拜訪他的阿姨?)

句型 直述句改疑問句 (p. 5)。

解析 由於 is visiting 為 Be 動詞型態,改為以疑問詞 where 為首的問句時,必須將 is 提至主詞之前,形成 Where + Be + S + Ving 倒裝句型。

④ "Has Joanne passed the exam?" Ask her.

Ask Joanne if _____.

ANS **Ask Joanne if she has passed the exam.**

(跟瓊恩說她已經通過考試了。)

句型 直接問句改間接問句 (p. 18)。

解析 首先須刪除直接問句之引號與問號;其次,由於直接問句為 Yes-No 問句,因此如要作為 ask 之直接受詞則必須加連接詞 if。另,祈使句型之間接問句不需更改原直接問句之動詞時態。

Words & Phrases

inform〔ɪnˋfɔrm〕v. 通知;告知

⑤ Whether being vegetarian is good for one's health is being discussed.

It is being discussed _____.

ANS **It is being discussed whether being vegetarian is good for one's health.**

（吃素是否有益健康廣為人們所討論。）

句型 改爲虛主詞的句型 (p. 25)。

解析 本題改以虛主詞it爲首，將眞主詞（名詞子句whether being vegetarian is good for one's health）移至句尾。

Words & Phrases

vegetarian〔ˌvɛdʒəˋtɛrɪən〕*adj./n.* 素食的 / 素食者

health〔hɛlθ〕*n.* 健康

⑥ Harry does not study hard.

His sister studies very hard.

Harry _____ study as _____ as his sister does.

ANS **Harry does not study as hard as his sister does.**

（亨利不如他姐姐用功。）

句型 用比較句型合併 (p. 99)。

解析 本句係原級比較句型【as ＋原級 adj./adv.＋ as】之合併。兩句重複處爲 study hard，副詞爲 hard，故以 as hard as 合併兩句，形成 Harry does not study as hard as his sister studies.。因 as hard as 所連接之第二句動詞 studies 與第一句 study 重複，故以 does 取代 studies。

⑦ Carol took an umbrella.

The umbrella was from her friend's house.

Carol took _____ her friend's house.

ᴬᴺˢ **Carol took an umbrella from her friend's house.**

（凱洛從她朋友那兒帶回了一把傘。）

句型 用介系詞合併 (p. 107)。

解析 介系詞 from 表 took 此動詞之來源／地點，將以上兩句合併。

---

⑧ My teacher asked me to do something.

I rewrote the report.

My teacher had me _____.

ᴬᴺˢ **My teacher had me rewrite the report.**

（我的老師叫我重寫這份報告。）

句型 用使役動詞合併 (p. 113)。

解析 合併句中出現使役動詞 have，其後之受詞與受詞補語間之關係為主動之動作，該受詞補語因而採用原形動詞 rewrite。

---

⑨ The police saw something on the street.

A man and a woman were fighting.

The police saw _____ on the street.

ᴬᴺˢ **The police saw a man and a woman fighting on the street.**

（警方看見一男一女在街頭打架。）

句型 用感官動詞合併 (p. 118)。

解析 以感官動詞 see 合併兩句，形成【感官動詞＋O＋OC】句型，其中 OC 可為原形動詞或 Ving 兩種型態。因第二句 were fighting 強調進行狀態，故合併後 saw 之 OC（受詞補語）以 Ving 型態呈現。

Words & Phrases
fight〔faɪt〕*v.* 打架

⑩ "Pocket Monster" is very popular.

Everyone knows it.

"Pocket Monster" is so _____ that _____.

ANS **"Pocket Monster" is so popular that everyone knows it.**

（「神奇寶貝」非常流行，男女老少皆知。）

句型 用特殊句型合併 (p. 122)。

解析 本題合併後爲特殊句型【so adj./ adv....that S＋V】，表「如此……所以」。其中，副詞 so 之後接形容詞 popular，而 that 爲連接詞以引導「表結果」之副詞子句 everyone knows it。

⑪ The girl _____ when _____.

(crying/her bike/when/burst out/from/she/fell down)

ANS **The girl burst out crying when she fell down from her bike.**

（這個女孩從腳踏車上跌下來時，放聲大哭。）

句型 副詞子句的重組 (p. 153)。

解析 組合句中出現表時間之連接詞 when。字串中兩動詞片語 burst out crying 及 fell down，經判斷應分別爲主要子句及附屬子句之動詞。When 所引導之附屬字句主詞爲 she，動詞爲 fell down，from her bike 爲受詞表動作發生之地點。

Words & Phrases
burst out crying *v. phr.* 突然間嚎啕大哭

fall down *v. phr.* 跌倒

⑫ The weather is _____ for us _____ .

(camping/go/bad/too/to)

ANS **The weather is too bad for us to go camping.**

（天氣太差了，以致我們無法露營。）

句型	特殊句型的重組 (p. 157)。
解析	動詞 is 後原接形容詞 bad，在此將副詞 too 置於 bad 之前以修飾之；動詞的執行對象 for us 後接不定詞 to go camping，組合而成【too adj./ adv....to V】之特殊句型，表「太……以致於不能……」。

Words & Phrases

go camping *v. phr.* 去露營

⑬ Bill _____ when he studied _____ .

(many letters/in the U.K./his girlfriend/wrote)

ANS **Bill wrote his girlfriend many letters when he studied in the U.K.**

（比爾在英國念書時寫了許多信給他的女朋友。）

句型	授與動詞的重組 (p. 127)。
解析	字串中出現 wrote，卻無介系詞，為授與動詞【write＋I.O.（間接受詞）＋DO（直接受詞）】之重組。句中之 I.O. 為 his girlfriend，D.O. 為 some letters；in the U.K. 為地方副詞，置於 studied 之後。

⑭ Jeff is _____ .

(in/going/big project/invest/the/to)

ANS **Jeff is going to invest in the big project.**

（傑夫即將投資這個大案子。）

句型	時態的重組 (p. 131)。
解析	合組後動詞應為 is going；經判斷其受詞為不定詞片語 to invest in；the big project 則為介系詞 in 之受詞。

Words & Phrases

invest〔ɪnˋvɛst〕v. 投資

⑮ Is _____ France?

(most beautiful/the/in/Paris/city)

ANS Is Paris the most beautiful city in France?

（巴黎是法國最漂亮的城市嗎？）

句型	疑問句的重組 (p. 135)。
解析	經判斷，本句主詞應為 Paris，而 most beautiful、the 與 city 組合而成 the most beautiful city，作為 is 之後之主詞補語；而 in France 為地方副詞，置於句尾。

第二部份：段落寫作

參考範文

Kate's family makes it a rule to do housework together on weekends. They all have their duties. For example, Kate is responsible for ironing clothes; her brother sweeps the floors. Dishwashing is Kate's mother's job, and mopping the floor for her father. After a day's hard work, the four of them usually go out to dinner. They enjoy working together very much.

中文翻譯

　　凱特的　人習慣在週末一起做家事。他們各有職份，比方說凱特負責燙衣服，她哥哥則負責掃地；洗碗是媽媽的工作，爸爸則分配到拖地

板。經過一天的辛勤工作後，他們四人通常會外出吃晚餐。他們非常喜
歡一起做事。

結構分析

　　本篇為描寫文，重點在於如何表達四人的工作分配狀況。在時態
上均採現在簡單式，以表達事實與習慣性的動作。段落首句點名本篇
主旨，而後以列舉的方式說明每個人的職責。最後以共同做打掃工作
的感受作為結尾。

在句型運用方面，包含：

（1）make it a rule to＋V（使……成慣例）。

（2）dishwashing 及 mopping 等動名詞當主詞，動詞採單數型態。

（3）enjoy 後以動名詞當受詞。

Words & Phrases

duty〔`dutɪ〕 *n.* 責任；任務

be responsible for *v. phr.* 負責

iron〔`aɪɚn〕 *n.* 鐵；熨斗

　　　　　　 v. 燙衣服

第三回 全真模擬試題

第一部份：單句寫作

　　請將答案寫在答案紙上對應的題號旁，如有文法、用字、拼字、標點符號、大小寫等之錯誤，將予扣分。

第1-5題：句子改寫

　　請依題目之提示，將原句改寫成指定型式，並將改寫的句子完整地寫在答案紙上（包括提示之文字及標點符號）。

> **範例**
>
> **Q** I like to sing songs.
>
> → Ted _____.
>
> **A** Ted *likes to sing songs.*

① Karen: Do you have any plan for this weekend?

　　Kudy: I am going mountain climbing.

　　Judy plans _____ this weekend.

② No other girl in Sally's family is as tall as she is.

　　Sally is _____ girl in her family.

③ Albert has bread for breakfast everyday.

　　Albert _____ yesterday morning.

④ Sylvia cannot afford to go to college.

　　Sylvia _____ enough money to _____ college.

⑤ John's uncle encouraged him to take a swimming lesson.

　　Who __ _____?

第6-10題：句子合併

　　請依題目之提示，將兩句合併成一句，並將合併的句子完整地寫在答案紙上（包括提示之文字及標點符號）。

範例

Q Sophia has a dog.

The dog is black and white.

→ Sophia has a _____.

A Sophia has a *black and white dog*.

⑥ Sutter sometimes drives his car to work.

He sometimes takes the subway to his office.

Sutter _____ or _____ to work.

⑦ Maybe working too hard caused his illness.

Maybe the cold weather caused his illness.

Either _____ or _____ caused his illness.

⑧ There is a problem.

I forgot to buy a newspaper on my way home.

The problem is that _____.

⑨ The DVD player doesn't work.

Michelle bought it yesterday.

The DVD player _____ doesn't work.

⑩ Davyne moved to Taiwan.

She has been studying Chinese since then.

Davyne _____ since she _____ to Taiwan.

第11-15題：重組

請將題目中所有提示 Words & Phrases 整合成一有意義的句子，並將重組的句子完整地寫在答案紙上（包括提示之文字及標點符號）。答案中必須使用所有提示 Words & Phrases，且不能隨意增加 Words & Phrases，否則不予計分。

範例

Q Would _____?
(like/some/you/coffee)

A Would *you like some coffee*?

⑪ Mr. White _____.
(an/expensive/bought/diamond ring/his wife)

⑫ Both Kevin _____.
(are/good/Kate/my/friends/and)

⑬ I _____ the speaker _____ I won the prize.
(ran/as soon as/that/to the stage/announced)

⑭ Fernando is so _____ to exercise.
(time/that/never/busy/he/has)

⑮ A stranger asked _____ her.
(could/beside/Karen/sit/if/he)

第二部份：段落寫作

題目：May 是一名國三女生。昨天 May 的父母親有事情外出，交代她照顧三歲大的弟弟。請根據以下圖片，寫一篇約 50 字的短文，描述 May 照顧弟弟的一天。

第三回 解析

第一部份：單句寫作

① Karen: Do you have any plan for this weekend?

Judy: I am going mountain climbing.

Judy plans ＿＿＿＿＿＿＿＿＿＿＿＿＿＿＿ this weekend.

ANS **Judy plans to go mountain climbing this weekend.**

（裘蒂打算這個週末去爬山。）

句型 不定詞片語當受詞 (p. 30)。

解析 Plan 作動詞時，意為「打算」，其後之受詞須採不定詞，即【plan + to 原形 V】句型。因而將第二句動詞 is going mountain climbing 改為不定詞片語 to go mountain climbing。

② No other girl in Sally's family is as tall as she is.

Sally is ＿＿＿＿＿＿＿＿＿＿＿＿＿＿＿ girl in her family.

ANS **Sally is the tallest girl in her family.**

（莎麗是家中個兒最高的女生。）

句型 比較級與最高級的句型切換 (p. 38)。

解析 本句係原級與最高級的切換，亦即將排他性之比較句型【No other + 單數 S + V + as adj./adv. as + N】改寫為最高級句型【N + V + the 最高級 + 單數 N】。原句為「莎麗家中沒有其他女生像她那麼高」，改寫為「莎麗是家中個兒最高的女生」。形容詞 tall 之最高級為 tallest，加定冠詞後為 the tallest girl。

③ Albert has bread for breakfast everyday.

Albert _____ yesterday morning.

ANS **Albert had bread for breakfast yesterday morning.**

（亞伯特昨天早上吃了些麵包。）

句型 時態的切換 (p. 43)。

解析 改寫句中出現 yesterday morning，時態改採過去簡單式表達。

④ Sylvia cannot afford to go to college.

Sylvia _____ enough money to _____ college.

ANS **Sylvia does not have enough money to go to college.**

（希薇亞沒有足夠的錢唸大學。）

句型 用特定片語改寫 (p. 48)。

解析 本句係【cannot afford to ＋ V】與【do not have enough money ＋ to V】兩句型之切換，意為「負擔不起（做……事）」。改寫句後之【to V】仍為不定詞片語 to go to college。

Words & Phrases

afford〔ə`ford〕 v. 負擔得起

⑤ John's uncle encouraged him to take a swimming lesson.

Who _____ ?

ANS **Who encouraged John to take a swimming lesson?**

（是誰鼓勵約翰學游泳的？）

句型 直述句改疑問句 (p. 5)。

解析 改寫後之疑問詞 who 為主詞（＝原句之主詞 John's uncle），其後應接動詞 encouraged，句尾改為問號。

⑥ Sutter sometimes drives his car to work.

He sometimes takes the subway to his office.

Sutter _____ or _____ to work.

ANS **Sutter drives his car or takes the subway to work.**

（沙特開車或搭地鐵上班。）

句型 用對等連接詞合併 (p. 58)。

解析 以對等連接詞 or 將兩句合併為 Sutter drives his car to work or he takes the subway to his office.。由於兩句主詞相同，即 Sutter＝he 為 drive 與 take 兩動詞之行使者，因而省略第二個主詞 he。同時 to his office 與 to work 意思相同，保留其一即可。

---

⑦ Maybe working too hard caused his illness.

Maybe the cold weather caused his illness.

Either _____ or _____ caused his illness.

ANS **Either working too hard or the cold weather caused his illness.**

（工作過重或天氣太冷導致他生病了。）

句型 用對等相關連接詞合併 (p. 62)。

解析 合併句中出現「對等相關連接詞」Either...or，題目兩句相同之處為 caused his sickness，因此可知 Either...or 所連接者為兩主詞 working too hard 及 the cold weather。

---

⑧ There is a problem.

I forgot to buy a newspaper on my way home.

The problem is that _____.

ANS **The problem is that I forgot to buy a newspaper on my way home.**

（問題是我忘了在回家路上買份報紙。）

> **句型** 用名詞子句合併 (p. 68)。
>
> **解析** 第一句所指之 problem＝第二句，因此合併句 The problem 之主詞補語＝以連接詞 that 引導之名詞子句＝ that I forgot to buy a newspaper on my way home。

Words & Phrases

on one's way home *phr.* 在某人回家路上

⑨ The DVD player doesn't work.

Michelle bought it yesterday.

The DVD player _____ doesn't work.

ANS **The DVD player (which/that) Michelle bought yesterday doesn't work.**

（蜜雪兒昨天買的影碟機故障了）

> **句型** 用形容詞子句合併 (p. 80)。
>
> **解析** 第一句主詞 the DVD player＝第二句 bought 之受詞 it。合併時以表事物之關係代名詞 which 來取代 it，將第二句改爲形容詞子句 which Michelle bought，置於 the DVD player 之後以修飾之。另，關代 which 可用 that 取代，同時由於 which/that 在此爲受格，可予以省略。

⑩ Davyne moved to Taiwan.

She has been studying Chinese since then.

Davyne _____ since she _____ to Taiwan.

ANS **Davyne has been studying Chinese since she moved to Taiwan.**

（黛芬自從搬來台灣後就一直在學中文。）

句型	用副詞子句合併 (p. 91)。
解析	本句係以「表時間持續度」之從屬連接詞 since 合併兩句。主要子句 She has been studying Chinese. 表「持續性的行為」,為現在完成式;since 之後之附屬子句 since Davyne moved to Taiwan 表「時間起點」。注意,因改寫後主要子句置前,故將主詞改為 Davyne(= she)。

⑪ Mr. White _____.

(an/expensive/bought/diamond ring/his wife)

ANS **Mr. White bought his wife an expensive diamond ring.**

(白先生買了一只昂貴的鑽戒給他老婆。)

句型	授與動詞的重組 (p. 127)。
解析	字組中出現授與動詞 bought 但無介系詞,可知本句為授與動詞【buy + I.O.(間接受詞)+ D.O.(直接受詞)】之重組。句中之 I.O. 為 his wife,D.O. 為 an expensive diamond ring,注意二者不可顛倒。

⑫ Both Kevin _____.

(are/good/Kate/my/friends/and)

ANS **Both Kevin and Kate are my good friends.**

(凱文與凱特都是我的好朋友。)

句型	對等相關連接詞的重組 (p. 148)。
解析	凡看見 both 其後必搭配 and。本句係以「對等相關連接詞」both...and 連接兩主詞;字組中 Kate 為專有名詞,經判斷 Kate 應為主詞之一,組合後主詞應為 Both Kevin and Kate。本句動詞為 are,而 good 與 my 和 friends 組合為 my good friends 作為主詞補語。

⑬ I _____ the speaker _____ I won the prize.

(ran/as soon as/that/to the stage/announced)

ANS **I ran to the stage as soon as the speaker announced that I won the prize.**

（當主席一宣佈我得獎，我立刻就衝上台去。）

句型 副詞子句的重組 (p. 153)。

解析 經判斷本句主要子句之動詞應爲 ran to the stage。而字組中出現表時間之從屬連接詞 as soon as，合併句中之副詞子句型態爲【as soon as ＋ S ＋ V】。即 as soon as the speaker announced...；而 announced 爲及物動詞後須接受詞（即名詞子句 that I won the prize）組成 as soon as the speaker announced that I won the prize。

Words & Phrases

stage〔stedʒ〕*n.* 舞台；台上

announce〔əˋnaʊns〕*v.* 宣佈

win the prize *v. phr.* 贏得獎項；得獎

⑭ Fernando is so _____ to exercise.

(time/that/never/busy/he/has)

ANS **Fernando is so busy that he never has time to exercise.**

（費南多忙得沒有時間運動。）

句型 特殊句型的重組 (p. 157)。

解析 本句係特殊句型【so adj./ adv....＋that S ＋ V...】（如此……以致於）之重組，以 that 連接之子句表「結果」。So 後接形容詞 busy，that 子句之主詞爲 he，動詞爲 has time，副詞 never 爲頻率副詞，應置於一般動詞之前（has 在此爲一般動詞），形成 that he never has time。

⑮ A stranger asked _____ her.

(could/beside/Karen/sit/if/he)

ANS **A stranger asked Karen if he could sit beside her.**

（一位陌生人問凱倫他是否可以坐在她旁邊。）

句型 間接問句的重組 (p. 143)。

解析 本句 if 為連接詞，形成間接問句【if＋S＋V（＋受詞）】句型。其中主要子句動詞 asked 之受詞應為 Karen，間接問句主詞為 he，動詞為 could sit，介系詞 beside 後加受詞 her 置於句尾。

第二部份：段落寫作

參考範文

May was asked to baby-sit her three-year-old brother because her parents had to go out. May took her brother to a park where there were a pond, a slide and a seesaw. They played and played until both were tired. When their parents came home, they found May and her brother had fallen asleep on the sofa.

中文翻譯

梅的父母有事要外出，所以要她代為照顧三歲的弟弟。梅帶弟弟到公園去玩。公園裡有個池塘，一座滑梯和一個翹翹板。他們倆一直玩，玩到精疲力盡。梅的爸媽回家時，發現梅和弟弟已經在沙發上睡著了。

結構分析

　　本篇爲記敘文，涉及時間與空間的轉換。在時間的處理方面，敘述梅照顧弟弟的過程，採過去簡單式，如：帶弟弟到公園去玩。段落首句點出本篇的主旨——梅的父親有事外出，要梅代爲照顧小弟。隨即描寫照顧的過程，與如何度過這令人疲憊的一天。在空間方面，則涵括了公園及家裡。

在句型運用方面，包含：

（1）被動語態句型：May was asked to baby-sit her brother.

（2）表原因之附屬子句：because her parents had to go out。

（3）關係副詞爲首之形容詞子句：where there are a pond, a slide and a seesaw。

Words & Phrases

baby-sit〔ˋbebɪˌsɪt〕 v. 當臨時褓姆

slide〔slaɪd〕 n. 溜滑梯

seesaw〔ˋsiˌsɔ〕 n. 蹺蹺板

fall asleep v. phr. 睡著

第四回 全真模擬試題

第一部份：單句寫作

　　請將答案寫在答案紙上對應的題號旁，如有文法、用字、拼字、標點符號、大小寫等之錯誤，將予扣分。

第1-5題：句子改寫

　　請依題目之提示，將原句改寫成指定型式，並將改寫的句子完整地寫在答案紙上（包括提示之文字及標點符號）。

範例

Q	I like to sing songs.
→	Ted ＿＿＿＿＿＿＿＿＿.
A	Ted *likes to sing songs.*

① Bob told his wife, "Can you bring me some tea?"

　　Bob asked his wife if she ＿＿＿＿＿＿＿＿＿＿＿＿＿＿.

② To choose a major you like is very important.

　　It is very important ＿＿＿＿＿＿＿＿＿＿＿＿＿＿.

③ Eva: Did you get your money back?

　　Elaine: No, I didn't.

　　Elaine failed ＿＿＿＿＿＿＿＿＿＿＿＿ her money back.

④ Nobody treats me as well as Danny does.

　　Danny ＿＿＿＿＿＿＿ than any other ＿＿＿＿＿＿ does.

⑤ Bill lives in Los Angeles.

　　Bill ＿＿＿＿＿＿＿＿＿＿＿＿＿＿ for 10 years.

第6-10題：句子合併

　　請依題目之提示，將兩句合併成一句，並將合併的句子完整地寫在答案紙上（包括提示之文字及標點符號）。

> **範例**
>
> **Q** Sophia has a dog.
>
> The dog is black and white.
>
> → Sophia has a _____.
>
> **A** Sophia has a *black and white dog.*

⑥ John is short.

　His brother is very tall.

　John's brother is much _____ than he is.

⑦ Bob lifted the heavy box.

　His friend helped him.

　Bob lifted the heavy box _____ his friend's _____.

⑧ My friend told a joke.

　I laughed.

　_____ joke made me _____.

⑨ Tony had a feeling.

　The earth was moving under his feet.

　Tony _____ the earth _____.

⑩ Albert can do one thing.

　The thing is to give up the project.

　All Albert can do is _____.

請將題目中所有提示 Words & Phrases 整合成一有意義的句子，並將重組的句子完整地寫在答案紙上（包括提示之文字及標點符號）。答案中必須使用所有提示 Words & Phrases，且不能隨意增加 Words & Phrases，否則不予計分。

範例

Q Would ＿＿＿＿＿＿＿＿＿？

(like/some/you/coffee)

A Would *you like some coffee*?

⑪ The TV ＿＿＿＿＿＿＿＿＿＿＿＿＿＿＿＿＿.

　　(playing/favorite cartoon/channel 66/is/on/my)

⑫ How ＿＿＿＿＿＿＿＿＿＿＿＿＿＿＿＿＿？

　　(Cathy's/do/often/her/parents/call)

⑬ Go ask Mom ＿＿＿＿＿＿＿＿＿＿＿ at this station.

　　(get off/we/the train/whether/should)

⑭ Neither ＿＿＿＿＿＿＿＿＿＿＿ after the crash.

　　(were/nor/alive/the passengers/the driver)

⑮ Bill ＿＿＿＿＿＿ while he was ＿＿＿＿＿＿ in Europe.

　　(to/many/studying/traveled/countries)

第二部份：段落寫作

題目： Gina 幼年時的朋友 David 打電話告知他即將從美國回台灣過暑假，為了避免 Gina 在機場認不出他，David 於是寄了一張照片給她。請根據以下圖片，寫一篇約50字的短文。

第四回 解析

第一部份：單句寫作

① Bob told his wife, "Can you bring me some tea?"

Bob asked his wife if she _____.

ANS **Bob asked his wife if she could bring him some tea.**

（鮑伯問他妻子是不是能倒杯茶給他。）

句型 直接問句改間接問句 (p. 18)。

解析 本題為一般問句型之直接問句改為間接問句，即將 "Can you bring me some tea?" 改為【if＋S＋V】之名詞子句。首先須刪除直接問句之引號與問號，句尾更改為句點；其次將主詞改為 she，然後將原助動詞 can 改為 could，置於主詞 she 之後，最後把原受詞 me 改成 him。

② To choose a major you like is very important.

It is very important _____.

ANS **It is very important to choose a major you like.**

（選你所喜歡的科系是很重要的。）

句型 改為虛主詞的句型 (p. 25)。

解析 本題改以虛主詞 it 為首，將真主詞不定詞片語 to choose a major you like 移至句尾。

Words & Phrases

major〔`medʒɚ〕 *n., v.* 主修

221

③ Eva: Did you get your money back?

Elaine: No, I didn't.

Elaine failed _____ her money back.

ᴀɴꜱ **Elaine failed to get her money back.**

（伊蘭的錢拿不回來。）

句型 不定詞片語當受詞 (p. 30)。

解析 本句改以動詞 fail 表達時，fail 後需接不定詞為受詞。亦即在 get 前加上 to，形成不定詞片語 to get her money back，作為 fail 之受詞。

Words & Phrases

fail〔fel〕v. 失敗；（考試）被當；無法達成

---

④ Nobody treats me as well as Danny does.

Danny _____ than any other _____ does.

ᴀɴꜱ **Danny treats me better than any other person does.**

（丹尼對我比任何人都好。）

句型 比較級與最高級的句型切換 (p. 38)。

解析 本句係將原級比較句型即【as＋adj./adv.＋as】改為比較級句型【比較級＋than any other＋單數 N】。原句副詞 well 之比較級為 better，因此原句可改為 Danny treats me better than any other person treats me.。因 treats me 重複，故以 does 替代之。

Words & Phrases

treat〔trit〕v. 對待

⑤ Bill lives in Los Angeles.

Bill _____ for 10 years.

ANS **Bill has lived in Los Angeles for 10 years.**

（比爾已經在洛杉磯住了十年了。）

句型	時態的切換 (p. 43)。
解析	本句係將現在事實的陳述，改以持續狀態 (for 10 years) 來表達，因而時態須改採現在完成式【have＋Vpp】。

⑥ John is short.

His brother is very tall.

John's brother is much _____ than he is.

ANS **John's brother is much taller than he is.**

（約翰的哥哥／弟弟比約翰高多了。）

句型	用比較句型合併 (p. 99)。
解析	short 的相反詞為 tall；合併句中出現 than 顯然意味前面有比較級，因此將 tall 改為 taller，再將 John's brother（＝his brother）與 he（＝John）置於 taller than 兩端作為比較之對象。注意，修飾比較級不可用 very 而用 much。

⑦ Bob lifted the heavy box.

His friend helped him.

Bob lifted the heavy box _____ his friend's _____.

ANS **Bob lifted the heavy box with his friend's help.**

（有了朋友的幫忙，鮑伯舉起了這個重箱子。）

句型	用介系詞合併 (p. 107)。
解析	中文的「有」，在英文中可以介系詞 with 一字表達。合併後 with 後須接名詞 his friend's help 作為受詞。

Words & Phrases

lift〔lɪft〕*v.* 舉起

⑧ My friend told a joke.

I laughed.

_____ joke made me _____.

ANS My friend's joke made me laugh.

（我朋友講的笑話讓我覺得好笑。）

句型	用使役動詞合併 (p. 113)。
解析	合併句中出現使役動詞 make，其後因屬主動之動作，所以受詞補語採用原形動詞 laugh；主詞為名詞型態之 my friend's joke。

⑨ Tony had a feeling.

The earth was moving under his feet.

Tony _____ the earth _____.

ANS Tony felt the earth moving under his feet.

（湯尼覺得世界運轉在他腳下。）

句型	用感官動詞合併 (p. 118)。
解析	合併句中所缺者為動詞，因而將 had a feeling 改為動詞 felt；因 felt（原形為 feel）屬感官動詞，句型為【感官動詞＋O＋OC】，其中 OC 可為原形動詞 V 或 Ving 兩種型態。因第二句中的 was moving 強調進行狀態，故合併後 feel 之 OC（受詞補語）以 Ving 型態呈現。

⑩ Albert can do one thing.

The thing is to give up the project.

All Albert can do is _____.

ANS All Albert can do is give up the project.

（亞伯特所能做的就是放棄這個案子。）

句型 用特殊句型合併 (p. 122)。

解析 本題為特殊句型【All one can do is＋V】之合併。one thing＝the thing＝to give up the project；因 All one can do is 句型後採用原形動詞，故在 All Albert can do is 後加上 give up the project 以合併之。

Words & Phrases

give up *v. phr.* 放棄

---

⑪ The TV _____.

(playing/favorite cartoon/channel 66/is/on/my)

ANS **The TV is playing my favorite cartoon on channel 66.**

（電視第六十六頻道正在播放我最愛看的卡通。）

句型 時態的重組 (p. 131)。

解析 主詞後尋找適當之動詞。將 is 與 playing 結合形成進行式之動詞型態；my 之後則搭配名詞 favorite cartoon；「在第六十六頻道」以介系詞 on＋channel 66 表達之。

---

⑫ How _____?

(Cathy's/do/often/her/parents/call)

ANS **How often do Cathy's parents call her?**

（凱西的爸媽多久打一次電話給她？）

句型 疑問句的重組 (p. 135)。

解析 字串中出現頻率副詞 often，因此在疑問副詞 how 之後加上 often，形成以 How often 為首之問句句型。字串中有助動詞 do 與 call，故採【疑問詞＋助動詞＋S＋本動詞（＋受詞）?】句型。因助動詞為 do（複數），故 Cathy's parents 為主詞，而 her 為受詞。

⑬ Go ask Mom _____ at this station.

(get off/we/the train/whether/should)

ANS Go ask Mom whether we should get off the train at this station.

（去問媽媽我們是否該在這站下車。）

> **句型** 間接問句的重組 (p. 143)。
>
> **解析** 本句 whether 為連接詞，引導間接問句【whether ＋ S ＋ V（＋受詞）】，其中主詞為 we，動詞為 get off，前加助動詞 should，成為 should get off，其受詞為 the train。

⑭ Neither _____ after the crash.

(were/nor/alive/the passengers/the driver)

ANS Neither the driver nor the passengers were alive after the crash.

（撞車後，司機跟乘客無人生還。）

> **句型** 對等相關連接詞的重組 (p. 148)。
>
> **解析** 凡看見 neither 其後必搭配 nor。本題之 neither...nor 所連接者為主詞（the driver 與 the passengers）。特別注意，在【Neither ＋ S_1 ＋ nor ＋ S_2 ＋ V】的句型中，動詞單複數取決於較近動詞之主詞，即 S_2。因字串中動詞為 were，顯見 the passengers 必為 S_2。另，alive 為形容詞，置於 were 之後作主詞補語。

Words & Phrases

passenger〔`pæsṇʤɚ〕 *n.* 乘客

alive〔ə`laɪv〕 *adj.* 生還的；活的

⑮ Bill _____ while he was _____ in Europe.
(to/many/studying/traveled/countries)

ANS **Bill traveled to many countries while he was studying in Europe.**

（比爾在歐洲念書時曾到過許多國家遊玩。）

句型	副詞子句的重組 (p. 153)。
解析	組合句中含有表時間之附屬子句【while＋S＋V】，且主要子句及附屬子句各缺動詞。由於附屬子句動詞位置出現was，顯然應搭配studying，traveled則為主要子句之動詞。此外，traveled後接to，再接地點，表「到……旅遊」。

Words & Phrases

travel〔ˋtrævḷ〕v. 旅遊
Europe〔ˋjʊrəp〕n. 歐洲

第二部份：段落寫作

參考範文

　　Gina's childhood friend, David, is coming back to Taiwan soon. They are talking on the phone right now. Gina remembers that David was very slim, with short hair and heavy glasses. But David has changed a lot. Now, he is tall and strong, and has a beard. Besides, he now wears very fashionable clothes.

中文翻譯

　　芝娜幼年時的朋友大衛即將回台灣。他們現在正在講電話。芝娜記得大衛以前很瘦，留短髮、戴厚重的眼鏡。但是大衛已經變了許多。現在的他，又高又壯，且留了鬍子。此外，他現在的衣著也相當地入時。

結構分析

　　本篇為描寫文，涉及時間與空間的轉換。在時態的處理方面變化較大。用未來式（以 Be＋Ving 呈現），表「即將……」；用簡單過去式表達 David 過去的模樣；用現在完成式說明 David 的改變；至於大衛現在的外型與衣著則以現在簡單式表達。除此之外，在電話上交談，以現在進行式處理。

Words & Phrases

to talk on the phone　*v. phr.* 以電話交談
slim〔slɪm〕*adj.* 瘦弱
heavy〔ˈhɛvɪ〕*adj.* 粗重；厚重
beard〔bɪrd〕*n.* 鬍鬚
fashionable〔ˈfæʃnəb̩l〕*adj.* 流行的；時髦的

第五回　全真模擬試題

第一部份：單句寫作

　　請將答案寫在答案紙上對應的題號旁，如有文法、用字、拼字、標點符號、大小寫等之錯誤，將予扣分。

第1-5題：句子改寫

　　請依題目之提示，將原句改寫成指定型式，並將改寫的句子完整地寫在答案紙上（包括提示之文字及標點符號）。

> **範例**
>
> **Q**　I like to sing songs.
>
> →　Ted ＿＿＿＿＿＿＿＿＿＿＿＿.
>
> **A**　Ted *likes to sing songs.*

① My nephew is not old enough to tell the time.

My nephew ＿＿＿＿＿＿＿ too ＿＿＿＿＿＿＿＿＿＿ tell the time.

② Joanne is saving money to buy a cell phone.

Why ＿＿＿＿＿＿＿＿＿＿＿＿＿＿＿＿＿＿＿＿＿＿＿＿＿＿＿＿?

③ Prof. Chen asked, "When will you hand in the final report?"

Prof. Chen asked me ＿＿＿＿＿＿＿＿＿＿＿＿＿＿＿＿＿＿＿.

④ To show your friendliness to people around you is very important.

It is very important ＿＿＿＿＿＿＿＿＿＿＿＿＿＿＿＿＿＿＿＿.

⑤ Lily: You should spend some time with our children.

Dennis: I will play basketball with them.

Dennis will spend some time ＿＿＿＿＿＿＿＿＿ with his children.

第6-10題：句子合併

請依題目之提示，將兩句合併成一句，並將合併的句子完整地寫在答案紙上（包括提示之文字及標點符號）。

範例

Q Sophia has a dog.

The dog is black and white.

→ Sophia has a _____.

A Sophia has a *black and white dog.*

⑥ Sean drove more slowly.

The reason was that he was asked to slow down.

Sean _____ , so he _____.

⑦ Julia's parents were not satisfied with her performance.

Her teacher was not, neither.

Neither Julia's parents _____ her teacher _____ with her performance.

⑧ Jeff told me something.

He came up with a great idea while taking a shower.

Jeff told me that _____.

⑨ The tall guy is Jill's husband.

His suit is gray.

The tall guy _____ is gray _____ Jill's husband.

⑩ Celina has three jobs.

She has to support her family.

Celina _____ because she _____.

第11-15題：重組

請將題目中所有提示 Words & Phrases 整合成一有意義的句子，並將重組的句子完整地寫在答案紙上（包括提示之文字及標點符號）。答案中必須使用所有提示 Words & Phrases，且不能隨意增加 Words & Phrases，否則不予計分。

範例

Q Would _____?
(like/some/you/coffee)

A Would *you like some coffee*?

⑪ Susan _____ until she _____.
(broke up/Tom/the secret/didn't/know/with)

⑫ Maria _____ as a gift.
(her daughter/a teddy bear/for/bought)

⑬ Ted _____.
(on-line games/was/his classmates/with/playing)

⑭ Does _____?
(speak/Mandarin/Taiwanese/your boss/or)

⑮ Jonathon showed us _____.
(house/was/his/large/how/country)

第二部份：段落寫作

題目：有了捷運後，台北人的交通方式有了很大的改變。請根據以下圖片，寫一篇約50字的短文，描述捷運所帶來的改變。

第五回 解析

第一部份：單句寫作

① My nephew is not old enough to tell the time.

My nephew _____ too _____ tell the time.

ANS **My nephew is too young to tell the time.**

（我的外甥還太小，不會看時間。）

句型 用特定片語改寫 (p. 48)。

解析 本句係將【not + adj./adv. + to V】切換為【too + adj./adv. + to V】。not old enough 所表達亦即 too young。

② Joanne is saving money to buy a cell phone.

Why _____?

ANS **Why is Joanne saving money?**

（瓊恩為什麼要存錢？）

句型 直述句改為疑問句 (p. 5)。

解析 本題係改為以疑問詞 why 為首之疑問句。將 Be 動詞 is 提至主詞 Joanne 之前，形成倒裝，並在句尾加上問號。

Words & Phrases

cell phone〔ˋsɛl ˌfon〕 n. 手機；大哥大

③ Prof. Chen asked, "When will you hand in the final report?"

Prof. Chen asked me _____.

ANS **Prof. Chen asked me when I would hand in the final report.**

（陳教授問我何時會交期末報告。）

句型	直接問句改為間接問句 (p. 18)。
解析	本題係改為以疑問詞 when 為首的間接問句。首先將逗號、引號、問號去除，其次將直接問句之動詞與主詞對調，還原為 S + V 型態；此外，須特別注意主要子句與間接問句時態的一致性，即，將助動詞 will 改為 would。

Words & Phrases

hand in *v. phr.* 繳交

④ To show your friendliness to people around you is very important.
It is very important _____.

ANS **It is very important** to show your friendliness to people around you.

（對你週遭的人表示友善是件很重要的事。）

句型	改為虛主詞的句型 (p. 25)。
解析	將原句主詞（真主詞）to show your friendliness to people around you 移至 important 之後，並以虛主詞 it 取代之，即形成【It is important to + V】之句型。

Words & Phrases

friendliness〔`frɛndlɪnɪs〕*n.* 友善

⑤ Lily:　You should spend some time with our children.
Dennis: I will play basketball with them.
Dennis will spend some time _____ with his children.

ANS **Dennis will spend some time** playing basketball **with his children.**

（丹尼斯會花些時間跟他的孩子打球。）

句型	動名詞片語當受詞 (p. 30)。
解析	本句重點在動詞片語 spend time 後須接 Ving。因此，兩句組合後成為 Dennis will spend some time playing basketball with his children。

⑥ Sean drove more slowly.

The reason was that he was asked to slow down.

Sean _____ , so he _____ .

ANS **Sean was asked to slow down, so he drove more slowly.**

（尚恩被要求減速，所以他把車的速度放得比較慢。）

句型	用對等連接詞合併 (p. 58)。
解析	表因果之對等連接詞 so 之前為「原因」：Sean was asked to slow down.，而 so 之後表「結果」，即 he drove more slowly。

⑦ Julia's parents were not satisfied with her performance.

Her teacher was not, either.

Neither Julia's parents _____ her teacher _____ with her performance.

ANS **Neither Julia's parents nor her teacher was satisfied with her performance.**

（裘莉亞的爸媽和老師對她的表現都不滿意。）

句型	用對等相關連接詞合併 (p. 62)。
解析	本題係改為以對等相關連接詞 neither...nor 合併的句型。兩句重複部份為 be satisfied with her performance，故合併時以 neither...nor 連接兩主詞。須特別注意此時動詞之單複數，取決於較靠近動詞之主詞（本句為 her teacher），因而 Be 動詞採單數型態之 was。

satisfied〔ˋsætɪsˏfaɪd〕*adj.* 滿意的
performance〔pəˋfɔrməns〕*n.* 表演;表現

⑧ Jeff told me something.

He came up with a great idea while taking a shower.

Jeff told me that _____.

ANS **Jeff told me that** he came up with a great idea while taking a
shower.

（傑夫告訴我他在洗澡時想到一個好點子。）

句型 用名詞子句的合併 (p. 68)。

解析 第一句之 something ＝第二個句子,合併時在第二句前方加上連
接詞 that,形成名詞子句 that he came up with a great idea while
taking a shower。

come up with *v. phr.* 想出來

⑨ The tall guy is Jill's husband.

His suit is gray.

The tall guy _____ is gray _____ Jill's husband.

ANS **The tall guy whose suit is gray is Jill's husband.**

（那個西裝是灰色的高個兒是吉兒的丈夫。）

句型 用形容詞子句合併 (p. 80)。

解析 第二句中的所有格 his 指第一句中的 the tall guy's。合併時以關係
代名詞所有格 whose 來表示,將第二句改為形容詞子句 whose
suit is gray 接在第一句主詞 The tall guy 之後。

⑩ Celina has three jobs.

She has to support her family.

Celina _____ because she _____.

ANS **Celina** has three jobs **because she** has to support her family.

（因為要養家，所以瑟麗娜身兼三個工作。）

句型 用副詞子句合併 (p. 91)。

解析 本句係以表原因之從屬連接詞 because 合併兩句。主要子句為「結果」She has three jobs.，because 之後之附屬子句表「原因」She has to support her family.。

Words & Phrases

support〔sə`port〕*v.* 支撐；支持；養家活口

⑪ Susan _____ until she _____.

(broke up/Tom/the secret/didn't/know/with)

ANS **Susan** didn't know the secret **until she** broke up with Tom.

（直到跟湯姆分手後，蘇姍才知道這個秘密。）

句型 特殊句型的重組 (p. 157)。

解析 本句為【not...until（直到……某人才……）】句型。主要子句動詞為否定之 didn't，其後須接原形動詞 know；其次，名詞 the secret 與 Tom 分別為 know 及 with 之受詞，不可顛倒，因為 Susan 不會 broke up with the secret。

Words & Phrases

break up with sb. *v. phr.* 與某人分手

⑫ Maria _____ as a gift.

(her daughter/a teddy bear/for/bought)

ANS **Maria bought a teddy bear for her daughter as a gift.**
（瑪莉娜送給她女兒一隻泰迪熊。）

句型　授與動詞的重組 (p. 127)。

解析　字串中出現 bought 與介系詞 for，因此本句為授與動詞【buy ＋ D.O.（直接受詞）＋ for ＋ I.O.（間接受詞）】之重組。句中之直接受詞（D.O.）為 a teddy bear，間接受詞（I.O.）為 her daughter，注意二者不可顛倒。

---

⑬ Ted _____.
(on-line games/was/his classmates/with/playing)

ANS **Ted was playing on-line games with his classmates.**
（泰迪在跟他同學玩線上遊戲。）

句型　時態的重組 (p. 131)。

解析　主詞之後尋找動詞，即 was playing；接下來判斷 was playing 之受詞。字串中有兩名詞組，分別為 on-line games 及 his classmates。顯然 one-line games 應為 was playing 之受詞，而 his classmates 則為 with 之受詞。

---

⑭ Does _____?
(speak/Mandarin/Taiwanese/your boss/or)

ANS **Does your boss speak Mandarin or Taiwanese?**
（你的老闆講國語或台語？）

句型　疑問句的重組 (p. 135)。

解析　由字串判斷出有兩個名詞組：your boss 和 Mandarin or Taiwanese。由動詞 speak 可知其主詞應為 your boss，其受詞應為 Mandarin or Taiwanese。

---

⑮ Jonathan showed us _____.

(house/was/his/large/how/country)

ANS **Jonathan showed us how large his country house was.**

（瓊納森讓我們見識他的村舍有多大。）

句型 間接問句的重組 (p. 143)。

解析 間接問句之詞序應為 S＋V。依判斷，間接問句之主詞應為 his country house，動詞為 was，而疑問副詞 how 則接形容詞 large，表規模、程度，置於間接問句句首。

第二部份：段落寫作

參考範文

Taipei's MRT has brought convenience and comfort to its citizens. I used to go to work by bus. The bus was always crowded with passengers. Everyone sweated and showed impatience. Now, I travel by MRT because it is clean and comfortable. In addition, I spend less time waiting. There are other benefits too. For example, you can shop in the underground mall.

中文翻譯

台北的捷運帶給了它的市民方便與舒適。我以前都是搭公車上班。公車上總是擠滿了人，每個人都汗流浹背，顯得很不耐煩。現在我搭乘捷運，因為既乾淨又舒適。此外，等車時間減少了。捷運系統還有其它的好處，比方說，你可以在地下商店街逛街購物。

結構分析

　　本篇爲描寫文，涉及時間與空間的轉換。在時間的處理方面，包括表事實之現在式（如：捷運乾淨、舒適，可在地下商店街逛街購物），及表過去的狀況之過去簡單式（如：過去搭乘公車的苦處）。在空間方面，則涵蓋了捷運、公車與地下商店街三個地方的切換。

Words & Phrases

be crowded with　*v. phr.* 擠滿著……中
passenger〔ˋpæsṇʤɚ〕*n.* 乘客
impatience〔ɪmˋpeʃəns〕*n.* 不耐煩
benefit〔ˋbɛnəfɪt〕*n.* 好處；利益
underground〔ˋʌndɚˋgraʊnd〕*adj.* 地下的
mall〔mɔl〕*n.* 購物中心；商場

第六回 全真模擬試題

第一部份：單句寫作

　　請將答案寫在答案紙上對應的題號旁，如有文法、用字、拼字、標點符號、大小寫等之錯誤，將予扣分。

第1-5題：句子改寫

　　請依題目之提示，將原句改寫成指定型式，並將改寫的句子完整地寫在答案紙上（包括提示之文字及標點符號）。

> **範例**
>
> **Q**　I like to sing songs.
> →　Ted _____.
> **A**　Ted *likes to sing songs.*

① No other city in Taiwan has as many temples as my city does.

　　My city _____ temples than all the other _____ in Taiwan.

② Mark says he likes beef and seafood.

　　Yesterday Mark _____.

③ The weather is so hot that we don't do any outdoor activities.

　　The weather is too _____ for us _____ activities.

④ Ted went fishing in the forest this morning.

　　When _____?

⑤ My cousin asked, "Are you going to get married this year?"

　　My cousin asked me if _____ this year.

第6-10題：句子合併

請依題目之提示，將兩句合併成一句，並將合併的句子完整地寫在答案紙上（包括提示之文字及標點符號）。

範例

Q Sophia has a dog.

The dog is black and white.

→ Sophia has a _____.

A Sophia has a *black and white dog.*

⑥ Lily has two kids.

Her brother has the same number of children as she does.

Lily has as _____ kids as _____.

⑦ Karen won a prize in the contest.

Her parents were proud.

Karen's parents were proud _____ her _____ a prize in the contest.

⑧ Jack said something to his friends.

His friends were very angry.

Jack's words made _____.

⑨ I saw something on the wall.

A spider was climbing.

I _____ a spider _____ on the wall.

⑩ My grandmother had a rule.

She avoided eating meat in the morning.

My grandmother used to _____ in the morning.

第11-15題：重組

　　請將題目中所有提示字詞整合成一有意義的句子，並將重組的句子完整地寫在答案紙上（包括提示之文字及標點符號）。答案中必須使用所有提示字詞，且不能隨意增加字詞，否則不予計分。

範例

Q Would _____?

(like/some/you/coffee)

A Would *you like some coffee*?

⑪ The one-way tickets _____.

(both/sold out/the round-trip tickets/and/are)

⑫ Most _____ only after they _____ ill.

(become/health/the importance/people/of/realize)

⑬ What _____ is _____ with my problems.

(has/my sister/help/done/me)

⑭ Sean _____ as her birthday gift.

(some/girlfriend/sent/his/flowers)

⑮ Ivy _____ near his office.

(her/waited/boyfriend/a café/has/for/at)

第二部份：段落寫作

題目：班上同學似乎忘了今天是 Emma 的生日，她很不開心 。放學後 Emma 才發現原來事有蹊蹺。請根據以下圖片，寫一篇約50字的短文，描述 Emma 的生日。

第六回 解析

第一部份：單句寫作

① No other city in Taiwan has as many temples as my city does.

My city ＿＿＿＿＿＿ temples than all the other ＿＿＿＿＿ in Taiwan.

ANS **My city has more temples than all the other cities in Taiwan.**

（我住的城市廟宇比台灣其他城市來得多。）

句型 比較級與最高級的句型切換 (p. 38)。

解析 本句係將原級比較句型【as＋adj./adv.＋as】改為比較級句型【比較級＋than all the other＋複數N】。原句形容詞原級 many 之比較級為 more，因此將 as many temples as... 改為比較級句型後為 more temples than all the other...。

Words & Phrases

temple〔ˋtɛmpḷ〕 n. 寺廟

---

② Mark says he likes beef and seafood.

Yesterday Mark ＿＿＿＿＿＿＿＿＿＿＿＿＿＿＿＿＿＿＿＿＿＿.

ANS **Yesterday Mark said he liked beef and seafood.**

（馬克說他喜歡牛肉跟海鮮。）

句型 時態的切換 (p. 43)。

解析 因出現 yesterday，改寫句中主要動詞應改成 says 之過去式 said，名詞子句中之動詞 likes 亦用過去式 liked。

---

③ The weather is so hot that we don't do any outdoor activities.

The weather is too ＿＿＿＿＿ for us ＿＿＿＿＿＿＿＿＿ activities.

245

ANS **The weather is too hot for us to do any outdoor activities.**
（天氣太熱了，我們無法做任何戶外活動。）

> **句型** 用特定片語改寫 (p. 48)。
>
> **解析** 本句係【so＋adj./adv.＋that＋S＋V...】與【too＋adj./adv.＋to
> ＋V】（太……以致／不能……）兩句型之切換。切換時，too之
> 後接形容詞hot，後接不定詞【to＋V】。特別注意的是，原句中
> that子句後否定的don't do，切換為【too...to】句型時，需改為
> 肯定的to do。

④ Ted went fishing in the forest this morning.
When _____?

ANS **When did Ted go fishing in the forest?**
（泰迪何時到森林去釣魚的？）

> **句型** 直述句改疑問句 (p. 5)。
>
> **解析** 由於went為一般動詞型態，改為以疑問詞when為首的問句時，
> 必須在主詞之前加上助動詞did，形成 When＋did＋S＋V?之
> 句型。

⑤ My cousin asked, "Are you going to get married this year?"
My cousin asked me if _____ this year.

ANS **My cousin asked me if I was going to get married this year.**
（我表姊問我是否會在今年結婚？）

> **句型** 直接問句改為間接問句 (p. 18)。
>
> **解析** 首先須刪除直接問句之引號與問號；其次，原直接問句中並無
> 疑問詞，改為間接問句時須加上連接詞if，同時回復倒裝句，改
> 為【if＋S＋V】的名詞子句，作為主要子句動詞asked之受
> 詞。

⑥ Lily has two kids.

Her brother has the same number of children as she does.

Lily has as _____ kids as _____.

ANS **Lily has as many kids as her brother does.**

（麗莉的小孩跟她哥哥的一樣多。）

句型 用比較句型合併 (p. 99)。

解析 本句係原級比較句型【as＋many＋N＋as】之合併。兩句重複
處為 two kids 和 the same number of children，故以 as many kids as
合併兩句，形成 Lily has as many kids as her brother has.。另，因
her brother has 與第一句動詞 has 重複，故以 does 取代 has。

⑦ Karen won a prize in the contest.

Her parents were proud.

Karen's parents were proud _____ her _____ a prize in
the contest.

ANS **Karen's parents were proud of her winning a prize in the contest.**

（凱倫的爸媽因為她在比賽中得獎而感到很光榮。）

句型 用特殊句型合併 (p. 122)。

解析 本題合併後為特殊句型【be proud of＋N/Ving】，表「以……為
榮」。因而將 won 改為原型 win，再改為動名詞 winning。

Words & Phrases

win a prize *v. phr.* 贏；獲獎

⑧ Jack said something to his friends.

His friends were very angry.

Jack's words made _____.

ANS **Jack's words made his friends angry.**
（傑克所說的話讓他的朋友們很生氣。）

句型	使役動詞的合併 (p. 113)。
解析	題目中出現的 made 為授與動詞，因此本句為【make ＋ O.＋ O.C.（受詞補語）】之合併。句中之受詞補語為形容詞 angry。

⑨ I saw something on the wall.

A spider was climbing.

I _____ a spider _____ on the wall.

ANS **I saw a spider climbing on the wall.**
（我看到一隻蜘蛛在牆上爬著。）

句型	用感官動詞合併 (p. 118)。
解析	第一句的動詞為 saw 感官動詞，第二句動詞為進行式 was climbing。合併時採【感官動詞＋ O ＋ Ving】句型。

⑩ My grandmother had a rule.

She avoided eating meat in the morning.

My grandmother used to _____ in the morning.

ANS **My grandmother used to avoid eating meat in the morning.**
（我祖母以前總是盡量少在早上吃肉。）

句型	用特殊句型合併 (p. 122)。
解析	第一句 had a rule，表過去有的習慣，本題合併後為特殊句型【used to ＋ V】。注意，used to ＋ V 與 be used to+Ving 之間不同，後者表「習慣於……」。

⑪ The one-way tickets _____.
(both/sold out/the round-trip tickets/and/are)

ANS **The one-way tickets** and the round-trip tickets are both sold
out.

（單程跟來回票都賣完了。）

句型 對等相關連接詞的重組 (p. 148)。

解析 原本 both 應與 and 搭配以連接兩名詞（both the one-way tickets
and the round-trip tickets）作爲主詞，但本提示第一個字並非
both，故將其後移至動詞 are 之後，表「兩者皆……」。

Words & Phrases

one-way tickets *n. phr.* 單程票
round-trip tickets *n. phr.* 來回票
be sold out *v. phr.* 賣光

⑫ Most _____ only after they _____ ill.
(become/health/the importance/people/of/realize)

ANS **Most** people realize the importance of health **only after they**
become ill.

（大部份的人都是在生了病後才瞭解健康的重要性。）

句型 副詞子句的重組 (p. 153)。

解析 組合句中出現表時間之連接詞 only after，引導時間副詞子句。
字串中兩動詞 know 及 become，經判斷應分別爲主要子句及附屬
子句之動詞。主要子句主詞應爲 Most people，動詞爲 know，受
詞爲 the importance of health。附屬子句動詞片語爲 become ill。

Words & Phrases

realize〔ˋriə͵laɪz〕*v.* 理解；領悟
unhealthy〔ʌnˋhɛlθɪ〕*adj.* 有病的；不健康的

⑬ What _____ is _____ with my problems.
(has/my sister/help/done/me)

ANS **What my sister has done is help me with my problems.**
（我妹妹所做的就是幫我解決問題。）

句型 特殊句型的重組 (p. 157)。
解析 本題為【What sb. do＋is＋V＋(O)】。其中，主詞為以what為首之名詞子句，該名詞子句之主詞為my sister，動詞為has done；help me為主要子句動詞後之原形動詞，後接介系詞片語with my problems。

⑭ Sean _____ as her birthday gift.
(some/girlfriend/sent/his/flowers)

ANS **Sean sent his girlfriend some flowers as her birthday gift.**
（尚恩送了些花給他的女友當生日禮物。）

句型 授與動詞的重組 (p. 127)。
解析 重組字串中出現授與動詞sent，但並無介系詞，由此可知句型應為【授與動詞send＋人（I.O.）＋物（D.O.）】。句中直接受詞（D.O.）為some flowers，間接受詞（I.O.）為his girlfriend。

⑮ Ivy _____ near his office.
(her/waited/boyfriend/a café/has/for/at)

ANS **Ivy has waited for her boyfriend at a café near his office.**
（艾薇一直在她男友辦公室附近的一家咖啡店等他。）

句型 時態的重組 (p. 131)。
解析 主詞之後尋找動詞。本句動詞為has waited for，其受詞為her boyfriend；at a café為地方副詞，置於句尾。

Words & Phrases

café〔kəˋfe〕*n.* 西式小餐館、咖啡館

第二部份：段落寫作

參考範文

Today was Emma's birthday, but everyone in her class seemed to have forgotten it. Her classmates neither talked about it nor gave any presents to her. After school, Emma went home alone, disappointed. However, as she entered her house, something unexpected happened. All her good friends were at her home, and everyone shouted, "Surprise!" How special and lovely today was!

中文翻譯

艾瑪今天生日，但是班上同學好像都忘了這件事情。沒有人提及她的生日，也沒人送禮物給她。下課後艾瑪黯然地一個人回家。當她進門時，發生了令人意料不到的事。她的好朋友都在她家，每個人都對她大叫：「想不到吧！」今天真是既特別又可愛的一天！

結構分析

本篇主角為 Emma，配角為她的同學。文體屬於記敘文，涉及時間與空間的轉換。在時間的處理方面，為流水帳描述法，敘述在學校的情境及回家發生的事，均採過去式。在空間方面，則涵蓋學校及家裡。文中表時空的副詞片語（或子句）為 After school 及 as she entered her house。段落第一句表達本文的主題：Today was Emma's birthday.，而中文以轉折語 however 表達意境的轉變，最後再以感嘆句 How special and lovely today was! 做為結尾，以呼應首句。

在句型運用方面，包括：

（1）對等相關連接詞【neither...nor】句型：

　　Her classmates neither talked about it nor gave any presents to her.

（2）授與動詞句型：...gave any presents to her

（3）感嘆句 How special and lovely today was!

Words & Phrases

seem〔sim〕 *v.* 似乎

disappointed〔ˌdɪsəˋpɔɪntɪd〕 *adj.* 感到失望的

unexpected〔ˌʌnɪkˋspɛktɪd〕 *adj.* 預料之外的

第七回 全真模擬試題

第一部份：單句寫作

請將答案寫在答案紙上對應的題號旁，如有文法、用字、拼字、標點符號、大小寫等之錯誤，將予扣分。

第1-5題：句子改寫

請依題目之提示，將原句改寫成指定型式，並將改寫的句子完整地寫在答案紙上（包括提示之文字及標點符號）。

範例

Q	I like to sing songs.
→	Ted _____.
A	Ted *likes to sing songs.*

① To be able to drive a car is very convenient for me.

It is convenient for me _____.

② John: You are going to study chemistry in college, aren't you?

Jill: Yeah, chemistry really interests me.

Jill is interested _____ in college.

③ Chinese New Year is the most important holiday for us.

Chinese New Year is _____ than any other _____

for us.

④ Joanne has a headache and a runny nose.

Joanne _____ last night.

⑤ I went home early so that I could catch my favorite TV program.

I _____ in order to _____ TV program.

第6-10題：句子合併

　　請依題目之提示，將兩句合併成一句，並將合併的句子完整地寫在答案紙上（包括提示之文字及標點符號）。

範例

Q　Sophia has a dog.

　　The dog is black and white.

→　Sophia has a _____.

A　Sophia has a *black and white dog*.

⑥ Allen did his laundry this afternoon.

　He also washed the dishes.

　Allen _____ and _____ this afternoon.

⑦ John speaks English very well.

　He can also speak good French.

　John _____ both _____ very well.

⑧ Something is still unknown.

　Who broke the window and stole the money?

　It is still unknown _____.

⑨ Dennis has dreamed of a place.

　There are plenty of butterflies there.

　Dennis has dreamed of a place where _____.

⑩ The architect will take the project.

　The condition is that the boss pays him well.

　The architect _____ if _____.

第11-15題：重組

　　請將題目中所有提示字詞整合成一有意義的句子，並將重組的句子完整地寫在答案紙上（包括提示之文字及標點符號）。答案中必須使用所有提示字詞，且不能隨意增加字詞，否則不予計分。

範例	
Q	Would _____?
	(like/some/you/coffee)
A	Would *you like some coffee*?

⑪ Have _____?

(tried/red shoes/you/on/these)

⑫ Show us _____.

(how many seats/are/at the restaurant/there)

⑬ Irene _____ on foot.

(by/either/bus/goes to/or/work)

⑭ Robin _____ to Japan _____ started the new job.

(a/before/he/on/vacation/went)

⑮ Judy _____ so that she can _____.

(at/afford/part-time/a new computer/night/works)

第二部份：段落寫作

題目：在 Sally 的回家途中，有隻流浪狗一直跟著她，最後她將這隻狗帶回家養。請根據以下圖片，寫一篇約 50 字的短文，描述 Sally 如何發揮她的愛心。

第七回 解析

第一部份：單句寫作

① To be able to drive a car is very convenient for me.

It is convenient for me _____.

ANS **It is convenient for me to be able to drive a car.**

（對我而言，會開車是很方便的。）

句型 改為虛主詞的句型 (p. 25)。

解析 本題改以虛主詞 it 為首，將真主詞，即不定詞片語 to be able to drive a car，移至句尾。

---

② John: You are going to study chemistry in college, aren't you?

Jill: Yeah. Chemistry really interests me.

Jill is interested _____ in college.

ANS **Jill is interested in studying chemistry in college.**

（吉兒對大學唸化學系感到很有興趣。）

句型 動名詞片語當受詞 (p. 30)。

解析 將第二句的動詞 interest 改以動詞片語 be interested in 表達，其後之受詞須採動名詞型態。亦即將原句之 study chemistry 改為 studying chemistry。

---

③ Chinese New Year is the most important holiday for us.

Chinese New Year is _____ than any other _____ for us.

ANS **Chinese New Year is more important than any other holiday for us.**

（農曆新年對我們來說比任何其他節日來的更重要。）

句型	比較級與最高級的句型切換 (p. 38)。
解析	本句係將最高級句型【the most ＋單數N】改爲比較級句型【比較級＋than any other ＋單數N】。原句形容詞最高級most important之比較級爲more important。

④ Joanne has a headache and a runny nose.

Joanne ＿＿＿＿＿＿＿＿＿＿＿＿＿＿＿＿＿＿＿＿＿＿ last night.

ANS **Joanne** had a headache and a runny nose **last night.**

（瓊恩昨晚頭痛、流鼻水。）

句型	時態的切換 (p. 43)。
解析	改寫句中出現過去時間last night，時態改採過去簡單式，因此將動詞has改爲had。

Words & Phrases

have a runny nose *v. phr.* 流鼻水

⑤ I went home early so that I could catch my favorite TV program.

I ＿＿＿＿＿＿＿＿＿＿ in order to ＿＿＿＿＿＿＿＿＿ TV program.

ANS **I** went home early **in order to** catch my favorite **TV program.**

（我提早回家，爲的是想及時看到我最愛的電視節目。）

句型	用特定片語改寫 (p. 48)。
解析	本句係【S ＋ V...＋ so that ＋ S ＋ V...】與【S ＋ V...＋ in order to ＋ V ＋(O)】兩句型之切換。切換時，in order to 後須接原形動詞，因此改寫後in order to catch my favorite TV program。

Words & Phrases

catch 〔kætʃ〕 *v.* 趕上

⑥ Allen did his laundry this afternoon.

He also washed the dishes.

Allen _____ and _____ this afternoon.

ANS **Allen did his laundry and washed the dishes this afternoon.**

（艾倫今天下午洗了衣服也洗了碗盤。）

句型 用對等連接詞合併 (p. 58)。

解析 以對等連接詞 and 連接兩句之動詞片語（did his laundry 和 washed the dishes）。時間副詞 this afternoon 置於句尾。

Words & Phrases

do the laundry *v. phr.* 洗衣服

wash the dishes *v. phr.* 洗碗盤

⑦ John speaks English very well.

He can also speak good French.

John _____ both _____ very well.

ANS **John speaks both English and French very well.**

（約翰的英文跟法文都講得很好。）

句型 用對等相關連接詞合併 (p. 62)。

解析 合併句中出現 both，因此本題為對等相關連接詞【both...and】的句型。兩句主詞與動詞相同，故以 both...and 連接兩句之受詞 English 與 French。

⑧ Something is still unknown.

Who broke the window and stole the money?

It is still unknown _____.

ANS **It is still unknown who broke the window and stole the money.**

（目前無法得知是誰打破窗戶並偷了錢。）

句型	用名詞子句合併 (p. 68)。
解析	第一句 something 指第二個句子,因此將第二句改為名詞子句以 合併之。此名詞子句以虛主詞 it 代替,形成虛主詞為首的句型。

⑨ Dennis has dreamed of a place.

There are plenty of butterflies there.

Dennis has dreamed of a place where _____.

ANS **Dennis has dreamed of a place where** there are plenty of butterflies.

(丹尼斯夢見一個滿是蝴蝶的地方。)

句型	用形容詞子句合併 (p. 80)。
解析	第二句句尾的 there 為第一句所提到的 place,合併時將第二句併 入第一句,亦即將第二句改為以關係副詞 where 為首之形容詞子 句,形成 where there are plenty of butterflies。

Words & Phrases

plenty of　*phr.* 許多

⑩ The architect will take the project.

The condition is that the boss pays him well.

The architect _____ if _____.

ANS **The architect** will take the project **if the boss pays him well.**

(如果老闆付給他的酬勞夠高,這名建築師就會承接這個案子。)

句型	用副詞子句合併 (p. 91)。
解析	合併句中出現從屬連接詞 if,其後子句表條件,即第二句中之 the boss pays him well。

Words & Phrases

project〔`prɑdʒɛkt〕n. 方案;規劃
condition〔kən`dɪʃən〕n. 條件

⑪ Have _____?

(tried/red shoes/you/on/these)

ANS **Have you tried on these red shoes?**

(你試穿過這些紅色的鞋子了嗎?)

句型 疑問句的重組 (p. 135)。

解析 此句子爲助動詞 have 爲首的 Yes/No 問句,句構爲【Have + S + Vpp + (O)?】。句中主詞爲 you,Vpp 爲 tried。「these red shoes」爲動詞片語 have tried on 之受詞。

Words & Phrases

try on v. phr. 試穿

⑫ Show us _____.

(how many seats/are/at the restaurant/there)

ANS **Show us how many seats there are at the restaurant.**

(讓我們看看餐廳裡有多少位子。)

句型 間接問句的重組 (p. 143)。

解析 本句爲祈使句型之間接問句。原直接問句應爲 How many seats are there at the restaurant?,更改爲間接問句時,how many seats 保持不變,但應將 are there 改回成直述句的結構 there are。時間副詞 at the restaurant 置於句尾。

⑬ Irene _____ on foot.

(by/either/bus/goes to/or/work)

ANS **Irene goes to work either by bus or on foot.**

(愛玲搭公車或走路上班。)

| 句型 | 對等相關連接詞的重組 (p. 148)。 |
| 解析 | 對等相關連接詞 either...or 連接同性質之介系詞片語 by bus 及 on foot。動詞為 goes to work。 |

⑭ Robin _____ to Japan _____ started the new job.
(a/before/he/on/vacation/went)

ANS **Robin** went on a vacation **to Japan** before he **started the new job.**

（羅賓在開始做新工作前，前往日本渡假。）

| 句型 | 副詞子句的重組 (p. 153)。 |
| 解析 | 字串中出現連接詞 before，以用來引導表時間之副詞子句，其主詞為 he。主要子句動詞應為不及物的 went，其後接介系詞 on，其後再接 a vacation 做為受詞。 |

⑮ Judy _____ so that she can _____.
(at/afford/part-time/a new computer/night/works)

ANS **Judy** works part-time at night **so that she can** afford a new computer.

（裘蒂晚上兼差，以便能買得起一部新電腦。）

| 句型 | 特殊句型的重組 (p. 157)。 |
| 解析 | 本句為【...so that S＋V】特殊句型，so that 後接「目的」。重組字串中有兩個動詞，其中 works 應與副詞 part-time 搭配；afford 則與名詞 a new computer 搭配。Work part-time at night 之「目的」即為 afford a new computer。 |

第二部份：段落寫作

參考範文

A dog followed Sally on her way home. Sally tried but couldn't get rid of the dog. All she could do was ask people if they knew its owner. Nobody had an idea. So, she decided to take the dog home. To her surprise, Sally's mother allowed her to keep the dog. Since then, the dog has become her best friend.

中文翻譯

在莎麗回家的路上，有隻狗兒一直跟著她。莎麗試著擺脫，但是卻擺脫不了這隻狗。她所能做的就是問路人是否知道狗主人是誰。不過，沒有人知道。於是她決定將這隻狗帶回家。令人意外的是，莎麗的媽媽居然肯讓她養這隻狗。從此之後，這隻狗就變成了莎麗的好朋友。

結構分析

本篇主角為 Sally 與一隻小狗，其他人物包括路人與媽媽。文體屬於記敘文，文章同時涉及時間與空間的轉換。在時間的處理方面，敘述回家路上發生的事件以及回家後的情況，均採過去式。在空間方面，則涵蓋回家路上及家裡。段落首句點出 Sally 與狗的初識。發展至 So, she decided to take the dog home. 為本文重點。而末句說明這隻小狗自此變成 Sally 的好朋友，與首句形成對比。

在句型運用方面，包括：

（1）特殊句型【All sb. can do is V】句型：

All she could do was ask people if they knew its owner.

（2）間接問句 if 及授與動詞 ask 句型：

All she could do was ask people if they knew its owner.

寫作破關 ▶ 初級

（3）以不定詞片語當受詞補語：

Sally's mother allowed her to keep the dog.

（4）since 句型：【have Vpp ＋ since 過去特定時間點】：

Since then, the dog has become her best friend.

Words & Phrases

get rid of *v. phr.* 擺脫

owner〔`onɚ〕*n.* 擁有者

allow〔ə`lau〕*v.* 允許

264

第八回 全真模擬試題

第一部份：單句寫作

請將答案寫在答案紙上對應的題號旁，如有文法、用字、拼字、標點符號、大小寫等之錯誤，將予扣分。

第1-5題：句子改寫

請依題目之提示，將原句改寫成指定型式，並將改寫的句子完整地寫在答案紙上（包括提示之文字及標點符號）。

範例

Q	I like to sing songs.
→	Ted _____.
A	Ted *likes to sing songs.*

① Miss Smith moved to Thailand two years ago.

When _____?

② Mei is wondering, "Where can I find the answer to the question?"

Mei is wondering where _____.

③ Regretting what you have done is no use.

It is no use _____.

④ Amy is excited that she attends piano classes.

Amy is excited about _____.

⑤ Happiness is the best medicine for Rita.

Happiness is _____ than any other _____ for Rita.

第6-10題：句子合併

　　請依題目之提示，將兩句合併成一句，並將合併的句子完整地寫在答案紙上（包括提示之文字及標點符號）。

範例

Q　Sophia has a dog.

　　The dog is black and white.

→　Sophia has a _____.

A　Sophia has a *black and white dog.*

---

⑥ Phil smokes a pack of cigarettes every day.

　　Jessie smokes the same number of cigarettes as Phil does.

　　Jessie _____ as _____ as Phil does every day.

⑦ Fred was very worried about something.

　　He couldn't win the game.

　　Fred was very worried about _____.

⑧ Sonia cooked dinner for her boyfriend.

　　Her boyfriend asked her to do it.

　　Sonia's boyfriend got her _____ for him.

⑨ Tom heard something.

　　The girl was playing his favorite songs.

　　Tom heard the girl _____.

⑩ Mr. Jones quit his job.

　　He wanted to live with his grandchildren.

　　Mr. Jones _____ so that he could _____.

第11-15題：重組

　　請將題目中所有提示字詞整合成一有意義的句子，並將重組的句子完整地寫在答案紙上（包括提示之文字及標點符號）。答案中必須使用所有提示字詞，且不能隨意增加字詞，否則不予計分。

範例

Q Would _____?

(like/some/you/coffee)

A Would *you like some coffee*?

⑪ Mel _____.

(his good friends/his old car/one/sold/of)

⑫ I _____ since I first _____.

(the meaning/learned it/have/of the word/misunderstood)

⑬ How _____?

(had/today/much/you/coffee/have)

⑭ Mei asked _____.

(the office/thirty minutes/if/could/leave/she/early)

⑮ The twin sisters _____ and tea.

(in/good taste/both/have/coffee)

第二部份：段落寫作

題目： Vicky 在某個雨天的上班途中，遭遇了一連串不愉快的遭遇。請根據以下圖片，寫一篇約50字的短文，描述 Vicky 倒楣的一天。

第八回 解析

第一部份：單句寫作

① Miss Smith moved to Thailand two years ago.

When _____ ?

ANS **When did Miss Smith move to Thailand?**

（史密斯小姐何時搬去泰國的？）

句型	直述句改疑問句 (p. 5)。
解析	由於原句動詞moved為一般動詞型態，改為以疑問詞when為首之問句時，須在主詞之前加上助動詞did，並將moved改為原形之move；此外，two years ago應刪除，並於句尾加上問號。

② Mei is wondering, "Where can I find the answer to the question?"

Mei is wondering where _____ .

ANS **Mei is wondering where she can find the answer to the question.**

（梅不知道在那兒才能找到這個問題的答案。）

句型	直接問句改間接問句 (p. 18)。
解析	首先須刪除直接問句之引號與問號；其次，將主詞與動詞之順序調換，形成以where為首之名詞子句where she can find the answer to the question。

③ Regretting what you have done is no use.

It is no use _____ .

ANS **It is no use regretting what you have done.**

（後悔你所做的事是沒有用的。）

句型	改為虛主詞的句型 (p. 25)。
解析	本題改以虛主詞it為首，句型為【It is no use Ving】；因此，將真主詞（＝動名詞片語regretting what you have done）移至句尾。

Words & Phrases

regret〔rɪ`grɛt〕v. 後悔

④ Amy is excited that she attends piano classes.

Amy is excited about _____.

ANS **Amy is excited about** attending piano classes.

（艾咪對上鋼琴課感到很興奮。）

句型	動名詞片語當受詞 (p. 30)。
解析	改寫句動詞片語為be excited about，介系詞about後之受詞為動名詞，因而將第一句動詞改為attending。

Words & Phrases

attend〔ə`tɛnd〕v. 上課；參加（比賽、會議）

⑤ Happiness is the best medicine for Rita.

Happiness is _____ than any other _____ for Rita.

ANS **Happiness is** better than any other **medicine for Rita.**

（對芮塔來說，沒有任何別的藥比快樂來得好。）

句型	比較級與最高級的句型切換 (p. 38)。
解析	本句係最高級與比較級之切換，亦即將最高級句型【the best ＋單數N】改寫為【比較級＋than＋any other 單數N】。原句為形容詞最高級best之比較級為better，改寫後為better than any other medicine。

⑥ Phil smokes a pack of cigarettes every day.
Jessie smokes the same number of cigarettes as Phil does.
Jessie ＿＿＿＿＿＿ as ＿＿＿＿＿＿ as Phil does every day.

ANS **Jessie smokes as many cigarettes as Phil does every day.**
ANS **Jessie smokes as much as Phil does every day.**
（潔西跟菲兒每天所抽的煙一樣多。）

句型 用比較句型合併 (p. 99)。
解析 本句係原級比較句型【as＋原級 adj./adv.＋as】之合併。兩句重
複處為動詞 smoke，第二句表【Jessie 吸的煙跟 Phil 一樣多包，
亦即 Jessie 煙癮跟 Phil 一樣重】，故以 smoke as many cigarettes as
合併兩句，其中 many cigarettes 為 smoke 之受詞。或可改為
smoke as much as，而 much 為副詞，修飾動詞 smoke。

⑦ Fred was very worried about something.
He couldn't win the game.
Fred was very worried about ＿＿＿＿＿＿＿＿＿＿＿＿.

ANS **Fred was worried about not winning the game.**
（弗烈得非常擔心他無法贏得比賽。）

句型 用介系詞合併 (p. 107)。
解析 第一句之 something 指第二句，合併後介系詞 about 後應接動名
詞 winning。注意，表否定的 not 則加於該動名詞之前。

⑧ Sonia cooked dinner for her boyfriend.
Her boyfriend asked her to do it.
Sonia's boyfriend got her ＿＿＿＿＿＿＿＿＿＿＿ for him.

ANS **Sonia's boyfriend got her to cook dinner for him.**
（桑妮亞的男友要她替他準備晚餐。）

句型 用使役動詞合併 (p. 113)。

解析 合併句中出現與使役動詞類似用法之 get，觀察其後之受詞 her 與受詞補語間 cook dinner 之關係為主動，因而將受詞補語改為不定詞 to cook 型態。

⑨ Tom heard something.

The girl was playing his favorite song.

Tom heard the girl _____.

ANS **Tom heard the girl playing his favorite song.**

（湯姆聽見這個女孩在彈奏他最愛的曲子。）

句型 用感官動詞合併 (p. 118)。

解析 以感官動詞 heard 合併兩句，形成【感官動詞＋O＋OC】句型，其中 OC 可為原形動詞或 Ving 兩種型態。因第二句 was playing 強調進行狀態，故合併後 heard 之 OC（受詞補語）以 Ving 型態呈現。

⑩ Mr. Jones quit his job.

He wanted to live with his grandchildren.

Mr. Jones _____ so that he could _____.

ANS **Mr. Jones quit his job so that he could live with his grandchildren.**

（瓊斯先生把工作辭掉以便能跟孫子們住在一起。）

句型 用特殊句型合併 (p. 122)。

解析 本題合併後為特殊句型【...so that S＋V】，表「以便於」。而 so that 之後應接表「目的」之子句，亦即 he could live with his grandchildren。

Words & Phrases

quit〔kwɪt〕*v.* 辭職；戒除

⑪ Mel _____.

(his good friends/his old car/one/sold/of)

ANS **Mel sold one of his friends his old car.**

（梅爾把他的舊車賣給他的好友之一。）

句型 授與動詞的重組 (p. 127)。

解析 字串中出現 sold（爲 sell 之過去式）卻無介系詞，爲授與動詞【sell＋I.O.（間接受詞）＋DO（直接受詞）】之重組。重組字串中 one of 應搭配複數可數名詞 his good friends，形成 one of his good friends 爲間接受詞。直接受詞爲 his old car。

---

⑫ I _____ since I first _____.

(the meaning/learned it/have/of the word/misunderstood)

ANS **I have misunderstood the meaning of the word since I first learned it.**

（從我一開始學到這個字，就一直誤解它的意思。）

句型 時態的重組 (p. 131)。

解析 句中出現表時間之連接詞 since（自從），其時態爲：主要子句採現在完成式，since 後之附屬子句爲過去特定時間點或過去式動詞。因此，字串中之 have misunderstood 爲主要子句動詞，而 learned it 爲附屬子句動詞。介系詞片語 of the word 所修飾者爲名詞 the meaning，形成 the meaning of the word，作爲 misunderstood 之受詞。

Words & Phrases

misunderstand〔͵mɪsʌndɚˋstænd〕*v.* 誤解

meaning〔ˋminɪŋ〕*n.* 意義

⑬ How _____?

(had/today/much/you/coffee/have)

ANS **How** much coffee have you had today**?**

（今天你喝了多少咖啡？）

句型 疑問句的重組 (p. 135)。

解析 本句主詞為 you，動詞為完成式之 have had，而 much 與 coffee 應與疑問詞 how 搭配，形成 how much coffee 置於句首。而將時態助動詞 have 移至主詞 you 之前，時間副詞 today 置於句尾，並加上問號（?）。

---

⑭ Mei asked _____.

(the office/thirty minutes/if/could/leave/she/early)

ANS **Mei asked** if she could leave the office thirty minutes early**.**

（梅詢問她是否可以提前三十分鐘離開辦公室。）

句型 間接問句的重組 (p. 143)。

解析 本句 if 為連接詞，形成間接問句【if＋S＋V（＋受詞）】句型。間接問句主詞為 she，動詞 could leave，受詞為 the office，時間副詞 thirty minutes early 意思是「提早三十分鐘」，置於句尾。

---

⑮ The twin sisters _____ and tea.

(in/good taste/both/have/coffee)

ANS **The twin sisters** have good taste in both coffee **and tea.**

（這對雙胞胎姊妹對咖啡與茶有獨到的品味。）

句型 對等相關連接詞的重組 (p. 148)。

解析 本句係對等相關連接詞【both A and B】重組句型。句中之 B 為名詞型態之 tea，依對等相關連接詞之特性可知 A 必為名詞。本句動詞為 have，受詞為 good taste；對等連接詞所連接者為兩名詞 coffee 與 tea。另注意，表示對某事物有品味，用介系詞 in。

第二部份：段落寫作

參考範文

Vicky had a bad day today. It started in the morning when it poured but she forgot to take an umbrella. She got all wet. Then, when she arrived at the bus stop, the bus had just left. What's worse, Vicky was thirty minutes late for work and was called to her boss's office. What a bad day Vicky had!

中文翻譯

薇琪今天很倒楣。一早就運氣不佳。下大雨，卻忘了帶雨傘出門，結果全身都淋濕了。到公車站時，車子已經開走了。更糟的是，她遲到了三十分鐘，被老闆叫進辦公室。薇琪今天實在有夠倒楣！

結構分析

本篇主角 Vicky，文體屬於記敘文，文章同時涉及時間與空間的轉換。在時間的處理方面，敘述一早出門到辦公室所發生的一連串倒楣事件，均採過去式。在空間方面，則涵蓋了上班路上及辦公室。

在句型運用方面，包括：

（1）以 when 引導之時間副詞子句句型：

It started in the morning when it poured but she forgot to take an umbrella.

（2）過去兩動作一前一後發生（過去完成式與簡單過去式之搭配）：

When she arrived at the bus stop, the bus had just left.

公車離開發生較早，用過去完成式；抵達公車站牌較晚發生，用過去簡單式。

Words & Phrases

pour〔por〕*v.* 傾倒；下傾盆大雨

第九回 全真模擬試題

第一部份：單句寫作

　　請將答案寫在答案紙上對應的題號旁，如有文法、用字、拼字、標點符號、大小寫等之錯誤，將予扣分。

第1-5題：句子改寫

　　請依題目之提示，將原句改寫成指定型式，並將改寫的句子完整地寫在答案紙上（包括提示之文字及標點符號）。

範例

Q　I like to sing songs.

→　Ted _____.

A　Ted *likes to sing songs.*

① You can buy lottery tickets at any ticket booth.

　Where _____?

② Bill asked his daughter, "Did you have a good time on Grandpa's farm?"

　Bill asked his daughter _____ on her Grandpa's farm.

③ Swimming during the summer is a good idea.

　It is a good idea to _____.

④ My friends are playing basketball.

　My friends _____ since 7 p.m.

⑤ Serena always does very well on math and English.

　Serena is good _____.

第6-10題：句子合併

　　請依題目之提示，將兩句合併成一句，並將合併的句子完整地寫在答案紙上（包括提示之文字及標點符號）。

範例

Q　Sophia has a dog.

　　The dog is black and white.

→　Sophia has a ＿＿＿＿＿＿＿＿＿＿.

A　Sophia has a *black and white dog.*

⑥ Sam's mother asked Sam to do his homework.

　　He still watched TV.

　　Sam's mother ＿＿＿＿＿＿＿＿＿＿ , but he ＿＿＿＿＿＿＿＿＿＿.

⑦ Angela has a talent for languages.

　　She is good at cooking, too.

　　Angela not only ＿＿＿＿＿＿＿＿＿＿＿ is good at cooking.

⑧ I am not sure about something.

　　Who cleaned the house for me?

　　I am not sure who ＿＿＿＿＿＿＿＿＿＿＿＿＿＿.

⑨ Yoshio cannot forget those days.

　　He had good times with Angela then.

　　Yoshio cannot forget those days when ＿＿＿＿＿＿＿＿＿.

⑩ Julie's parents felt very disappointed.

　　Julie failed the entrance exam.

　　Julie's parents ＿＿＿＿＿＿＿＿＿＿ because she ＿＿＿＿＿＿＿.

第11-15題：重組

請將題目中所有提示字詞整合成一有意義的句子，並將重組的句子完整地寫在答案紙上（包括提示之文字及標點符號）。答案中必須使用所有提示字詞，且不能隨意增加字詞，否則不予計分。

範例

Q Would _____?

(like/some/you/coffee)

A Would *you like some coffee*?

⑪ Laura _____ she was _____.

(college/teach English/student/used to/when/a)

⑫ Dancing _____.

(of/one/hobbies/is/Ming's)

⑬ I _____.

(easy questions/asked/in class/some/my students)

⑭ Nancy _____ since she was _____.

(has devoted/to/in college/teaching English/herself)

⑮ Could _____?

(you/me/the pepper/pass/to)

第二部份：段落寫作

題目： Charles 與另外兩名同學相約明天要出去玩。請根據以下圖片，寫一篇約 50 字的短文，描述他們計劃的三種可能玩法。

第九回 解析

第一部份：單句寫作

① You can buy lottery tickets at any ticket booth.
Where _____?

ᴬᴺˢ **Where can you buy lottery tickets?**
（到那兒可以買到彩券？）

句型 直述句改疑問句 (p. 5)。

解析 由於 can 為模態助動詞，改為以疑問詞 where 為首之問句時，必須將 can 提至主詞之前，形成 Where ＋ can ＋ S ＋ V 倒裝句型。而 where 所問即原句表地點之介詞片語 at any ticket booth，改寫時須刪除。

---

② Bill asked his daughter, "Did you have a good time on Grandpa's farm?"
Bill asked his daughter _____ on her Grandpa's farm.

ᴬᴺˢ **Bill asked his daughter if she had a good time on her Grandpa's farm.**
（比爾問他女兒在爺爺的農場是否玩得開心。）

句型 直接問句改間接問句 (p. 18)。

解析 首先須刪除直接問句之引號與問號，其次將主詞與動詞之詞序調換，動詞還原為過去式之 had，而 you 所指為主要子句動詞之受詞（his daughter），改寫間接問句時主詞應改為 she。因原問句為 Yes/No 型式，故應改用 if 引導之間接問句，形成 if she had a good time。

Words & Phrases

have a good time *v. phr.* 玩得愉快

③ Swimming during the summer is a good idea.

It is a good idea to _____.

ANS **It is a good idea to swim during the summer.**

（夏天時游泳是個好點子。）

句型 改為虛主詞的句型 (p. 25)。

解析 本題改以虛主詞 it 為首，將真主詞（原為動名詞片語 swimming during the summer，改寫成不定詞片語型式 to swim during the summer）移至句尾。

---

④ My friends are playing basketball.

My friends _____ since 7 p.m.

ANS **My brothers have been playing basketball since 7 p.m.**

（從七點開始，我的朋友們就一直在打籃球。）

句型 時態的切換 (p. 43)。

解析 改寫句中出現 since ＋特定時間，表時間之持續性，時態應改為現在完成式。但因將原句為現在進行式 are playing，所以採用現在完成進行式 have been playing 強調此刻仍在發生。

---

⑤ Serena always does very well on math and English.

Serena is good _____.

ANS **Serena is good at math and English.**

（瑟琳娜數學跟英文都很好。）

句型 用特定片語改寫 (p. 48)。

解析 本句係【be good at ＋ N/ Ving】句型，意為「擅長……」。改寫句後介系詞可直接接「擅長的科目＝ math and English」。

⑥ Sam's mother asked Sam to do his homework.

He still watched TV.

Sam's mother _____ , but he _____.

ANS **Sam's mother** asked Sam to do his homework, **but he** still watched TV.

（山姆的媽媽要他去做功課，他卻在看電視。）

句型 用對等連接詞合併 (p. 58)。

解析 本題以對等連接詞 but 合併兩句。兩句之主詞與動詞均不同，不須做任何改變或省略。

---

⑦ Angela has a talent for languages.

She is good at cooking, too.

Angela not only _____ is good at cooking.

ANS **Angela not only** has a talent for languages but also **is good at cooking.**

（安琪拉不只對語言有天份，她對烹飪也很拿手。）

句型 用對等相關連接詞合併 (p. 62)。

解析 合併句中出現 not only 顯然為對等相關連接詞【not only...but also】句型。兩句主詞相同（Angela＝She），因此以 not only...but also 連接 has a talent for languages 與 is good at cooking 兩動詞片語。

Words & Phrases

have a talent for *v. phr* 對……有天份

---

⑧ I am not sure about something.

Who cleaned the house for me?

I am not sure who _____.

ANS **I am not sure who** cleaned the house for me.

（我不確定是誰幫我整理房子的。）

句型 用名詞子句合併 (p. 68)。

解析 第一句 something 指第二個句子，因此將第二句改為名詞子句以合併之。因 who 在原句中為主詞，故改為間接問句時動詞部分不須做改變，字序亦不變。

⑨ Yoshio cannot forget those days.

He had good times with Angela then.

Yoshio cannot forget those days when ＿＿＿＿＿＿＿＿＿＿＿.

ANS **Yoshio cannot forget those days when** he had good times with Angela.

（善夫無法忘懷那段跟安琪拉在一起的快樂時光。）

句型 用形容詞子句合併 (p. 80)。

解析 第二句的 then 為第一句所指之時間，合併時將第二句併入第一句，亦即將第二句改為以關係副詞 when 為首之形容詞子句，形成 when he had good times with Angela。

⑩ Julie's parents felt very disappointed.

Julie failed the entrance exam.

Julie's parents ＿＿＿＿＿＿＿ because she ＿＿＿＿＿＿＿.

ANS **Julie's parents** felt very disappointed **because** she failed the entrance exam.

（因為裘莉沒通過入學考試，所以她爸媽感到很失望。）

283

句型	用副詞子句合併 (p. 91)。
解析	合併句中出現表因果之從屬連接詞 because，後接表「原因」之子句，即 Julie failed the entrance exam.；主要子句則為 Julie's parents felt very disappointed.。此外，因 Julie 已於主要句中出現，因此附屬子句中之主詞以代名詞 she 替代 Julie。

Words & Phrases

entrance exam〔ˋɛntrəns ɪgˋzæm〕*n. phr.* 入學考試

⑪ Laura _____ she was _____.
(college/teach English/student/used to/when/a)

ANS **Laura** used to teach English when **she was** a college student.
（蘿拉上大學時曾教過英文。）

句型	副詞子句的重組 (p. 153)。
解析	字組中出現表時間之從屬連接詞 when，後須接子句（when she was a college student）。Used to 後應接原形動詞 teach，組成主要子句 Laura used to teach English。

⑫ Dancing _____.
(of/one/hobbies/is/Ming's)

ANS **Dancing** is one of Ming's hobbies.
（明的嗜好之一是跳舞。）

句型	特殊句型的重組 (p. 157)。
解析	本句係【one of＋複數可數 N】句型之重組。動詞為 is，所有格 Ming's 後接名詞 hobbies，one of 則應置於 Ming's hobbies 之前，表「……之一」。

Words & Phrases

hobby〔ˋhɑbɪ〕*n.* 嗜好

⑬ I _____.

(easy questions/asked/in class/some/my students)

ANS I asked my students some easy questions in class.

（我在課堂上問了學生一些簡單的問題。）

> **句型** 授與動詞的重組 (p. 127)。
>
> **解析** 重組字串中出現授與動詞 asked 但並無介系詞，由此可知本句爲【授與動詞 ask ＋人（I.O.）＋物（D.O.）】的重組。本句間接受詞應爲 my students，直接受詞爲 some easy questions，二者不可顛倒。而地方副詞 in class 置於句尾。

⑭ Nancy _____ since she was _____.

(has devoted/to/in college/teaching English/herself)

ANS Nancy has devoted herself to teaching English since she was in college.

（南希從大學開始就致力於英文教學的工作。）

> **句型** 時態的重組 (p. 131)。
>
> **解析** 句中出現表時間之連接詞 since（自從），其時態爲：主要子句採現在完成式，since 後之附屬子句爲過去特定時間點或過去式動詞。字組中 has devoted 爲主要子句之動詞，後接反身代名詞 herself 和介系詞 to（表「獻身於」），而 teaching English 則爲其受詞。In college 置於附屬子句 she was 之後，形成表時間之副詞子句 since she was in college。

Words & Phrases

devote oneself to *v. phr.* 致力於；獻身於

⑮ Could _____?

(you/me/the pepper/pass/to)

ANS **Could you pass the pepper to me?**

（你可以遞胡椒粉給我嗎？）

句型 時態的重組 (p. 131)。

解析 模態助動詞 could 之後接主詞，you 為本句主詞，動詞為 pass，其受詞為 the pepper，to me 表接受對象。

Words & Phrases

pepper〔ˋpɛpɚ〕n. 辣椒；胡椒粉

第二部份：段落寫作

參考範文

Charles and his friends are planning tomorrow's activities. They have three options for different weather conditions. If it rains, they will have to play video games at home. If it is a cloudy day, they plan to play basketball on the playground. They will go swimming if tomorrow is sunny and hot.

中文翻譯

查爾斯跟他的朋友正計劃著明天的活動。對於不同的天氣狀況，他們有三種不同的計劃。如果下雨他們就必須待在屋內打電動；假如是陰天，他們打算到操場去打籃球；如果明天出大太陽又熱，就去游泳。

結構分析

　　本篇主角為 Charles 和他的朋友，文體屬於描寫文。本文描述在不同的天氣條件下可能規劃的活動，因此時間與空間的轉換一致。在時態上，條件句用現在式表達，而可能的活動則採未來式。首句 Charles and his friends are planning tomorrow's activities. 點出本段落之重點。而後分別描述三種條件下的活動內容。

在句型運用方面主要是 if 子句的變化：

If it rains, ...

If it is a cloudy day, ...

... if tomorrow is sunny and hot.

Words & Phrases

option〔ˋɑpʃən〕 *n.* 選項

playground〔ˋpleˏgraʊnd〕 *n.* 操場；遊樂場

第十回 全真模擬試題

第一部份：單句寫作

請將答案寫在答案紙上對應的題號旁，如有文法、用字、拼字、標點符號、大小寫等之錯誤，將予扣分。

第1-5題：句子改寫

請依題目之提示，將原句改寫成指定型式，並將改寫的句子完整地寫在答案紙上（包括提示之文字及標點符號）。

範例

Q I like to sing songs.

→ Ted _____.

A Ted *likes to sing songs.*

① Lily: Did you do your math homework?

Ray: No. I don't want to do it.

Ray avoided _____.

② No other animal in the zoo is as cute as the penguin.

The penguin is the _____ in the zoo.

③ Sue and Sam went on a trip to Africa.

_____ next month.

④ Ben doesn't have any interest in running a business.

Ben _____ interested in _____ at all.

⑤ No other girl in Janet's class works as hard as she does.

Janet _____ than all the other _____ in her class.

第6-10題：句子合併

請依題目之提示，將兩句合併成一句，並將合併的句子完整地寫在答案紙上（包括提示之文字及標點符號）。

範例

Q Sophia has a dog.

The dog is black and white.

→ Sophia has a _____.

A Sophia has a *black and white dog.*

⑥ Joanne's family is very big.

There are not many members in Kate's family.

Joanne's family _____ than Kate's.

⑦ Kiki traveled to Southern Taiwan.

Kiki rode a motorcycle.

Kiki _____ by _____.

⑧ Arthur went to the hospital yesterday.

The doctor checked his eyesight.

Arthur had his eyesight _____ yesterday.

⑨ Anne saw something.

Her roommate cried in her room.

Anne saw _____ in her room.

⑩ Debby enjoys water sports.

She likes swimming, water skiing, and diving.

Debby likes _____ , such as _____.

第11–15題：重組

　　請將題目中所有提示字詞整合成一有意義的句子，並將重組的句子完整地寫在答案紙上（包括提示之文字及標點符號）。答案中必須使用所有提示字詞，且不能隨意增加字詞，否則不予計分。

範例

Q Would _____?
(like/some/you/coffee)

A Would *you like some coffee*?

⑪ Tell the shopkeeper _____.
(item/want/which/to/you/buy)

⑫ The food _____ tasted delicious.
(at/nor/looked/the Italian restaurant/neither/good)

⑬ Albert _____ for _____.
(worked/three months/has/his report/on)

⑭ Rose _____ she is _____.
(her mother/trouble/whenever/turns to/in)

⑮ Alan left home _____ now.
(in/living/is/school dormitory/and/the)

第二部份：段落寫作

題目： Debby 在逛街途中遇到兩名外國人向她問路。請根據以下圖片，寫一篇約50字的短文，描述 Debby 如何幫助他們。

第十回 解析

第一部份：單句寫作

① Lily: Did you do your math homework?

Ray: No. I don't want to do it.

Ray avoided _____.

ANS **Ray avoided doing his math homework.**

（雷故意不做數學作業。）

句型 動名詞片語當受詞 (p. 30)。

解析 Avoid 後之受詞須採動名詞型態，即【avoid ＋ Ving】句型。形成 avoided doing his math homework。

Words & Phrases

avoid〔ə`vɔɪd〕v.（故意）避免

---

② No other animal in the zoo is as cute as the penguin.

The penguin is the _____ in the zoo.

ANS **The penguins is the cutest animal in the zoo.**

（企鵝是動物園內最可愛的動物。）

句型 比較級與最高級的句型切換 (p. 38)。

解析 本句係原級與最高級的切換，亦即將排他性之原級比較句型【No other N ＋ V ＋ as adj./adv. as ＋ N】改寫為最高級句型【N ＋ V ＋ the 最高級 ＋ N】。形容詞 cute 之最高級為 cutest，改寫後為 the cutest animal。原句為「動物園中沒有任何動物像企鵝那麼可愛」，改寫後為「企鵝是動物園中最可愛的動物」。

③ Sue and Sam went on a trip to Africa.

_____ next month.

ANS Sue and Sam **will go on a trip to Africa** next month.

ANS Sue and Sam **are going on a trip to Africa** next month.

（蘇跟山姆準備下個月到非洲去玩。）

句型	時態的切換 (p. 43)。
解析	改寫句中出現未來時間，時態改採未來式。本句有兩種改法，一為加模態助動詞will表「將要」或用be going to表「即將」。

④ Ben doesn't have any interest in running a business.

Ben _____ interested in _____ at all.

ANS Ben **is not** interested in **running a business** at all.

（班對經營一個事業興趣缺缺。）

句型	用特定片語改寫 (p. 48)。
解析	本句係【be interested in＋N/Ving】句型。介系詞in之後之受詞為running a business。

Words & Phrases

run a business *v. phr.* 做生意

⑤ No other girl in Janet's class works as hard as she does.

Janet _____ than all the other _____ in her class.

ANS Janet **works harder** than all the other **girls do** in her class.

（珍妮比班上其他女生都用功。）

句型	比較級與最高級的句型切換 (p. 38)。
解析	本句係原級與比較級的切換，亦即將排他性之原級比較句型【No other N＋V＋as adj./adv. as＋N】改寫為比較級句型【比較級＋than all the other＋複數N】。原句副詞 hard 之比較級為 harder，改寫後為 harder than all the other girls。原句為「珍妮班上沒有任何女生像她那麼用功」，改寫後為「珍妮是班上最用功的女生」。

⑥ Joanne's family is very big.

There are not many members in Kate's family.

Joanne's family _____ than Kate's.

ANS **Joanne's family is bigger than Kate's.**

（瓊恩家的人比凱特家的人來得多。）

句型	用比較句型合併 (p. 99)。
解析	因題目中出現 than，本句須用比較級句型【原級-er/more 原級＋then】合併。第二句表示 Kate 家中成員不是很多，換句話說，Joanne 家中的人數比較多。 Big 之比較級為 bigger。

⑦ Kiki traveled to Southern Taiwan.

Kiki rode a motorcycle.

Kiki _____ by _____.

ANS **Kiki traveled to Southern Taiwan by motorcycle.**

（琪琪騎摩托車到台灣南部去玩。）

句型	用介系詞合併 (p. 107)。
解析	介系詞 by 表交通方式，將第二句之 rode a motorcycle 改為介系詞片語 by motorcycle 以合併兩句。

⑧ Arthur went to the hospital yesterday.

The doctor checked his eyesight.

Arthur had his eyesight _____ yesterday.

ANS **Arthur had his eyesight checked (by the doctor) yesterday.**

（亞瑟昨天〔讓醫生〕檢查眼睛。）

句型 用使役動詞合併 (p. 113)。

解析 合併句中出現使役動詞 have，其後之受詞 his eyesight 與受詞補
語 checked 間為被動關係，即 his eyesight was checked (by the doctor)。

---

⑨ Anne saw something.

Her roommate cried in her room.

Anne saw _____ in her room.

ANS **Anne saw her roommate cry in her room.**

（安看到她的室友在房間裡哭。）

句型 用感官動詞合併 (p. 118)。

解析 以感官動詞 see 合併兩句，形成【感官動詞＋O＋OC】句型，
其中 OC 可為原形動詞或 Ving 兩種型態。因本題中第二句動詞採
過去簡單式 cried，強調「事實」，故合併後 saw 之 OC（受詞補
語）以原形動詞型態呈現。

Words & Phrases

roommate〔ˋrum͵met〕 *n.* 室友

⑩ Debby enjoys water sports.

She likes swimming, water skiing, and diving.

Debby likes _____ , such as _____.

ANS **Debby likes** water sports, **such as** swimming, water skiing, and diving.

（黛比喜歡水上運動，諸如：游泳、滑水及潛水。）

句型 用特殊句型合併 (p. 122)。

解析 本題合併後爲特殊句型【...such as...】，以列舉方式說明Debby所喜歡的water sports。Such as之後分別列出運動項目。

---

⑪ Tell the shopkeeper _____.

(item/want/which/to/you/buy)

ANS **Tell the shopkeeper** which item you want to buy.

（告訴店員你要買什麼東西。）

句型 間接問句的重組 (p. 143)。

解析 本句間接問句係以疑問詞which引導的名詞子句，其後應爲S＋V型態。在此主詞爲you、動詞爲want，動詞之受詞爲不定詞片語to buy。

Words & Phrases

shopkeeper〔`ʃɑpˏkipɚ〕n. 店主

item〔`aɪtəm〕n. 項目

---

⑫ The food _____ tasted delicious.

(at/nor/looked/the Italian restaurant/neither/good)

ANS **The food** at the Italian restaurant neither looked good nor tasted delicious.

（那家義大利餐廳的菜，看起來既不怎麼樣，嚐起來亦不美味。）

> **句型** 對等相關連接詞的重組 (p. 148)。
>
> **解析** 字組中出現 neither 及 nor，為【neither A nor B】句型。介系詞片語 at the Italian restaurant 為形容詞修飾 food，字組中有動詞 looked，重組句中出現另一個動詞 tasted，按對等相關連接詞之特性，可知 neither...nor 連接此兩個動詞，形成 neither looked good nor tasted delicious。

Words & Phrases

taste〔test〕*v.* 嚐起來

⑬ Albert _____ for _____.
(worked/three months/has/his report/on)

ANS **Albert** has worked on his report **for** three months.
（亞伯特已經花了三個月寫他的報告。）

> **句型** 副詞子句的重組 (p. 153)。
>
> **解析** 組合句中出現 for，其句型為【現在完成式＋for＋一段時間】。本句動詞為現在完成式之 has worked，for 之後則接 three months。由於動詞 has worked 為不及物，後須接介系詞 on，再接受詞 report。

Words & Phrases

work on *v. phr.* 從事某事

⑭ Rose _____ she is _____.
(her mother/trouble/whenever/turns to/in)

ANS **Rose** turns to her mother whenever **she is** in trouble.
（只要蘿絲遇到困難，都會找她媽媽幫忙解決。）

句型 副詞子句的重組 (p. 153)。

解析 字組中出現 whenever，爲表時間之連接詞，故將之置於 she is in
trouble 之前，形成時間副詞子句 (whenever she is in trouble)。主
要子句的動詞爲 turns to，其受詞爲 her mother。

Words & Phrases

turn to *v. phr.* 向……請求幫助

whenever〔hwɛn`ɛvɚ〕*conj.* 不論何時

be in trouble *v. phr.* 遇到困難或麻煩

⑮ Alan left home _____ now.

(in/living/is/school dormitory/and/the)

ANS **Alan left home and is living in the dormitory now.**

（艾倫離開了家裡，現在住在宿舍裡。）

句型 時態的重組 (p. 131)。

解析 本題句尾出現 now，故爲現在進行式時態之重組。字組中 is 與
現在分詞 living 搭配，後接 in the school dormitory 表地點。Left
home 與 is living in the school dormitory 兩動作之間以 and 連接。

Words & Phrases

dormitory〔`dɔrmə͵torɪ〕*n.* 宿舍

第二部份：段落寫作

參考範文

　　Two foreigners were asking Debby for directions to the
SOGO department store. One of them had a map in his hand
and was pointing at the map. On the map were some places,

including a post office and the SOGO department store. After talking for a while, Debby showed them how to get there. She then felt a sense of achievement because she could communicate with foreigners in English.

中文翻譯

　　有兩個外國人向黛比問到太平洋崇光百貨的路怎麼走。其中一人手拿地圖，並指著圖。圖上標示了幾個地方，包括郵局跟太平洋崇光百貨公司。黛比跟他們說了一會兒話，然後指點他們怎麼去。之後她覺得很有成就感，因為她能用英語跟外國人溝通。

結構分析

　　本篇主角為Debby與兩名外國人；文體屬於描寫文，描寫Debby遇到外國人問路的情景，而發生地點則在百貨公司附近。由於事情發生於過去，全篇採過去時態。重點描寫事項為兩位外國人手持地圖（有形描述），以及事後Debby感到很有成就感（無形描述）。
在句型運用方面，包括：
（1）特殊句型【..., including...】：
　　On the map were some places, including a post office and the SOGO department store.
（2）間接問句句型：
　　Debby showed them how to get there.
（3）表因果之副詞子句【結果＋because 原因】：
　　She then felt a sense of achievement because she could communicate with foreigners in English.

Words & Phrases

ask...for directions　*v. phr.* 向……問路
a sense of achievement　*n. phr.* 成就感

國家圖書館出版品預行編目資料

全民英檢寫作破關─初級 = Master GEPT
writing. elementary / 艾菱作 -- 初版. -- 臺北市：貝
塔語言，2003〔民92〕
　　面；　　公分
　ISBN 957-729-305-0（平裝）

1.英國語言─作文

805.17　　　　　　　　　　　　　　　92000404

全民英檢寫作破關─初級
Master GEPT® Writing: Elementary

作　　者／艾菱
總 編 審／王復國
執行編輯／陳家仁
插 畫 家／林家德

出　　版／貝塔語言出版有限公司
地　　址／台北市 100 館前路 12 號 11 樓
電　　話／(02)2314-2525
傳　　真／(02)2312-3535
郵　　撥／19493777 貝塔出版有限公司
客服專線／(02)2314-3535
客服信箱／btservice@betamedia.com.tw

總 經 銷／時報文化出版企業股份有限公司
地　　址／桃園縣龜山鄉萬壽路二段 351 號
電　　話／(02) 2306-6842

出版日期／2005 年 9 月初版二刷
定　　價／320 元
特　　價／260 元
I S B N：957-729-305-0

Master GEPT® Writing: Elementary
Copyright 2003 by 艾菱
Published by Beta Multimedia Publishing

貝塔網址：www.betamedia.com.tw

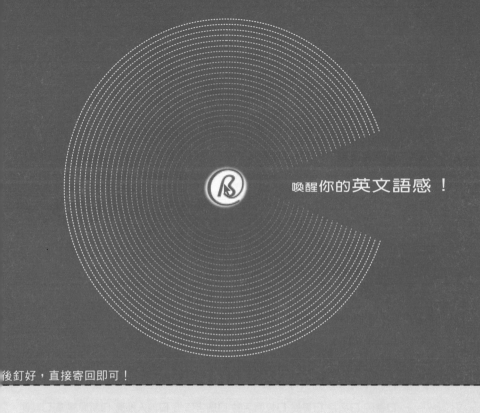

喚醒你的英文語感！

後釘好，直接寄回即可！

100 台北市中正區館前路12號11樓

 貝塔語言出版 收
Beta Multimedia Publishing

寄件者住址 ☐☐☐

謝謝您購買本書！！

貝塔語言擁有最優良之英文學習書籍，為提供您最佳的英語學習資訊，您可填妥此表後寄回（免貼郵票）將可不定期收到本公司最新發行書訊及活動訊息！

姓名：＿＿＿＿＿＿＿＿＿＿＿＿＿　性別：□男 □女　生日：＿＿＿年＿＿＿月＿＿＿日

電話：(公)＿＿＿＿＿＿＿＿＿＿(宅)＿＿＿＿＿＿＿＿＿＿(手機)＿＿＿＿＿＿＿＿＿

電子信箱：＿＿＿＿＿＿＿＿＿＿＿＿＿＿＿＿＿＿＿＿＿＿＿＿＿＿

學歷：□高中職含以下　□專科　□大學　□研究所含以上

職業：□金融　□服務　□傳播　□製造　□資訊　□軍公教　□出版

　　　□自由　□教育　□學生　□其他

職級：□企業負責人　□高階主管　□中階主管　□職員　□專業人士

1. 您購買的書籍是？＿＿＿＿＿＿＿＿＿＿＿＿＿＿＿＿＿＿＿

2. 您從何處得知本產品？(可複選)

　　　□書店 □網路 □書展 □校園活動 □廣告信函 □他人推薦 □新聞報導 □其他

3. 您覺得本產品價格：

　　　□偏高 □合理 □偏低

4. 請問目前您每週花了多少時間學英語？

　　　□ 不到十分鐘 □ 十分鐘以上，但不到半小時 □ 半小時以上，但不到一小時

　　　□ 一小時以上，但不到兩小時 □ 兩個小時以上 □ 不一定

5. 通常在選擇語言學習書時，哪些因素是您會考慮的？

　　　□ 封面 □ 內容、實用性 □ 品牌 □ 媒體、朋友推薦 □ 價格 □ 其他＿＿＿＿＿＿＿

6. 市面上您最需要的語言書種類為？

　　　□ 聽力 □ 閱讀 □ 文法 □ 口說 □ 寫作 □ 其他＿＿＿＿＿＿＿＿

7. 通常您會透過何種方式選購語言學習書籍？

　　　□ 書店門市 □ 網路書店 □ 郵購 □ 直接找出版社 □ 學校或公司團購

　　　□ 其他＿＿＿＿＿＿＿＿＿

8. 給我們的建議：＿＿＿＿＿＿＿＿＿＿＿＿＿＿＿＿＿＿＿＿＿＿＿＿＿＿＿＿

＿＿＿＿＿＿＿＿＿＿＿＿＿＿＿＿＿＿＿＿＿＿＿＿＿＿＿＿＿＿＿＿＿＿＿＿＿

喚醒你的英文語感！

Get a Feel for English !

喚醒你的英文語感！

Get a Feel for English !